THE COMING OF A NEW MILLENNIUM

HEIDI NEALE & NICK MANOLUKAS

BERKELEY, CALIFORNIA

THE COMING OF A NEW MILLENNIUM

©1998 HEIDI NEALE & NICK MANOLUKAS

PUBLISHED BY:

LABRYS
2425 B Channing Way #574
Berkeley, CA 94704
labrysx@earthlink.net

All rights reserved, except for the inclusion of brief quotations in a review. Please address all inquiries to Labrys.

ISBN 0-9659778-2-X
Library of Congress Catalog Card Number 97-94360

Cover design and illustration by Lightbourne Images ©1997
Printed with soy ink on recycled paper in the USA by Gilliland Printing

For our dear Mothers
Marie and Joanna

Thank you for giving us sweet Life!

ACKNOWLEDGMENTS AND GRATITUDES

Our sincerest thanks to Sam, our dear friend, mentor and spiritual guide. We are eternally grateful for your wisdom and unwavering support.

We also owe a great debt to many scholars and authors whose research and insight helped make the book possible: Riane Eisler, Marija Gimbutas, Carl Sagan, Joseph Campbell, Costis Davaras, Spyridon and Nanno Marinatos, Christos Doumas, Anne Baring, Jules Cashford, Carol Christ, Judith Plaskow and Starhawk. We're grateful to the Corvallis Public Library for their excellent collection, friendly service and very generous grace periods.

A heartfelt thanks to those friends who helped us develop the book by reading the manuscript and providing their helpful comments: Jenny Lorang, Randy Chakerian, Mary Ellard-Ivey, Margaret J. Anderson, Jeni Wells-Whitney, Trell Anderson and Gaelyn Larrick. We also appreciate the help of our friends Frank Harris, Bill Moses and Monika Ivancic.

We are extremely fortunate and thankful to have a loving, supportive family whom we cherish with all our hearts: Elsie Belding, Marie Manolukas, Joanna Neale, John Manolukas, Katy, Jamie and Joey Kline, Hal, Tao and Cecelia Neale, Howard Neale and little Howie.

For making the actual book production and publishing possible, our sincere thanks to Lightbourne Images, Gilliland Printing and Bleu Turrell for his awesome artwork. Thanks also to Dan Poynter, for helping us find our way through the labyrinth of the publishing world.

And finally, a special thanks to Julia and Ernesto for their magical inspiration.

With hope for a better world,
Heidi & Nick
Corvallis, Oregon
August 26, 1997

THE COMING OF A NEW MILLENNIUM

KNOSSOS
o
THE OLD CITY
o
THE POWERS THAT BE
o
SEEK AND YE SHALL FIND
o
A VOICE FROM THE PAST
o
HOPE FINALLY ESCAPES FROM THE BOX
o
FIRE ON THE MOUNTAIN
o
KEFTEA
o
THE MESSAGE

CHAPTER ONE
KNOSSOS

Two goats nibbled their way around the small whitewashed house, to a spot just under Zoee Nikitas' window. The little white one jumped up, stretched its neck way out, and with all its might tried to get the last purple clover peeking out through a crack in the wall. Its tiny bell ringled and jingled until she awoke. She flung the covers aside and started getting dressed, selecting her favorite crimson shirt and well worn blue jeans from the old oak armoire. She sat down in front of the mirror and gently combed her long, black curly hair. As she slowly worked out the knots and tangles, she looked herself straight in the eye. *Where will this excavation take us today? How far back in time?* Her deep brown eyes stared back.

Suddenly, that sensation of weightlessness welled up and surged through her again. The reflection faded away and scenes from her life appeared in the mirror – her Cretan grandparents at the church picnics along the Chicago lakefront, sailing into the sea-filled caldera of Santorini twenty years ago and seeing the ruins at Akrotiri, her first Minoan excavation, her recent discovery of the Knossos Cave – the memories glided simultaneously over the glass, each singing its part in melodious resonance. She could just barely see the rhythm, the current of dimmer, more distant images flowing swiftly beneath.

Her reflection returned and the images swirled away. When she came back into focus, she sat calmly for a moment, centering herself. She'd had similar experiences throughout her life, but recently, they'd become more frequent and much more intense. She took a long, slow, breath, and when she released it, a cloud of butterflies rose in her stomach, fluttering fast. They lifted her up and carried her out the door in their flurry; she barely managed to grab her jacket, tool kit and micro computer on the way.

A red-orange sun was just creeping over Mt. Ida's purple ridgeline as she walked past the taverna and down the quiet road. Fine silver mist rose from the vineyards and olive groves, glistening in the early rays, and a few high clouds glowed pink. She plucked an orange from her favorite roadside tree, peeled it, and savored the sweet citrus as she went.

She crossed through the empty parking lot, and even though the first of many tourist busses had not yet arrived, Yanni's souvenir stand was set up and ready to go. He sold everything, from sun glasses and sweatsocks, to miniature pithoi and King Minos ashtrays. His impressive collection of Greek worry beads were draped around the kiosk. She waved.

He held up a decorative plate with a sparkling Palace of Knossos emblazoned across the front and grinned. "Kali medda my friend, good morning!"

She walked over to him, and in her American Greek said, "Yanni, you have been trying to sell me this plate for three months. How can I convince you I don't want it?"

His eyes twinkled and he replied with a laugh, "you cannot. I can plainly see the spirit of Knossos is in your blood."

"That may be so, but I'm still not interested in the plate."

"We shall see."

"You keep trying, Yanni." She laughed, continuing on through a small grove of trees surrounding the entrance to the ruins. A cluster of little birds peeped wildly from some hidden perch in the branches right over Costa's head. There he was, opening up the gate as he'd done just about every day for the last fifty years. This short balding man had never said a word to Zoee, but today he tipped his cap and wished her good luck.

"It's a good day for it," he declared, picking up a coin from the dusty walkway.

"Thank you, Costa! Say, my associates will be here sometime this morning. Would you mind pointing them toward the dig?"

He nodded and waved her on.

She stepped through the gate and started across the broad, stone plaza, which rambled past the remnants of the once great palace. It had been uncovered and partially restored at the turn of the century, and today, the red and black pillars and reconstructed rooms rose like ghosts from the buried bricks and rubble. She'd excavated many ruins and caves throughout the Aegean, but she could hardly believe she was about to explore a new site so close to the heart of the Minoan civilization, in the back yard of the Palace at Knossos.

Though it existed over three millennia ago, its futuristic design and dazzling use of light, water, color and earth would be a fantastic work of architecture in any time. Set on a hill near the north shore of the island of Crete, Knossos was a crossroads between the continents and cultures of what became Europe, Africa and the Middle East.

The Classical Greeks believed it had been the center of a powerful kingdom ruled by King Minos, and the home of the dreaded Minotaur, a half man, half bull creature who lived in a vast underground labyrinth beneath the palace. As a tribute to Minos, every eighth year King Aegeus of Athens was forced to send seven girls and seven boys as sacrifices to the Minotaur, for as long as the beast was alive. One year, Aegeus sent his son Theseus, in the hope that he could slay the Minotaur and end their humiliation once and for all. King Minos' daughter Ariadne took one look at the boy and fell in love. She couldn't bear to lose Theseus to the horrible beast, so she made him a deal: she'd help him complete his task if he promised to take her with him. He readily agreed. She gave him a ball of thread and told him to fasten one end to the labyrinth entrance, and let it unravel as he combed the hellish maze. He searched the winding pathways, found the Minotaur and slew it with his sword, then followed the magic thread safely back into the light of day.

Theseus and Ariadne fled the palace, narrowly escaping King Minos' legion of soldiers. They ran for the harbor, found his ship and set sail for Athens immediately. Unfortunately, Theseus' love for Ariadne was not undying, and he deserted her on the island of Naxos on his way home. But woe, in his haste, he forgot to lower the black sail and raise the white as a sign to his father he'd survived his Herculean task. Upon seeing the black sail, King Aegeus threw himself into the sea in misery, thinking his son was dead.

Zoee believed there was a kernel of truth in the old Greek myths, but she also knew they were written 1,000 years after the Minoans had vanished. Through archeology, she could go beyond the tales and interpret the past from the artifacts themselves. The statuary, frescoes, pottery and architecture painted a very different picture of this lost civilization.

She moved on past the ruins and started down a gentle slope. Dew drops sparkled on the field of dark green brush, and course dirt crunched beneath her feet. Up ahead, a morning dove landed on a limestone boulder and welcomed her with a "coo."

At the sound of its song, she froze in her tracks. For an instant, she was surrounded by a dense grove of lush green trees. A creek bubbled through a cavern far beneath her feet, and bright sunlight illuminated giant green ferns. The dove was perched on a knobby old oak nearby. When it cooed once again, it broke the spell, returning to the limestone boulder.

"No wait!" she called out. But the trees disappeared and she was back on the rocky hillside, staring at the small gray bird.

"Coo!"

"Thank you Bird, for bringing me a glimpse," she said, trying to ground herself. "What more can you show me today?"

The dove just blinked and flew away.

"That's okay, Bird." She looked past the big rock to the dig site, which at this point was nothing more than a roped-off area thirty feet in diameter. "I know where the answers lie. Down there, in that cave."

"Kali medda!" a low voice resounded from behind.

She spun around to see Vasilios, a husky, middle-aged Greek with a bushy graying mustache. He was an old friend who'd been her crew leader on digs throughout the islands. As usual, he was dressed in his traditional Cretan attire – a black sailor's cap, black shirt and black knee-high leather boots.

"So, today is the big day!" he said, setting down his equipment and giving her a big kiss on both cheeks. "And the sea has brought a fresh, warm wind. It is a good sign!"

"It's a great sign!" she agreed, hugging the burly man.

"That's the spirit, Zoee." He patted her shoulder. "Now, let's get to work. The rest of the crew is on their way. I have a few more things to get from my truck, but I will be back shortly."

He soon returned with five local men, who were loaded down with pickaxes, shovels and assorted digging gear. A large canvas worktent teetered on two bouncing wheelbarrows, and a rattling pile of metal furniture was precariously lashed to a third. The whole rambling mass came clambering down the hill, chattering loudly over the din.

One of the crew yelled, "Zoee!"

Another waved, and shouted his good morning greeting. "Kali medda, Professor!"

"It's a wonderful morning!" she called back. "Welcome!"

They put down their stuff, and one by one, greeted her with

wholehearted hugs.

"Now we can begin," Vasilios boomed. He barked out some directions and the crew began their tasks.

Seven feet of compacted earth blocked the entrance to the cave, and even though the X-rays revealed no artifacts, Zoee wanted to be cautious. So they started with the picks, carefully loosening and sifting through the soil....

Only three months had passed since she confirmed the cave's existence, and in that time she'd been able to secure funding and assemble a highly qualified team. Dr. Nizam Adalat was a veteran, having worked in the region for over 40 years. He'd spent his life studying the cultures of recent prehistory, focusing on the period between 10,000 and 1500 b.c.e. And though he'd been raised and educated in England with his mother's family, his professional interests led him east, to the Neolithic site of Catal Huyuk in his father's homeland of Turkey. From there, he went on to explore sites throughout the Mediterranean, including the Minoan dig at Akrotiri. Shortly thereafter, he completed one of his doctoral dissertations on Minoan frescoes, and became renowned for his *Catalogue of Minoan Pottery*. Dr. Adalat was also Professor Emeritus at Oxford.

Zoee felt honored when he'd asked to be part of her team, but she couldn't figure out why he was so motivated to be involved. He certainly didn't need another feather in his cap at this point in his career. She'd read his books and heard him lecture on a number of occasions, but she'd only met him once, at a conference in Athens last year.

On the other hand, Dr. Fiona Deegan had been one of her closest friends and colleagues for 15 years. They met on a dig at Sesklo in northern Greece when they were grad students, and from the very beginning, they knew they were birds of a feather. Over the years, they'd attended conferences and symposia together and collaborated on a number of digs. Fiona had become an expert on the cultures of Old Europe. Through her research, she'd established that a thriving transcontinental civilization existed throughout Europe between 7000 and 1500 b.c.e. Like Zoee, she had successfully broken into the archeological establishment, challenging long held assumptions and interpreting data with a fresh eye.

They'd be here any time now.

"How are ya' keepin' Dr. Nikitas?" rang a familiar Irish voice.

"Have we missed anything?"

Zoee whirled around to see the tall woman with unruly red curls coming down the hill. She was so excited, she ran over and hugged Fiona enthusiastically, without noticing the reserved Dr. Adalat following a few yards behind.

"Hullo, *Doctor* Nikitas," said the elder man in a wide-brimmed hat, white shirt and khaki pants.

Zoee squeezed Fiona's arm and stepped forward to greet the imposing figure. "Dr. Adalat, it is my honor to welcome you to Knossos."

He softly grasped her outstretched hand, and shook it ever so gently. "The pleasure is mine."

"Ahh, Dr. Deegan," Vasilios boomed, walking over to greet them. "It is good to see you again!"

"How many times have I asked you to call me *Fiona*?" She smiled and patted his broad, solid shoulder. "I'm glad to see you too!"

"Vasilios," Zoee said after a moment, "I'd like to introduce you to Dr. Nizam Adalat. Vasilios Koulouris."

"Doctor," Vasilios nodded.

"Mr. Koulouris."

"Well, shall we begin?" Zoee said, as she started walking back toward the crew. "I haven't made any changes to the plans I sent you last month, so let me show you the site."

"Splendid," Dr. Adalat agreed.

"I was wishin' we could!" Fiona added excitedly.

Zoee introduced her colleagues to the crew and they spent a

few minutes walking around the grounds. Dr. Adalat nonchalantly wandered away from the others to survey the perimeter and compare the site area to his map.

"Enough of this looking around," Fiona announced. "I want to feel that Cretan Earth again. Where's my shovel Zoee?"

"Right next to mine."

The two women walked over to the worktent and when they were finally alone, Zoee put her arm around Fiona's shoulder and lowered her voice. "I'm so glad you're here, Fiona. It happened again, like at Sesklo, when we were brushing the dirt from that buried tile basin, and all of a sudden it was completely restored and filled with water..."

Fiona's eyes glazed over as she remembered the experience. "...and the candle light was surrounding us..."

"Yeah, but this time I was in a rainforest, surrounded by old, old trees."

"Jaysus," Fiona barely whispered. "When?"

"This morning, on my way here. I also had another one of those flashbacks just after I woke up today – more vivid scenes of my life."

"Are you all right?"

"Yeah, I'm fine. I'm *great*! And totally psyched we're exploring this cave together."

"Me too." Fiona gave her a squeeze, then picked up two shovels and handed one to her. "Looks as though we had better be getting started then!"

Zoee took it, smiling warmly at her dear friend.

They went back outside and joined Vasilios and the crew. The work was slow but steady as they sifted and hauled wheelbarrows full of rocky dirt. By midday, they'd gotten through several feet of compacted soil, with no sign of any artifacts. As expected, they reached a layer of volcanic ash, which then gave way to limestone boulders of various sizes. The pace started to pick up a bit as the crew removed stone after stone.

Dr. Adalat eventually emerged from the tent, and came over

to what was now a hole in the ground eight feet wide and five feet deep. Without saying a word, he picked up a full wheelbarrow and took it away to the rockpile. Zoee and Fiona took note, secretly exchanging expressions of surprise.

They worked together for another couple of hours, taking turns digging up and carting away the camouflage. Zoee remained in the hole throughout, picking and chipping out rocks. She'd been working on a small pointy one for about twenty minutes, trying to free it from the ground. She wiggled it back and forth, round and round, until it finally let loose. A cool, musty scent rose from an opening, pulling her closer in. She reached inside as far as she could and felt the hollow space. Then she turned her elbow, lowered her hand and touched the earthen floor.

Vasilios caught a whiff and leaned over her shoulder. "We're in. We're in!" he yelled, loud enough for the whole crew to hear.

Two of the workers dropped their picks, huddling around them, and Fiona, Dr. Adalat and the others appeared at the crater rim.

Zoee pulled back her arm and looked up at the expectant faces. "Yes! We're in!"

The team cheered and the crew waved their handkerchiefs in the air.

"And I think we're at the base of the cave. I felt the floor."

"Bravo, Zoee! Bravo," Vasilios exclaimed, kneeling down beside her. "Let me give you a hand."

One by one they coaxed the stones free and cleared the dirt away, until they opened a narrow portal to carry them into the darkness.

"We enter this long forgotten cave," Zoee said softly, looking at each of her colleagues, "with great respect for those who came before us. Okay. Light beams on low." She crouched down and looked into the seemingly endless void. *Here we go.* She carefully squeezed through, and slowly stood up. The walls of the cavernous limestone chamber began to take vague form in the dim light. As each of her three colleagues entered, the light level grew, bringing more definition to the inner space. Their eyes began to adjust, and a rectangular shape gradually materialized out of the course contour of the rock.

Fiona gasped, "the gateway to the inner chamber!"

They took a few steps closer, and an elaborate spiral emerged from a huge stone slab resting against the back wall.

Zoee cautiously approached the mammoth doorway and gently touched it, tracing her finger around the smooth curve of the spiral carving. *A coiled snake.*

"I would have expected a more sophisticated design," Dr. Adalat commented cynically.

"That would be a matter of opinion," Zoee countered, "but I think we can all agree, it's our first indication that this is a Minoan cave. What do you think Vasilios, how should we move the stone?"

"We will need harnesses and hydraulic lifts. It will take some time to prepare."

"Okay. Can you be ready by morning?"

"Of course. At the break of day."

"Looks like we'll wait till morning then. Good job, Vasilios. You and your crew have done excellent work today. You've taken us to the threshold!"

Dr. Adalat looked disturbed. "Forgive me, I do not mean to be presumptuous, but I see no reason to wait until tomorrow. We have the equipment we need, and it should not take more than a few minutes to remove the stone once the lifts are in place."

"And I see no reason to rush through," Zoee responded gently. "This slab is not going *anywhere.*" She patted the thick rock. "We've all had a long day and the crew needs a break. We'll begin again at dawn."

Dr. Adalat nodded reluctantly and started back toward the opening.

Outside the cave, a purple blue Cretan twilight bathed the ruins of Knossos, which seemed timeless in the disappearing light.

Zoee and Fiona stood together, drinking in the spirit of the ancient site, lost in their own thoughts – even Dr. Adalat paused to appreciate the beauty. They enjoyed the last few minutes of spectacular sunset, then gathered their gizmos, secured the site and headed out.

Several of the crew agreed to stay behind, provided of course that Tasso, the owner of a local taverna, would prepare a decent carry out and have it delivered. Zoee arranged for Fiona and Dr. Adalat to rent rooms nearby, so they all had a chance to drop off their stuff and have a cold shower before they met at Tasso's for dinner.

Tasso offers some of the area's best hospitality. He is fond of telling tourists, and reminding locals, that "you've tried the rest, now try the best!" One could always count on spirited discussion and great food. Vasilios headed straight there.

"Yassou, Vasilios," Tasso boomed. "Tikannes?"

"I am well, Tasso," he replied, heading for his favorite table in the corner. "How are you my good friend?"

"Ehh, what's the use for complaining? Can I pour you some raki before dinner?" He was already halfway to the table with a large carafe.

Vasilios nodded appreciatively. "It's been a good day. We broke through!" He lifted his glass, took a sizable swig and dramatized the day for his friend.

About ten minutes later, Zoee walked in. "Ah, Professor, come in come in," Tasso said with a welcoming grin. "I hear you made it through. Bravo! Some raki to celebrate? Tonight, I'm pouring my finest blend." He handed her a glass and directed her to sit across from Vasilios.

"You're really pushing the raki tonight, Tasso," Vasilios quipped.

"Thanks," Zoee replied. "I'd love a little."

Vasilios raised his refilled glass and made a toast. "Yassou Zoee! May we have good fortune on this dig!"

She lifted her glass. "Yassou!" They clinked a hearty clink and she took a long, refreshing drink. "So Vasilios, has Nizam Adalat changed much since those Akrotiri days?"

Vasilios sat back and took a deep breath. "The year was 1967, and I remember it well. It was a very exciting time. Marinatos' discovery of the ancient Minoan site ignited the archeological world, and Nizam Adalat was one of the archeologists chosen to assist. His presence caused a tremendous uproar in the village. Though his professional reputation was not questioned, his heritage was – who was this Turk with a British accent, strolling in here as if he owned the place? Could he be trusted? We had all been taught to hate the Turks for the crimes of their forefathers. As you well know Zoee, our ancestors suffered terribly at the hands of the Turkish Empire for hundreds of years, and many could not let go of that hatred. But I could not hold on to it – I see no purpose to hate if we ever want to live in peace and enjoy the gift of life. Though I must be honest with you, regardless of the old vendettas, I still didn't like him. I have become a great admirer of his work over the years, but I found him to be a pompous, arrogant ass then, and he still seems too full of himself now."

"I'm hoping he'll come around."

"We will soon find out." Vasilios nodded toward the taverna door.

Zoee turned around to see Fiona and Dr. Adalat just coming in. "Hello!" she said, rising to greet them. "Please, join us."

"This place reminds me of the last time we were together, Zoee," Fiona said, turning a few heads as she crossed the taverna, "two years ago in New York. Remember, we went to that Greek restaurant to get into the spirit of the conference, and ended up discussing the legend of Atlantis all night?"

"It was all your fault," Zoee said, as the three of them sat down and two more glasses appeared. *You're* the one who ordered that second bottle of retsina..."

"Atlantis?" interrupted Nikos, an old local who was playing backgammon with a group of village men. "I hope you archeologists have finally realized what we on the island have always known. The legend of Atlantis is the story of our island ancestors. Call them what you want, Minoans, Atlanteans, Cretans – they're all the same."

Dr. Adalat smiled at the elderly man. "What do you mean, sir?"

Fiona looked at Zoe and shrugged. "Off we go again!"

Like many old Greeks, Nikos had a flair for the art of storytelling. He rose from his chair to take center stage, as the community spirit of a Greek taverna and the raki began to work their subtle magic. In his heavily accented English, he continued on.

"I mean exactly what I say. The legend of Atlantis is the story of the Minoan people. We learn this through the writings of Plato, who tells us of an enchanted island, a paradise of artistic achievement and magnificent architecture. A fantastic place, where whatever sweet fruit and fragrant flowers grow now upon our Earth, whatever roots and potent herbs, and essences we distill, grew and thrived in that wondrous land."

He paused dramatically, making sure he had everyone's attention.

"For thousands of years, people throughout the Mediterranean and throughout the world have been telling this story. Then, along came Schliemann, Sir Arthur, my good friend Spyridon Marinatos and all the rest of you archeologists. You were fascinated by the old stories, so you came with your picks and shovels and began digging up our old cities. As you uncovered our ancient world, you created your *own* constantly changing stories. The Minoan civilization, the Royal Palaces, the wealthy, powerful kings who commanded powerful navies, et-cetera, et-cetera, et-cet-era.

"It is obvious your stories are the same ones Plato wrote down 500 years before Christ was born. Some of the names and interpretations have changed, but you are all talking about the same people and the same place. I prefer to tell it this way."

Nikos took a hardy sip of raki before launching off again. "*Millions* of years ago, just ninety kilometers north of here, a volcanic island broke through the metallic blue waters of the Aegean Sea. The lava gurgled and boiled, spewing forth layer upon layer of new Earth, until a great cone rose up a mile high in the sky. Eventually, the wind and the sea brought life. Great forests grew, flowers bloomed and the swallows drank the sweet nectar. When it reached its most glorious point, our ancestors named it Kalliste – the beautiful one.

"They made the island their home. They became artisans and architects, and developed a gentle, yet sophisticated civilization which spread throughout the Aegean. They lived in three-story houses, painted with beautiful pictures from floor to ceiling. They even had indoor plumbing," he added with a particularly satisfied look on his face. "They were a peaceful, seafaring people who traded throughout the Mediterranean for *thouuuusands* of years – until their world exploded. As Plato said, it was swallowed up by the fearsome sea in a single day of great misfortune.

"The most cataclysmic event the world has ever seen occurred at the height of their magnificent civilization. Kalliste erupted with such force, the island was completely destroyed. Its cities were buried under ash, and tidal waves raced across the sea. The volcanic cloud spread death and darkness for hundreds of miles...and the swallow never returned," he concluded sadly, sitting back down.

"Atlantis is just a mythical place in the *Atlantic* ocean," some North American tourist piped up. "That's why Plato called it *Atlantis*."

Nikos dismissed the argument out of hand. "Plato confused being far away in time with being far away in space. Remember, he was writing about Kalliste more than 1,000 years after its destruction."

The tourist still looked skeptical, so Nikos pointed to Zoee. "If you do not believe me, ask the experts."

She took her cue.

"I can't tell you why he called it Atlantis, but I can tell you that what we've found in this region fits Plato's descriptions of an artistic and sophisticated culture. And like Atlantis, Kalliste, now called Santorini, erupted and was completely destroyed in a single day. This explosion was many, *many* times more powerful than Mt. St. Helens or Mt. Pinatubo. When Kalliste blew, it ejected a tremendous amount of rock, creating a giant hole deep in the Earth's crust. What was left of the volcano collapsed in on itself, and essentially sank to the bottom of the sea. I think it's highly possible Nikos is correct."

"Well, we went to the British Isles last year, and they all believe it's in the Atlantic Ocean," the tourist insisted.

"Well, you know," Fiona interjected, "I believe that's true. The people of Ireland have a legend about Atlantis, and they do place it in the Atlantic Ocean. But I believe this tradition has its roots here, in Greece. I've recently found evidence to suggest there was an influx of people from Asia Minor into Ireland within a few years of the eruption. They probably brought their tale with them."

"Well, we could go on with this again for hours and hours," Zoee winked at Nikos, "but I think it's time I propose a toast."

They lifted their glasses.

"Welcome! Thank you all for joining me here, on this beautiful island of Crete. I can't quite explain it, but since discovering this cave three months ago, I've been sensing this expedition will reveal extraordinary insights into this ancient world, and into ourselves. May tomorrow fulfill our wildest hopes and dreams!"

"Yassou! Bravo!" came the cheers from around the table, as each took a drink.

Even Dr. Adalat raised his twice filled glass. "Here, here!" Then, to everyone's surprise, he stood up and announced he would also like to propose a toast. "My deepest thanks to our hosts here in Crete, and to all the Greek people who have extended their festive hospitality to me over the years. It is a beautiful land, with a beautiful legacy in your Minoan ancestors." He looked at

Nikos. "And thank you sir, for your delightful account of their splendid civilization – from which we have much to learn. Drs. Nikitas and Deegan, Mr. Koulouris, my sincere gratitude for allowing me to participate in this event. To us all!"

The four enthusiastically brought their glasses together again, and Vasilios nodded approvingly. "To us all!"

Tasso soon came out with several loaves of crusty bread, a dish of thick, creamy, garlicky yogurt dip, stuffed grape leaves, and a tomato and cucumber salad in olive oil, lemon, dill and oregano. After the appetizers, a crispy spinach phyllo pie and a velvety eggplant mousakka appeared. The food was delicious and it just kept coming. They ate and they drank, and they ate and they drank, then Nikos picked up his bazoukia.

As he plucked the first few notes of Zorba the Greek, the sound shot straight to Vasilios' soul. He rose dramatically from the table, lifted both arms wide and began moving to the rhythm. "Ella! Ella!" he invited the whole taverna. "Come, join me, we must have a dance together to ensure good luck tomorrow. It's simple. Just follow my steps, then let the music take over."

Zoee and Fiona joined his hand and he danced them out to the patio. The air was mild and a little salty, and geraniums glowed silver red in the light of the rising full moon. Local Cretans, young and old, followed them without hesitation. Finally, even Dr. Adalat and the skeptical tourist couldn't resist the lure.

Vasilios pulled a red handkerchief from his boot and snapped it loudly in the air. "Ooooohpaaaah!" he sang, twisting the dancing thread in circles, spirals and figure eights – a ritual as old as the stars up high. He threw his head back and saw Taurus the Bull, leaping across the sky. The Bull looked back and dipped his horns, winking with the bright red star of his eye. Orion the Hunter pursued from the east, as Taurus ran toward the horizon....

The Zodiac sailed through the stillness of Night, till Virgo rose with Dawn. She sprinkled her light over Zoee, whispering, "awaken!"

Sun was just about up when Zoee reached the dig. She carefully climbed down the short rope ladder into the crater, and out of the corner of her eye, saw a bright light escaping out of the borough. She approached slowly, crawled through and found Vasilios and the crew securing the last of the harnesses around the massive stone. "Morning everyone!"

"Good morning Zoee! Kali medda," the crew welcomed her enthusiastically.

"Kali medda Zoee," Vasilios echoed. "We are just about ready. The lifts are in place and the stone is secure."

"Right on schedule. I appreciate *all* of your excellent work," she said, acknowledging each of the crew.

"Don't you start without me!" Fiona yelled from the crack in the rocks.

"Wouldn't dream of it," Zoee assured her, laughing.

Vasilios stepped a few feet back and aimed the remote control at his contraption.

"I'd like to wait for Dr. Adalat to arrive, Vasilios."

"No need to wait at all," Dr. Adalat said excitedly, as he squeezed through the narrow opening.

"Good morning, Doctor!" Zoee called out.

"Please, call me Nizam."

"Only if you call me Zoee."

"Agreed."

"Okay, Vasilios, whenever you're ready!"

He aimed the remote and the crew firmly took hold of the leather harness straps. "Okay, sigah sigah..."

The hydraulic lifts slowly raised the cyclopean stone, and the men carefully guided it away from the passage entrance.

"Bravo!" exclaimed Zoee. She tentatively moved toward the opening, and placed her hand on the cool limestone. She bowed her head, and silently asked, *Mother Earth, please allow us to enter this inner sanctum.* She patted the rock, held her breath and stepped through. Her cave light trickled down a ten-foot passage, and forms appeared on the walls.

"Frescoes!" she gasped. "The tunnel is completely covered with them, and they're intact. Antelopes, butterflies, birds and bees, cavorting in flowery plants and trees! This is fantastic!" She felt a tiny ripple of energy pass by in the surrounding space. "Jesus! A Linear A inscription! It leads down to a chamber at the bottom."

She cautiously led them down the broad greenstone steps, and into the inner chamber. It was about eight feet high, ten feet across and roughly circular. Tall red and white lilies were painted around the cave. In the center of the back wall, two golden bulls with long graceful horns attended a round marble chest, sparkling on the earthen floor between them. Five rock crystal lamps encircled the container, which stood about two feet high. As they tip toed closer, their beams illuminated a glittering gemstone butterfly inlaid on the lid.

Fiona clutched Zoee's arm. "It's magnificent!"

"Incredible," whispered Nizam. "The lamps are from the New Palace Period, but I've never seen anything like this vessel. It appears to have a removable lid!"

"Yes. It does," agreed Zoee, after analyzing it closely. "What do you think, Vasilios? Can we safely remove it?"

He scrutinized the artifact with an engineer's eye. "As long as we're careful, I don't see why not."

Zoee and Vasilios each firmly grasped it. As her fingers touched the cool stone, she thought she heard Echo singing, *set sail!* "Oh-kay. On the count of three. Enna, thio, tria."

They lifted it ever so slowly, and gently set it on the floor of the cave. Once it was safe in gravity's care, the four of them knelt around the archive and peered inside.

"It's a Linear A tablet!" Zoee whispered. She gingerly reached in, and carefully removed the marble disc. A long, gemstone snake spiraled around the stone, and in between each coil, were the symbols in gold relief. For a moment, they went out of focus and swirled toward the center of the tablet – a whirling vortex pulling her closer inward. In her heart she knew this was the key.

She gently passed it to Vasilios, who said a silent prayer and kissed the stone. He handed it to Nizam, who rested it on his lap and gently touched the inscription with his long, slender fingers. When Fiona received the tablet, she contemplated its delicate symbols, slowly rotating the disc in each direction. She then passed it back to Zoee.

"Here's a symbol I don't recognize, and here's another one! I need to get these into my database right away."

"You go on," Fiona suggested. "I'm going to have a look around here. See ya' later so!"

"Me too," Nizam agreed. "These frescoes are calling to me."

"I will go tell the crew of this stupendous find!" Vasilios announced enthusiastically.

Zoee carefully carried the tablet out of the depths of Earth and into the light of Day.

She placed the elegant disc on the worktent table, wishing the stone voices would speak. She'd been trying to decipher Linear A for almost a decade, extensively analyzing each of the 358 small stone and clay fragments which had preserved the ancient script. By comparing the 73 known characters to other ancient languages, she was able to create a series of five decryption matrices. She'd run the program a number of times and she knew she was close – if she could only find a few missing characters.

She stared into the tablet and scrutinized each one, counting a total of eleven she didn't recognize. Then she started again from the beginning. She came across a string of three characters and was suddenly stopped by a flash of understanding. Something about an emergence, she thought, tracing her finger over them. She quickly set up her micro computer, and using a hand held scanner, loaded the text into her database.

With a few more keystrokes, she logged on to the Yale University mainframe, downloaded the text file and ran her application. Her matrices appeared on the screen, and the Linear A characters streamed by, cycling through, cycling through....

The indicator light finally stopped flashing. "C'mon! Let's

see it!" she said out loud, as words appeared on the screen.

WE ARE THE PEOPLE OF KEFTEA....

Then, without warning, a diamond of light appeared in front of the screen. It suddenly expanded, completely engulfing her, and the words became a vague impression on her mind.

A harmonic ringing saturated the air, and Nizam and Fiona came scrambling out of the cave and up the ladder. They could see Zoee surrounded by an oval of light. Waves of energy emanated from the phenomenon, pulsating through them.

"What is it?" Nizam yelled.

"I haven't the faintest idea!" Fiona yelled back.

"We've got to save Zoee!" Vasilios cried. But before they could do anything, the oval suddenly collapsed, flashing out of existence. "Zoee! Zoee!" he called out frantically.

"Good God in heaven, she's gone!" Fiona gasped, "and so is the tent!"

They looked at Nizam, who was shaking his head in astonishment. "She just vanished. Incredible. What could have happened to her?"

"Is she dead?" Fiona asked, as tears welled up in her eyes. Vasilios gently put his arm around her shoulder.

"Look," Nizam pointed, "the artifact appears to be unharmed." He cautiously approached it and saw the screen. "And her computer is intact. Good Lord!"

"What is it?" Vasilios asked, walking over with Fiona.

"See for yourselves."

They peered over Nizam's shoulder.

"Jaysus! She's deciphered the tablet!" Fiona exclaimed, wiping the tears from her face.

"Holy Mother of Jesus! She's cracked the code!"

Fiona read the words aloud, "WE ARE THE PEOPLE OF KEFTEA. WE RECORD OUR WAY OF LIFE SO OUR DESCENDANTS MAY KNOW HOW WE LIVED...."

The three of them huddled around as Nizam scrolled down the screen. They continued reading the text, until the flash of a camera broke their train of thought.

Vasilios whirled around to see a wave of tourists descending upon them. "It's going to be a mob scene here in a matter of minutes!"

"We've got to protect the tablet," Nizam declared. "If it falls into the wrong hands, we could be facing a Return of the Dead Sea Scrolls!"

"We could take it to my grandmother's village," Vasilios suggested. "It's not far, and I think it would be safe there."

"That's a good idea," Fiona concurred. "Why don't I just go with it then. But first," she grabbed a blank disc, "we must save Zoee's data. Let's send a copy to our e-mail addresses too, just in case."

"All right," Nizam agreed. "I'll stay here with the crew and protect the site."

Inside the light, Zoee felt curiously peaceful as the phenomenon surged through her. She saw her colleagues emerge from the cave, but then they vanished, and she felt herself moving forward. Images of galaxies and nebulae filled her mind, and points of colored light appeared in the glow around her. They raced by, faster and faster, streaking together, becoming lines which curved and twisted, forming endless and self-similar shapes. She felt herself being swept up in the patterns, merging with the currents of the Cosmos.

CHAPTER TWO
THE OLD CITY

Amidst the glass and steel skyscrapers of New Jerusalem, a single date palm thrust upward from a square hole in the concrete sidewalk, its fronds rustling in a gentle breeze. A tall Arab-American woman with jet black hair leaned against the tree, soaking up the rays of morning sun as they danced across her face. She reached inside the pocket of her dark blue jacket, and retrieved a well-worn journal, turning to her last entry for the hundredth time:

December 17, 1999 - I saw Grandmother again in my dream last night. As I lay sleeping in my uncle's house, she gently touched my arm and whispered in my ear, "Shayda my dear, wake up! Come with me. I must show you something!" I slowly got up and she hurried me along. "Come. Come, we cannot be late," she said, opening my bedroom door. As we stepped through, the hallway transformed into a floor of solid gold, and all of a sudden,

we were standing beside the huge minaret on top of the Dome of the Rock! I could see the Old City below, and the mountains and the sea off in the distance.
   "You must come here as soon as you can," she said to me, squeezing both of my hands.
   "Why, Grandmother?" I asked. "What am I supposed to do?"
   "When the time comes, you will know," she answered, just before she vanished.
   I can still hear her voice in my mind. So real. And compelling. How can I not go?

   December 18 - And now I'm here, in Jerusalem, she wrote. *I don't know what I'm going to find in the Old City, so I guess I'll just have to go wherever the desert wind blows. Here comes the bus.*

   The city bus pulled up and everyone filed on. Shayda slipped the journal into her inside pocket, slung her hand-woven Persian bag over her shoulder and stepped up. The bus was packed with dozens of people in contemporary western dress, and a few who could have lived in biblical times; most were speaking Hebrew. There was one vacant seat in the back, next to two other women. One of them wore a starburst tie-dyed shirt and faded blue jeans ripped in both knees. The other was dressed in a heavy linen outfit and sported black tortoise shell sun glasses. She guessed they were both Americans.
   Shayda took the seat and when there was a break in their conversation, she chimed in. "I'd bet you're from New York," she said to the one with the glasses.
   "You got that right," the woman replied, peering over her frames.
   "But I don't recognize your dialect," she said to the other one. "Where are you from?"
   "Oregyn, sort of. How 'bout you?"
   "Dearborn, Michigan." Like any self-respecting Michigan-

der, she lifted her left hand and pointed to a spot near her thumb. "It's right here," she said, as if it were obvious her hand resembled the Lower Peninsula. "Well, it's nice to meet you New York and Oregahhn, my name is Shayda."

"I'm Simone," said the New Yorker.

"And I'm Regina."

"Are you two traveling together?"

Regina piped up. "Nope, we just met on this bus. I got in from Rome yesterday, and Simone here just spent the last six months on a kibbutz."

"Yeah," Simone confirmed. "What's your story?"

"I've been visiting relatives."

"Where do they live?" Regina asked.

"Jordan, but we're originally from Iran."

"When did you leave Iran?"

"In 1979."

"Were you fleeing the Ayatollah Khomeni?" asked Simone.

"Yes. We fled Tehran shortly after he came to power. My family was persecuted because we practiced Sufism – Islamic mysticism. When Khomeni's fundamentalists," she felt a knot tighten in her throat, "murdered my grandmother, we escaped across the desert into Pakistan. My two uncles went to Jordan and my parents took us to the U.S."

"How old were you?" Regina asked, visibly stunned.

"Eighteen."

Regina shook her head. "I can't even imagine that."

"Seems like we're always fleeing some oppression, doesn't it?" Simone said sadly. "My grandparents escaped Hitler's Nazis when my dad was a kid. They had to go into hiding for three months before they could get across the border into Switzerland. From there, they went to New York. They were luckier than most...."

"How 'bout your mom's side Simone?" asked Regina.

"They came from Russia in the mid-1800s. Where's your family from?"

"Ireland. My grandparents left in the 1840s, to escape the famine. They ended up in Chicago – there's a huge Irish Catholic community there. When I turned eighteen, I fled out West and never went back."

As the bus passed from the New City into the Old City, it seemed to pass through time. In a matter of minutes, the wide boulevards and highrises of modern Jerusalem gave way to the narrow, crowded streets and stone buildings of antiquity.

"It's hard to believe," Simone finally said, "that we come from the three cultures which have been killing each other here for thousands of years." She looked out the gritty bus window.

"Yeah," agreed Regina. "I guess being American kinda separates us from the old fights."

Shayda looked around the bus. "And most people forget how similar our traditions really are."

"Yeah," Simone agreed. "I seem to remember that Christians, Muslims and Jews *all* believe Jerusalem is the naval of the Earth."

"Until Mohammed moved it to Mecca," Shayda laughed, pausing a moment to think about it. "Isn't it interesting? The navel is the place where the umbilical cord attaches us to our mothers, yet these three religions revere an all-powerful male god. Makes you wonder what came before, huh?"

"Well, what did come before?" Regina asked.

Before Shayda could respond, the bus pulled up to the Jaffa Gate, one of the six ancient entrances into the Old City.

"Sorry to leave you hanging," Shayda apologized, "but I'm getting off here."

"Well, so are we," Regina said.

The three women grabbed their packs and got off. It was a glorious mid-December day – the sky was clear, and the morning sun cast a warm, golden light across the jumble of limestone walls and buildings behind the massive gate.

As Shayda looked through the archway, her eyes were drawn past the minarets and steeples to the gilded Dome of the Rock, shimmering like a floating egg of light. Just like in her dream.

She could hear the call of the muezzin rising above the din, summoning the men to prayer. She retrieved her micro digicam from her colorful bag and started taping. As a rule, she tried to capture the essence of a place without boring her viewers with hours of rambling video. So she periodically took snippets of carefully selected scenes.

She took a nice wide shot of the top of the gate, and as she brought the camera down, Simone was walking through. She punched up her title and "The Old City – Here We Go" appeared over the Dome, waiting for her off in the distance.

As she was putting the camera away, she noticed Regina, standing with her back to the gate, staring up toward the Mount of Olives – the place where Jesus ascended to heaven. After a moment, Regina turned back around and faced the gate, then took a deep breath and stepped through. Shayda followed her in.

The sounds and smells of a noisy bazaar erupted around them. Little shops lined both sides of the crowded narrow street, and they sold everything – from beautiful replicas of Byzantine icons and fine silk garments, to mass produced crucifixes, plastic shields of David and blacklight posters of Mohammed on his flying horse.

Tourists haggled with local shopkeepers, trying in vain to get a little better deal on their souvenirs. A herd of Franciscan Monks dressed in hooded brown frocks slowly walked past them, their long rope belts swinging hypnotically with each measured step. Two Orthodox Jews in long black coats and tall hats were arguing passionately, thrusting their index fingers in each other's face. An Arab woman draped in black glared at them disapprovingly, before darting into a doorway. A group of colorfully dressed Ethiopians glided gracefully through the crowd.

Suddenly a young, anglo man emerged out of the throng and began shouting, "I'm John the Baptist, let me cleanse your sins! I'm John the Baptist, let me save your soul!"

When he finally moved on, Shayda joked, "if he's John the Baptist, then why does he sound like he's from Ypsilanti?"

"He's probably suffering from Jerusalem Syndrome," Simone

explained matter of factly.

The other two looked skeptical.

"No, it's true. It's a common occurrence in Jerusalem. People come here on vacation or on a pilgrimage, and presto, they become characters from the Bible. He was probably raised in a very religious household in some sprawling American suburb."

Regina looked incredulous. "You gotta be kiddin' me."

"No, I'm not. The Kfar Shaul Hospital treats hundreds of them every year. Most of them come around after a few days."

"They must be tripping."

"I think they are," Shayda said with a laugh. "It's just a question of their substance of choice. No doubt some of them smoked a big houka of hash and took off on their magic carpets. But, as we can see, some are definitely getting off on the Gospel of St. John."

They continued down David Street marveling at the sights until they came to a fork in the road. Shayda looked at her map. "We're here at the corner of David Street and Suq el-Lahhamin. I'd like to go to the Dome of the Rock, what about you two?"

"I was plannin' to see the Church of the Holy Sepulcher."

"I'm going to the Western Wall. No doubt they're each in a different direction."

"You got it. Do we split up or stay together?"

"Let's stick together!" exclaimed Regina. "We can go to all three places."

"It would be more interesting that way."

"We're agreed then," Simone announced.

"I have an idea," Shayda suggested. "Let's see the oldest places first. We can visit the Western Wall, the Church of the Holy Sepulcher and then finish up at the Dome of the Rock."

They meandered through the narrow old streets, slowly making their way to the security checkpoint which guarded the entrance to the Western Wall. Being a New Yorker well accustomed to waiting on line, Simone always came prepared with reading material. Today she just happened to have a brief history of the Wall, which she read out loud.

"In the twentieth year of the current era, Herod was King of Judea, at that time a minor tributary of the Roman Empire. During his rule, he completely fortified and renovated the Old City, building theaters, stadiums, harbors and other monuments to the Empire. He also extensively refurbished the Second Jewish Temple, constructing the Western Wall as a buttress.

"However, this small token of philanthropy did not make up for the excessiveness of Roman exploitation. By the year 66, Jews had had enough oppression, and this minor tributary was overflowing with rebellion. A spirit of freedom was in the air and the Great Revolt ensued. The Roman Emperor Titus sent in 60,000 troops to end the rebel uprising, and four years later his army broke through the Herodian walls of the Old City and destroyed the Second Temple. All that remains is the Western Wall." Simone closed the guidebook, but continued.

"For almost two thousand years, Jews have been lamenting the Temple's destruction, and praying for its restoration. Jews believe the Messiah will someday appear and the Jewish Holy Temple will rise for a third time, bringing with it peace throughout the world. However, the Islamic Dome of the Rock was built right on top of the Temple ruins, and its destruction would most definitely not bring peace."

"Maybe someday the Dome will be big enough to have a Jewish temple within it," Shayda responded optimistically.

"Hey, you might as well put a Christian church in there too. After all, the place is sacred to Christians – Jesus taught and worshipped there."

"Good idea," agreed Simone. "For the sake of peace, all three religious faiths should be represented."

"Do you think it's possible?" wondered Regina.

"Given the history, it doesn't seem likely," replied Simone. "But who knows? If we don't at least have hope, we may as well just bang our heads against the Wall."

"That's right," Shayda said. "And let's not forget, Israel has signed peace treaties with Egypt, Palestine *and* Syria. There was a time when no one believed that was possible."

At last they reached the front of the line. Several young Israeli soldiers frisked them with metal detectors, searched their bags and waived them through. They entered the crowded stone plaza and were immediately confronted with the colossal Western Wall, towering 70 feet high and stretching over 1,000 feet long. Ten layers of mammoth Herodian stones supported 20 layers of smaller Byzantine and Ottoman bricks. And that was only half of it! The other half was still buried under thousands of years of rubble. Along the top, a line of Israeli flags flapped in the unusually warm winter wind, and military sharpshooters crouched on nearby rooftops, peering through binoculars.

A sturdy metal barrier separated the plaza, dividing the worshippers by gender – men prayed on the left side and women on the right. Many of the male devotees were wearing the distinctive clothing of their 17th century eastern European ancestors – black overcoats, black fur hats, black woolen knickers and white stockings. Some of them had long, untrimmed beards and sidecurls, and quite a few were bobbing to and fro, chanting and reciting psalms in their trancelike state. One carried a beautifully decorated Torah scroll high above his head and others reached up to touch it. An old man, with a hunched back and sweet face raised a ram's horn to his lips and blew. The long, low note lingered in the air.

They wandered into the plaza, and Regina noticed a small group of people gathered around a rabbi. "Hey Simone, is that a bar mitzvah over there?"

"Looks like a bat mitzvah."

"*Bat* mitzvah?"

"Yeah. A young woman is participating in the ritual. I've heard a lot of wealthy American Jewish families have their children mitzvahed at the Wall."

"Did you go through the ritual?" asked Shayda.

"No. We almost never went to temple, except for special

events like weddings and funerals. My parents are both Jewish, but they're not very religious in the traditional sense. They do have a very close group of friends who've been getting together for years for their own Friday night seders. Most of these people are involved in some aspect of the performing arts, so you can imagine how the old stories get a new twist. That's how I got into acting.

"My twin sister Celeste, on the other hand, rebelled. She moved to Crown Heights and became part of the Hasidic community – an ultra orthodox sect which takes it way too far if you ask me. We've hardly had any contact since she made that choice; she won't have anything to do with me. I thought if I could learn more about Judaism, I'd be able to understand her decision and find some common ground. That's partly why I came here to live in a religious kibbutz."

"What was that like?" Regina wondered.

"It was, a learning experience. I studied hard and worked hard, and the communal atmosphere was positive. People really supported each other. There was a strong sense of community, but I must admit, I never really felt like I was part of it. I wasn't comfortable with all of the religious ritual and custom. Though I must say, there was a small group of women at the kibbutz who I did feel comfortable with. They believe the Halakhah, Jewish religious law, should be reinterpreted. They argued Halakhah is and always has been an organic, adaptable law, which is constantly changing with the surrounding culture. It strives for balance between the needs of the community and the needs of the individual. I believe in what they're trying to do, but they've encountered a lot of resistance. It'll take way too long to see significant change, and I don't have the patience.

"But for some reason, here I do feel part of the greater Jewish tradition. I look at that Wall and I see a place where thousands, if not millions, have come to offer hopeful prayers."

Just then a gust of wind blew through the plaza, dislodging a tiny scrap of paper from a crevice in the Wall. It shot high up into the air, did a couple of loop de loops, and gracefully drifted back down toward them. Simone reached out her hand and plucked it from thin air.

"Nice catch," Shayda said.

Simone read the Hebrew letters scrawled on the small wrinkled paper. "It says Shalom. Peace. Somebody offered a prayer for peace."

"Where did it come from?" Regina asked.

"The Wall," replied Simone. "It's sort of a mailbox to God. Jews write their prayers on paper and stick them in the cracks. They believe God is especially attentive to prayers here because this is where His Shekhinah, or Feminine Spirit, dwells. You'd probably guess there are companies in America who, for a nice price, will insert *personalized* messages for you."

They all laughed. Of course, it was a golden opportunity.

Simone reached into her satchel and pulled out a shiny piece of white linen paper neatly folded into a triangle. "This is the prayer I brought to put in the Wall. Would you like to read it?"

"Yeah!" replied Regina, taking the paper and carefully unfolding it. She held it out so Shayda could read it too.

Spirit of the Universe, I come to this Wall humbly mindful of the many who have come here to pray. I am only a link in that very long chain, but I am connected to it, part of it. I do lament the destruction of this temple, as I lament all destruction. Humanity has suffered terribly because of our hatred, dominance and greed, but it is my great hope that we can overcome the violence, and that peace and tolerance will one day prevail. I offer this prayer in memory of my dear Bubbie, who I miss so much. Please, hear our voices.

"That's beautiful, Simone," Shayda said, when she finished reading.

"Who's Bubbie?" Regina asked, handing her back the prayer.

"My grandmother. She always dreamed of coming to the Holy Land, but she died before she could make the journey. She always used to tell me that one day, I'd come and pray for the both

of us. Bubbie's been gone a long time now, and I still miss her...."
Simone's eyes misted over. "I'll be right back." She walked toward the special entrance marked for women, stopping at the shall stall on the way, to get a wrap to cover her shoulders and arms.

"Wanna go a little closer?" Regina asked.

"Sure."

As they approached the imposing structure, and the masses of people gathering, Shayda thought she could actually *feel* the messianic fervor around them. Intense, passionate voices rose, echoing off the gargantuan Wall, filling the air. They listened.

She pulled out her camera, and panned around the crowded plaza, past tour groups and supplicants, when a familiar form appeared in her screen. "Hey, there's Simone," she said into the mic. Simone waved, wiping away the last few tears, and Shayda faded out.

She faded back in on Regina, who was standing in front of the Church of the Holy Sepulcher, ready with her intro.

"This Church is built on the *very* spot where Jesus was crucified and where, three days later, he rose from the dead. Follow me and we'll go inside."

The aroma of myrrh wafted through the noisy basilica, crowded with hundreds of tourists, pilgrims, ministers, monks and priests. Chanters bellowed ancient hymns in voices ranging from horrendous to magnificent, and a dazzling array of Byzantine icons lined the walls.

Shayda resumed shooting, panning across the long row of icon stands, till suddenly, a waving middle-aged man filled her frame.

"Hello, my name is Demitri. Please, allow me to take you on a tour of the Church," he offered in his heavily accented voice.

Shayda stopped recording and put down the camera. "No, thank you."

"Ahh, but I can tell you about the Miracle of the Holy Fire," he persisted.

The three of them looked at each other and raised their eyebrows. Each had met numerous helpful guides throughout their travels.

He continued undaunted, "every year on Easter Sunday, the Holy Fire comes down from heaven and into the tomb of Christ. I have witnessed it myself many times. The priests say it is a supernatural sign marking the resurrection."

"How does it happen?" asked Regina.

"The Church is completely dark and filled with people anxiously waiting to see the Miracle. Inside the tomb, the Patriarch of the Greek Orthodox Church waits to receive the fire from God Himself. When it comes, the Holy Father lights a great torch and hands it out through a narrow opening in the wall. When they see the light emerge, the faithful rush forward to light their own candles. Within seconds, the whole Church is illuminated and everyone sings 'Christos Anesti,' which means Christ is Risen."

Simone looked skeptical. "And this happens *every* year?"

"Every year. Like clockwork."

"I'd like to see it."

"You will have to wait until Easter," he said with a wink.

"The Jews have a story like that. But it only happened *once*," she emphasized in Demitri's direction. "They believe a Holy Fire came down from heaven during the consecration of the First Jewish Temple."

"It's a common theme in many religions," Shayda explained. "Fire has often been used to link us to the spiritual world. Remember the Greek myth of Prometheus, who stole the flame from Zeus?"

"See what interesting discussion my comments have spurred?" Demitri announced with satisfaction. "Please, let me take you for a tour. It would be my pleasure and I assure you, you will not be disappointed."

They figured, what the hell.

"Okay," agreed Simone, "how much?"

"You give me what you think I deserve when we are done. Please, this way."

He led them toward the immense wall of icons. "In the Orthodox Christian church, icons are venerated for their symbolic connection to Christ."

As he spoke, an elderly woman approached the icon of the Virgin Mary and the infant Christ. She knelt down in front of the painting and began to pray.

"That woman is not worshipping the Virgin Mary, she is venerating Mary's *connection* to Christ."

"The Madonna and child," Shayda commented. "Oh, how the old symbols endure."

"What do you mean?" Simone asked.

"See how Mary holds the baby Jesus? It's a very old image which has appeared in many cultures. For example, Egyptian statuary shows the Goddess Isis holding her son Horus in her arms, just as Mary holds Jesus – and they were carved several thousand years before Christ was born."

"So, what are you saying?" asked Regina.

Demitri looked annoyed but Shayda continued anyway.

"Mary has her roots in the traditions of *many* older cultures. Fundamentally, however, she is another incarnation of the Great Mother Goddess, the central deity of our prehistory. To our ancestors, the Goddess was the Giver of Life; the Creatrix of All. She was the flowing energy of life itself from which everything came and to which everything returned. She was the manifestation of the mysterious forces of life, death and regeneration."

"So that's what you were getting at on the bus," commented Simone.

"Yes. The Goddess culture flourished for tens of thousands of years, peacefully spreading across the Middle Eastern, Mediterranean and Old European regions. Unfortunately, in the fourth millennium before Christ, the nomadic invasions began. Herders and hunters swept in from the cold hinterlands, bringing with them the gods of war. They worshipped the thunderbolt hurlers like Zeus, Jupiter and Yahweh, who ruled from the heavens above and claimed absolute power. The Goddess was displaced. Natural law was replaced by the law of conquest, and over many centuries, as the new order began to take hold, the old stories and symbols were changed to fit the new mythologies."

"What did they call the Goddess back then?" Regina asked.

"She had many names. The Sumerians knew her as Inanna or Ishtar; and the Babylonians called her Tiamat. Greek stories tell us of Hera, Gaia and Demeter. Jewish myth speaks of Eve, and to the Christians, she became Mary."

Demitri was nearly beside himself he was so uncomfortable. He raised his hands to interrupt the conversation. "I will hear no more of this. Goodbye." He walked away, shaking his head.

"So, what does it all mean?" Regina asked.

"It means the Goddess and her symbols have survived the millennia and are preserved in our religious stories," Shayda summed up quickly, not wanting to further monopolize the conversation.

"How do you know all this?"

"I'm a professor of comparative mythology at the University of Michigan."

"*That* explains it," Simone said, chiding her a little for her long windedness.

"Have you ever heard of Joseph Campbell?" Shayda didn't wait for an answer. "I was *really* lucky to be able to study under him. He wrote a whole *encyclopedia* of the mythologies of the world, and he spent his life analyzing the cultural and social patterns which have emerged over time. He believed the world was ready for a new mythology, perhaps one which could unite the entire planet."

"So who'll be the mythmakers this time?" wondered Simone.

"Good question."

Just then, the elderly woman who'd been praying to the Virgin let out a cry.

They all jumped at the high-pitched, piercing sound and

looked at the old, graying woman, dressed in black from head to toe. Her face was full of anguish and suffering as she wailed at the top of her lungs, the sound echoing across the basilica.

"I'll take *that* as a sign to move on," Simone said, looking a little spooked.

Regina got out a map of the inside of the church. "I suggest we go up these stairs. They should take us to Calvary, the place where Christ was crucified."

They followed her up the long steep stairs, and into the stark Franciscan Chapel. As they entered, they were confronted by a huge image of Christ being nailed to the cross. The Virgin Mary sadly looked on from another canvas.

Regina approached the altar and stared into the flame of a solitary candle. Without looking up she offered her prayer, speaking just loud enough for Shayda to hear. "Thank you for standing up for the ideals of peace, love and social justice, and for challenging oppression in the face of overwhelming odds. I'm so sorry you had to die for it," she paused. "The forces of greed have grown since your time, and it scares me for the future. But I'm grateful for your inspiration, it gives me strength. I will try hard to stand up for what's right, and continue the struggle."

She stepped away from the altar, and they quietly went next door to the Greek Orthodox Chapel, which marks the place where Christ died. In contrast to the Franciscan Chapel, this small room was ablaze with candle light, Byzantine paintings and gold. A dramatic portrayal of Christ on the cross dominated the room, and the Virgin Mary and baby Jesus again looked on.

Pilgrims filed in, lighting candles, kneeling and praying. A priest in a splendid gold-embroidered cloak walked through, swinging a clanky, smoky incense burner, to bless the icons and the people who came to worship. Regina took one look at the medieval image of Christ suffering on the cross, then bolted out the door and back down the stairs. The other two caught up with her near the Church entrance.

"Are you all right?" Shayda asked.

"No. I'm not. I'm sad for Christ's suffering and for all the people who suffered and died here. And I'm really pissed that Christ was murdered because he spoke up for the poor and challenged the religious leaders and the elite. He was just trying to make a more equal and just society, and it seems like his message has gotten totally lost."

"Maybe it's been pretty well buried, but not lost," Shayda said hopefully. "Look at Ghandi and Martin Luther King, Jr. They embraced Jesus' ideals of equality and justice through nonviolent action, and they've had a profound impact."

"Yeah, I know. It's just harder and harder to see."

"Do you want to take a break Regina?" Simone asked gently.

"No. I'm okay. Let's see the tomb – I wanna see it." She glanced at her map and motioned for them to follow.

A series of old stone arches led them through narrow halls, tiled with well worn mosaics. Long, bronze chandeliers hung low overhead, casting their flickering shadows across the smooth, ancient walls. The corridor widened a little, bringing them to a much taller archway, which finally ushered them into a cavernous rotunda, echoing with voices and sounds. Overhead, a brilliantly illuminated dome shrouded the majestic marble and gold mausoleum, resting before them in the center of the room. On either side of the tomb entrance, heavy gold pedestals held slender marble scrolls twenty feet high, and tiers of lighted candles arched over the glittering doorway. A large portrait of Christ rising from the dead rested on top of the Edicule. They slowly followed the black and white parquet floor inside.

Small candles illuminated the raised marble slab, covering the rock upon which Jesus' body had rested. *Out of death comes life*, Shayda thought to herself, touching the cool stone, *out of death comes life*.

At that moment, the old widow came in. She lit a candle, and made the sign of the cross three times, each time kissing the marble. She knelt down and began praying in a low soft voice. Her old, weathered face glowed magnificently in the candle light.

They stood quietly and watched as she slipped into another realm. Soon she began to cry, and then to wail again. Regina abruptly motioned for them to leave. As they walked out of the sepulcher, the old woman's wailing intensified, filling the rotunda with the sound of her pain. Regina just kept on going, until she was all the way outside the Church.

She turned to the others with tears in her eyes. "That's why I left the Catholic church – too much suffering and too much sorrow."

Simone put her arm around Regina's shoulder.

"I'm okay," she sniffed a couple times. "I'm okay. So, Shayda, I suppose people are always resurrecting from the dead in mythology, huh?"

"All the time! Just about every religion has a story about someone who overcomes death."

"What do you think they mean?"

"They remind us that death is not the end, but rather a natural part of the great cycle of life, death and rebirth. These stories are almost always linked to the changing of the seasons. That's why Jesus is born at the cold, dark time of the Winter Solstice, when the sun is just starting its slow return north. He dies and is resurrected near the Vernal Equinox, when everything is coming back to life after the long, cold winter."

"What are some of the other stories?" asked Simone.

"In Greek mythology, the Goddess Persephone is kidnapped by Hades, God of the Underworld, who forces her to live there half the year. However, every spring, and just in time for planting season, she returns to the world of the living. She's resurrected. Like Jesus, she symbolizes the regenerative powers of Mother Nature every spring."

"Yeah," Regina said, feeling a little better. "I see that."

"I will hear no more of this," Simone grumbled in a low gravelly voice, wrinkling her face.

They all laughed.

"Whatta ya say we head to the Dome?" Shayda suggested

enthusiastically.

"I am ready to go," Simone replied. "You know Shayda, I don't really know much about Mohammed. Maybe you could tell us about him on the way – in a *nutshell.*"

"I'd love to."

They started off down the road and Shayda began.

"In the sixth century, Mohammed lived in the city of Mecca, in what is now Saudi Arabia. Back then, Mecca was a desert crossroads connecting the continents and cultures of Asia, Europe and Africa. Transcontinental traders had to choose between two dangerous trade routes, one which involved a potentially perilous sea journey, and the other, a trip through the barren Arabian desert. Those merchants who preferred sand to sea had to go through Mecca. Consequently, a camel outfitter like Mohammed had plenty of work to keep him busy.

"Mohammed was a peaceful, honest man who was devoted to his wife, Khadija, herself a successful businesswoman. They were rumored to have had a more or less happy life, but this was a difficult time for Mohammed. Polytheism was still actively and openly practiced by many of Mecca's citizens. Mohammed however, believed in one all powerful God, whom he called Allah.

"Every day, Mohammed would go to the ancient temple called the Ka'aba, which incidentally was built by Adam, of Adam and Eve fame. Mohammed would try to offer his prayers to Allah at the temple, but he was constantly distracted by the other worshippers praying and sacrificing to all of their Gods and Goddesses. It was really nerve racking for the poor guy. Finally, one day in the year 615 he had had enough.

"On that memorable day, Mohammed climbed to the top of a nearby mountain and went into a spiritual trance, though some would no doubt describe it as a seizure. Mohammed believed he'd been visited by the Angel Gabriel. Whatever it was, it changed him forever.

"He came down from the mountain and told everyone about his divine encounter. People witnessed him being overtaken by the Holy Spirit and reciting the words of Allah. Before long, he had a small gathering of friends and followers who believed he was truly the Messenger of God. His revelations form the core of the Qur'an.

"When his followers began growing in numbers, conflict with the local polytheistic pagans eventually arose. The pagans believed Allah was a powerful God, but they refused to accept him as the only God. Rather, they believed he was the most powerful God of the pantheon of Gods and Goddesses, like Zeus was to the Greeks or Jupiter to the Romans. This difference of opinion finally exploded into war.

"Mohammed fled to Medina, where over the course of the next eight years, he solidified his power and returned to Mecca. He stormed the city and cleared the Ka'aba of all the pagan idols, leaving only the white rock which had been placed there by Abraham – yes, the same Abraham of Old Testament fame.

"Mohammed died a few years later, but his army did not die with him. In fact, they took advantage of the constant fighting between the Byzantines and the Persians, swept across the region, and ultimately conquered Jerusalem.

"In 690, less than 60 years after Mohammed's death, Ommayad Caliph Abdul Malik ibn Marwan built the Dome of the Rock on top of the Temple Mount, the place where the Jewish Temple once stood. A brazen move to be sure, however, the Dome of the Rock, or Haram Esh-Sharif, is said to be one of the most beautiful buildings ever built."

They approached the Moors gate near Wilson's arch, and of course, there was a line. They queued up and waited for the guards to get through all the bags.

"Hey Shayda, why did Abdul Ibimar build the Dome here?" Regina wondered.

"You've never heard the story of Mohammed's Miraj? His Night Ride to Mount Moriah?"

They both shook their heads.

"Oh, this is the site of one of Mohammed's most miraculous

journeys! One night, shortly after his beloved Khadija died, Mohammed was awakened by his favorite Angel Gabriel."

Her grandmother flashed across her mind. She hesitated, but went on.

"Gabriel floated Mohammed out the window and gently placed him on the back of a marvelous white animal, named Buraq. It could have been a pegasus, or some cross between a mule and a donkey with wings. The stories vary. Anyhow, with Gabriel by his side, he flew up into the star filled sky, to the Temple Mount at the summit of Mt. Moriah. When he arrived, everyone was there, Abraham, Moses, Jesus and a number of other remarkable figures. It was a virtual who's who of prophets.

"Then, a ladder miraculously appeared, and Mohammed climbed all the way up to the Gate of the Watchers. There he met the Angel Isma'il, a powerful angel who commanded an army of millions of angels. Isma'il allowed Mohammed to pass through the gate and approach Allah. Once through, Mohammed ascended through all of the spheres of creation, where he met with the other prophets again before finally meeting Allah face to face."

"Wow!" blurted out a wide-eyed Regina. "Just like Christ's transfiguration, when Elijah and Moses showed up!"

"Do Muslims believe those things actually happened?" Simone asked.

"Some do," answered Shayda, "just as some Christians believe in the physical resurrection of Christ, and some Jews believe the world was created in seven days. I like to think of these stories as metaphors. By meeting Abraham, Moses and Jesus, Mohammed acknowledges their status and establishes a clear link between these three monotheistic religions. He's only distinguished from the other prophets because he was the most recent one, and therefore, he had the latest word of God, to clear up all the misunderstandings which had developed since God first appeared to Abraham."

They approached the security checkpoint and Simone abruptly stopped. "The Temple Mount is off limits to religious Jews," she said hesitantly. "They believe only the upper echelon rabbis should have that honor and only on Yom Kippur, the Jewish Day of Atonement. Those little pangs of guilt still manage to find their way in, but I'm not going to let them sway me. Let's keep going."

They went through the gate, and were confronted by the massive stone platform upon which the Dome was built. A broad, steep staircase led them slowly up to the marble esplanade. At the top of the steps, freestanding stone arches stood like faithful sentries, guarding the entrance. As they passed underneath, they were momentarily blinded by an explosion of brilliant light radiating from the colossal golden egg, and reflecting off a field of smooth white marble. Heaven on Earth, precisely the intended effect. Shayda looked to the apex of the enormous Dome, and for an instant, felt the sensation of being up there again.

Out of the corner of her eye, she saw an elderly Islamic man sitting down at an old fountain. He wore a white cotton tunic and a gold patterned turban neatly wound around his head. He gracefully placed each bare foot in the fountain, gently cleansing them. She pulled out the digicam and panned around the esplanade, pausing a few moments on the old man. She didn't like to be intrusive with her camera, but she couldn't resist zooming in on that wrinkled bronze face preparing for deep spiritual contemplation.

They slowly made their way to the huge octagonal structure supporting the Dome. It was decorated with exquisite Persian tiles, which formed stars, diamonds, lilies and lotuses in turquoise, black, white, red, brown and green. Revelations from the Qur'an were inscribed all around, in white Arabic script delicately painted on cobalt blue trim.

They slipped off their shoes and walked slowly through a passageway and onto plush, hand woven Persian carpets covering the octagon floor. It took a few moments for their eyes to adjust, but then they began to see the intricate details and rich texture of the interior walls and ceilings. Botanical motifs, cornucopias and Mameluke stars mixed perfectly with geometric inlays, decorative gold inscriptions and the mosaic gemstone windows, which created changing reflections of surreal light. Three concentric circles of great marble pillars surrounded the expansive rotunda. Under the gleaming gold honeycomb mosaic in the center of the dome, was the summit of Mount Moriah, an exposed limestone rock 57 feet long.

"Mohammed left his footprint in this rock when he climbed up the ladder to meet Allah," Shayda said, walking toward it.

"Where?" Regina asked.

"Right here under this urn, which by the way, is supposed to contain a few of his hairs."

They inspected the indentation in the rock.

"I see it!" Regina whispered excitedly.

"I guess that could be a footprint," Simone reluctantly agreed.

Shayda leaned over. "Maybe...."

"It's hard to believe," Simone said seriously, "that this rock is the Jewish Holy of Holies. The most sacred spot on Earth – the place where Abraham almost killed his own child; and where the old Jewish Temple once held the Ark of the Covenant.

"I know," added Regina. "It's crazy. I can hardly believe this is really where Jesus taught, and prayed. I can almost feel his rage when he overturned the tables of those money changers, who were desecrating this sacred spot. I wonder what the world would be like if his revolution had been successful."

Shayda took a deep breath and closed her eyes, mindful of the Islamic tradition that a single prayer offered here is equal to a thousand prayers offered elsewhere. She placed her hand on the rock and concentrated. *Oh great spiritual power of the Universe, let there be an awakening of consciousness as we enter the 21st century – a global shift toward the values of justice, equality and peace. May the religions of the world find their common roots and unite, putting this long, cruel separation behind us. And please, help us to put down our weapons of destruction and lift up our voices in song. Help us to become whole.* She opened her eyes to see a man sprinkling flower-scented water on the rock.

She patted the solid stone, and took one more look around the impressive structure, before stepping outside to rejoin Simone and Regina. As she was walking toward them, she noticed an elderly woman looking directly at her, and pointing down a staircase. The woman started down the stairs, and without saying a word, Shayda went after her.

"Hey!" Simone called out. "Where are you going?"

"I don't know," Shayda called back, as she darted around the other people coming and going on the crowded steps. Shayda caught one more glimpse of her, but by the time she reached the bottom, the woman had disappeared. She looked around, but there was no sign of her – just a large tour group gawking at a mammoth gate.

"What's going on?" Regina asked, running up to her.

"I'm not sure," Shayda answered, turning on her camera. "She told me to come down here."

"Who told you?" Simone asked.

"Grandmother."

Simone and Regina just looked at each other and shrugged, while Shayda focused in on the gate.

"The Golden Gate is sacred to both Jews and Christians," a bored tour guide blurted out in a loud monotone. "Jews believe that when the Messiah comes, this is where He will enter the Temple Mount. Christians believe that when Christ returns, He too will come through the Golden Gate, just as he did on Palm Sunday nearly 2,000 years ago. However, as you can see, the gate has been blocked off. Islamic leaders sealed it in the seventh century to prevent either one of them from entering the Temple Mount. For added insurance, the Muslims situated a cemetery just on the other side..."

Suddenly, a blinding flash of light filled Shayda's screen, jolting her off balance. She tried to hold the camera steady and look up to see what was happening. A huge oval of golden light shrouded the entire gate, and a harmonic ringing sound filled the air. She felt a strange, almost electrical surge pass through her body; and then, to her amazement, a human figure appeared within the light. She looked to Simone and Regina, and the group of tourists. Everybody was staring at it, wide-eyed. She looked back through the viewfinder and tried to make some sense of what was happening. Seconds later, the phenomenon collapsed to a single point of light and popped out of existence, but the ringing lingered in their ears.

"Holy shit!" Simone exclaimed. "The blockade has disappeared. The Golden Gate is open!?"

The Gate was completely intact, but the stones which had blocked it were gone – nowhere in sight. They hadn't crumbled or slid or cracked. They'd simply vanished. A few old Muslim women who'd been visiting the cemetery timidly peered through from the other side. One of them ran away shrieking, and another fell to her knees and threw her arms forward in prayer.

Shayda stopped taping and looked around. Regina and Simone stood motionless, their mouths agape. Pilgrims and tourists dropped to the ground, praying feverishly. Some were just fixated, staring at the unblocked gate, and more started pouring down the stairs from the Temple Mount.

She looked at the camera. *This is why I'm supposed to be here.* Just then, a man nearly knocked her over as he rushed toward the Gate. "Simone. Regina," she said, recovering her balance. "I have to leave. I can't really explain it, but I was somehow meant to be here to record this, this, whatever it was. I have to protect the video."

"I think I should go with you," Simone said hesitantly. "What about you, Regina?"

"Well, I don't want to stay here by myself!"

The only way out was through the Gate, and as they crossed the threshold, they half expected to vanish into thin air.

There was so much commotion, they didn't notice they were being watched by a sunburnt man wearing an Izod sweater and dark shades. He pulled out his cellphone, and keeping his distance, followed them through.

CHAPTER THREE
THE POWERS THAT BE

Shayda clutched the digicam as she ran with Regina and Simone, through the cemetery and down the hill to Ha-Ofel Street. The usually busy thoroughfare had come to a stop. Motorists were out of their cars and rushing about, talking excitedly and blocking traffic in both directions. People streamed up the hill, running toward the gate, and more and more cars kept coming. Some of them stopped to join the hubbub, while others honked and slowly drove past on the narrow shoulder.

"There's a taxi!" Simone shouted, waving to get the cabbie's attention. "Shalom! Stop, please!"

They darted in between several abandoned cars and across the street to the northbound lane.

The cabbie stopped and leaned out the window. "What is going on?" he asked in a rough, husky English. "I saw a bright light."

"No time to explain," Simone said as they piled into the back seat. "Look, people are going nuts. We have to get out of here *now.*"

The cabbie looked around and quickly realized that if he didn't get out fast, he could kiss the rest of today's fares goodbye. "I think you are right." He floored it, jolting them backwards. "Where are you going?"

Shayda pulled herself up. "King George and Hillel Street."

A few cars back, a dark blue sedan with tinted glass inched its way forward through the metallic sea.

"Where are we going?" Regina whispered.

"The American Express office. I'm going to download this video to my mailbox, to be sure there's an extra copy."

"Good idea," affirmed Simone, "then what?"

"We should take it to the press," Shayda replied, putting the camera safely back in her bag. "The world needs to see this."

"What about ENN?" Simone suggested. "They have an office here in Jerusalem."

"That's a great idea!"

Regina's eyes were just about popping. "I think we saw a miracle!"

"What happened?" interrupted the cabbie. "A bomb?"

"That's a good question," responded Simone. "What was that?"

"I saw a brilliant oval of light, with a human figure inside of it," Shayda answered. "I hope I wasn't hallucinating."

"No. I saw it too," confirmed Regina.

"Un-be-lievable," Simone blurted out. "And what about the Golden Gate? The boulders just *vanished*."

The cabbie eyed them suspiciously in the rear view mirror, as he turned left onto Jericho Road.

"I also felt a weird vibration or something," added Regina.

"Yeah," Shayda agreed. "Like a pulse of energy."

They careened left on Sultan Suleiman Road, and wound around the Muslim Quarter on the north side of the Old City. By this time, most of the other drivers had left their cars and were flocking to Herod's Gate. The cabbie swerved to avoid hitting two old men, wobbling across the street on their bicycles. At the Damascus Gate, the crowd was so dense the cab was barely moving. Somehow they got through, but the throngs swallowed the empty space as soon as the car went by. The road opened up a little outside the Christian Quarter, and the cabbie picked up some speed and took a hard right onto HaNevi'im Street. He looked into the rearview mirror, narrowing his eyes.

"What's the matter?" Simone asked anxiously.

"We are being followed."

"Oh, shit!"

"Do you want me to lose 'em?" the cabbie grinned.

They all said "yes!" without hesitation. A second later, the cabbie pulled a tire screechin' u-ee, and Simone and Shayda were smashing Regina up against the car door; then before they could even get a grip, he flung them back against Simone with two hard rights. Stone walls rushed past the windows about six inches away from the car door, and a few more colorful expletives erupted from the back seat.

They nearly picked off an old woman, who reappeared in a doorway as the cab whizzed by, shaking her fists and shouting. After slowing imperceptibly at another intersection, he gunned it, once again plastering them against the seat.

Regina snuck a peek out the rear window. "I think we lost 'em."

"Who the hell was that?" Simone demanded.

"I have no idea," Shayda answered, tightening her grip on the bag. "But I bet I know what they want."

"And what is that?" the cabbie said, turning around and looking into the back seat.

Shayda pulled the bag in closer and Simone sat up and yelled at him. "Hey! Keep your eyes on the road would you?"

He nonchalantly turned back around and shrugged. "Ehh. I've been driving these roads for longer than you've been alive." He gave it more gas and they sped over the cobblelimestone.

In a few more minutes, they emerged onto a much wider paved

road. Shayda felt some relief when she recognized the area. "We're going to the American Express office."

"No problem."

They pulled up in front of the building, paid the cabbie and ran inside. Just as he drove away, the dark blue sedan came to a stop on the other side of the road.

The AmEx office was abuzz with lively discussion about what had occurred. One man told a teller the Golden Gate had been demolished. Two tourists butted in and said they heard it was a bomb. The three women hurried past them to the INET terminal and Shayda logged on. "I'm sending this footage to my office in Ann Arbor," she said excitedly, slipping in the disc.

"I have an e-mailbox," Simone said. "Should we send a copy there too, just in case?"

"Good idea."

Simone reached over the keypad and entered her address.

"Now we have to find out where the ENN office is. It should be in the phonebook file, here," Shayda said, making two selections from the pad. "It's on King David Street."

"Print out the address and let's *go*," Simone urged.

Shayda plucked the paper from the slot and they dashed out. From the other side of the office, the sunburnt man in the Izod sweater watched them leave. He punched a number into his cellphone, walked over to the window and peeked through the blinds. The women were trying to hail another cab.

"Yes?" A serious male voice answered.

"They accessed the AmEx INET terminal in Jerusalem. Find out what they did with that file and retrieve it. I'll pursue."

"You know, it's less than a mile from here. We could just walk," Regina suggested.

"Wait! There's a bus!" Simone yelled. They all broke into a run for the bus stop.

The Izod man lunged toward the door and got outside just in time to see them boarding the southbound. He jumped into his car and pursued.

The bus was chaotic – everyone had a version of what happened. Three oldtimers were arguing loudly in the back.

"It was a bomb I tell you."

"No, it was a fireball."

"I say it was an act of God!"

The bus made a couple more stops. Simone looked out the back window and saw the dark blue sedan. "Shit! It's that car again. We'll have to make a run for it when we get off."

The man's cellphone beeped and he picked up. "Did you retrieve the file?"

"They actually sent it to two locations, but yeah, I got 'em both. They also looked up the address of the ENN office."

"Damn, they're almost there. Send the file to New York." He abruptly disconnected the phone and looked up to see the light turn yellow.

Regina spotted the bright purple sign on the other side of the street. "Look, there's ENN!"

Shayda asked the driver to stop as close to the station as possible. He made it through the yellow light and pulled over about a block away.

"The car got stuck at the red, let's go!" Simone yelled, jumping off the bus. They took off across the street and Regina glanced back, just in time to see the man swerving out of the lane, running the red and driving through the intersection after them. "He's chasing us! Run!"

He sped by them, swerved up onto the curb, jumped out and stood between them and the ENN door. "Stop!" he ordered, holding out the side of his jacket to reveal a small gun sewn in a special pocket.

But Simone didn't even slow down. "Hyyyyyaahh!" she shrieked, launching into a slick karate kick to his lower midsection. As the spy doubled over they both looked at her, surprised.

"Hey, I live in New York," she shrugged as they bolted inside the door.

They clambered up to the front desk, startling the receptionist. Shayda looked at her squarely and calmly said, "some guy is chasing us and he has a gun. Please let us come inside."

The receptionist looked out the front door and saw the thug, who was just getting back to a standing position. Then she looked at the three frazzled women. "Okay, come around." They hurried past the counter and through the security door. When the receptionist looked back outside, the man was gone.

"May I help you?" an American voice said from an inner office.

"We need to see the executive producer immediately," Simone demanded, sizing up this tall dark-haired man and his sharp suit.

"I'm sorry, his office is in New York, but maybe I can help you. I'm Jonathan KenCairn, Chief Correspondent for Jerusalem and the Middle East." He shook each of their hands and they introduced themselves. "So, what can I do for you?"

"Can we sit down for a minute?" asked Regina.

"Sure, come in my office."

"Have you heard anything, unusual, today?" Shayda asked.

KenCairn's eyes narrowed ever so slightly. "What do you mean?"

"You know what I mean. The Temple Mount, the Golden Gate. The explosion of light everyone is talking about?"

"All I have at the moment are some pretty bizarre reports. Our mobile unit was dispatched about 20 minutes ago and they're still en route." He leaned forward over the desk. "Why don't you tell me what *you* know?"

Shayda pulled out the disc. "First, we'd like you to duplicate this disc, one for each of us, then we'll show you what's on it."

"Deal."

He retrieved two blank discs, used his desk terminal to make the copies and handed all three back to Shayda.

"Thanks," she replied, putting the original back in the bag and giving a copy to each of the other two. "I noticed you also downloaded the file onto your hard drive, so take a look. Cue it up to time index 11:11."

He cracked a sheepish grin, and the Golden Gate appeared on a large color monitor. At the sight of the flash he was out of his chair, clutching the edge of the desk. As the human form emerged out of the golden light, his jaw dropped another half inch. Without taking his eyes off the screen, he touched his computer pad and the image zoomed in. The form was still fuzzy, but he thought he could see a pair of dark eyes blinking though the glare. The recording ended and without saying a word, he replayed it and watched again. "What the hell is this?"

"We don't know," answered Regina. "It's *your* responsibility to find that out."

Shayda leaned forward in her chair and gave him a serious look. "That's why we brought the disc to you. We trust you to show what really happened and figure out what's going on."

"You know, about 40 minutes ago, I was in the uplink room talking with one of the engineers. All of a sudden the equipment went bananas. The lights surged, the monitors cut to static, our phone lines went dead and computers froze – all electronic systems were affected. And we actually felt something, some, energy pulse. I immediately called the power company, but they had no idea what it was. Though they did admit something unusual had happened. Ten minutes later all of the ENN affiliates got an e-mail from my producer in New York. She reported a system-wide power surge – the whole Earth News Net had been affected and they had no explanation. I reported back what I could, which until now, wasn't much. Whatever it was, it had a global effect."

"So, will you see this gets on your Net in its unadulterated form?" Shayda questioned.

He felt the intensity of their gazes. "Looks like I'd better," he replied, smiling. "But first, I need more information." He picked up his phone and pressed a button. "It's Jonathan. What's going on?" He paused for a few seconds, "uh huh, okay. Patch me through to the camera crew, will you? Thanks."

"Hey, can't you put that on speakerphone?" Simone interrupted.

Jonathan nodded, pressed another button, and a cacophony of voices and horns erupted from the speaker. "Hello?"

"Yair, it's Jonathan. Where are you?"

"The truck got stuck in traffic so Dorit and I left on foot to see if we could get through. Right now, we're in the Muslim Quarter. The place has gone mad. People are flocking to the Old City in droves."

"Go to the Golden Gate. There's been some sort of amazing light phenomenon, which somehow disintegrated the stone blockade and opened up the Gate. We've got it all on disc and I've seen it myself, but we need some live eyewitness reactions. Call me as soon as you get there and good luck."

"Ahhhh, right."

Jonathan hung up. "I'm gonna call my producer." He punched in another number, and within seconds he was on videophone with Angela Wright, a striking African-American woman with dark eyes and long, black beaded braids.

"Hey! Jonathan!" She raised her palms, put on her best Rasta voice and sang, "pos-i-tive vi-bray-shuns, yeah-ah, watchu got?" The notes of the melody seemed to dance on the tips of her fingers.

Jonathan was momentarily transfixed, then burst forth with his rendition of *Across the Universe* "...some-thin' that could chaange the world!"

She flashed a brilliant, wide grin. "And you've got it liiive on digitized video!" She looked off camera and called, "Ben! Come on over here, wouldja?"

Shayda, Regina and Simone all knew she was referring to Ben Gerrard, ENN's owner and executive producer. Gerrard became a celebrity when he took his vast computer software fortune and established the Earth News Network. He was a telecommunications guru who believed the power of technology was radically altering the world for the worse. His vision was to create a truly independent global network, not bound by corporate sponsorship and censorship. ENN was conceived to make technology a tool of truthful information, education and political liberation.

"I'll send it over the Hot Line," Jonathan said, punching up the encrypted channel.

A few seconds later, Ben joined Angela on the v-phone, flashing a peace sign. The camera automatically compensated, setting up a perfect two-shot. "Hey Jonathan! We've got it; hang on while we check it out."

Looking at Ben Gerrard, you'd never know he was one of the most influential people in the world. His blond, boyish appearance and trademark political tee-shirts solidly separated him from the rest of the corporate world. So did his lifestyle. He lived in a self-sufficient studio apartment on top of the ENN Tower – in downtown Manhattan. His rain catch and botanical garden provided for all of his nutritional needs, and solar panels heated his water and energized a few light bulbs and appliances in his apartment. He was currently developing an orbiting solar array to harness enough energy to power his entire network.

Ben had known Angela since 1967, when they were both student activists at Berzerkley. They spent many an hour reading and writing poetry, following the Grateful Dead and demonstrating against the Viet Nam war. Throughout the years, they'd collaborated now and again on computer graphics programs and children's television shows, and had a number of concert rendezvous. When Ben started up his network, he hired Angela as ENN's senior producer. That was only two years ago, and since that time they'd gained a significant following.

Once the network was up and running, Gerrard embarked on the next phase of his plan – to establish the Planet Earth Cooperative. This global network of interconnected public access stations linked information access with small-scale sustainable development. Each Co-op member organization was a locally based, environmentally sustainable industry, which supported its own ENN site. Members maintained local land ownership, and provided family wages and good housing for their workers. Each paid a fair percentage back into the Co-op, to create a reserve fund other members could access according to need. The Co-op was self sustaining, but profits from his software company helped it continue to grow. It was Gerrard's attempt to help cure the devastating global epidemic caused by the highly infectious Naftagatt virus.

"This is incredible!" Ben exclaimed. "We've got to get it on the Net as soon as possible. Do you have a mobile crew on location?"

"I've just spoken with them. They're trying to get through right now, but as you can imagine, the place has gone crazy. People are flooding the area. You should also know, the three eyewitnesses who recorded the event are sitting right here." Jonathan leaned back, allowing the camera to set up a wide shot. "We have them to thank for bringing us the footage."

"And we expect ENN to live up to its reputation, and tell the truth about what happened," Simone asserted.

Ben looked at her from the monitor and answered sincerely, "thank you for trusting us with this information. I promise not to let you down – the world deserves to see this! Jonathan, please call us immediately when the crew establishes a live feed. We'll run the footage, then cut to Jerusalem for reaction shots."

"If they'll agree, I'd like to do a studio interview with the eyewitnesses."

Simone jumped at the chance to be beamed around the globe and the other two also agreed.

"Excellent," Ben concluded. "Gotta go, but keep us informed and thanks for your great work."

"And Jonathan," Angela added, "loosen up that tie, wouldja?"

The channel cut to a fractal screen saver, and Jonathan ripped off his tie. A half second later, he was up and headed out the office door. "We'll be ready to go in five minutes. After the interview, I'll arrange for a driver to take you to...?"

"That could be a problem," Shayda replied. "Some thug must have seen us record the phenomenon, because he chased us and threatened us with a gun. He probably wanted to get the disc before we could give it to you, but he could still be lurking outside somewhere and I don't thing we're willing to take that chance. I think we should go to the American Embassy."

Simone and Regina agreed wholeheartedly.

"I have contacts at the Embassy. I'll arrange for them to come pick you up."

Meanwhile, in a penthouse board room, high atop the World Trade Center in New York City, the core of CHAOS had assembled. The chairmen of the largest, most powerful transnational corporations were discussing the latest threat to their global empire of free trade and profit. This elite group of upper echelon corporate execs represented global giants like Nabco, Morris Reynolds, DowPont, ExxoToyMitsu, Ruther Burdock Unlimited and DizzeyUniversal.

The Chairman of the chairmen, who controlled the defense behemoth WestLockMartBoMcDouglas, sat on an overstuffed black leather chair, his chubby diamond decorated fingers resting on the built-in remote control pad. With the touch of a button, he could summon gigaquads of information from the organization's vast computer network or interface with the CHAOS Satellite Comnet, directing the desired signals to a nine-foot monitor suspended from the vaulted ceiling.

"All right, let's get started," the Chairman announced, firing up his hand wrapped Havana. "This was recovered by our agents in Jerusalem. Unfortunately, the stupid idiots failed to destroy the original recording, and consequently, the video you are about to see has been delivered to that God damn Earth News Network. We expect they will be broadcasting it shortly." The rich old men lit up and watched in horror.

"Jesus H. Christ," Morris Reynolds exhaled, filling the room with a fresh cloud of Lucky smoke. "It looks like a Goddamned Spielberg movie."

"I don't like it," Nabco added. "If ENN broadcasts this, the consequences are unpredictable and I don't like unpredictable consequences. Their effect on The Margin could be negative, and we cannot take that risk. Have we figured out a way to jam their broadcasts yet?"

"Not yet," replied the Chairman. "Hell, those morons in engineering can't even explain the system-wide failure. Gerrard is a pretty sophisticated son of a bitch. My instinct tells me he engineered the whole God damn thing. He and his blasted network are turning out to be a royal pain in the ass."

"We should have taken him over when we had the chance," added Ruther Burdock. "He's nothing but an altruistic traitor, coddling the poor the way he does. And his naive pursuit of the truth. It goes against everything we believe in. Doesn't he understand that our way is the best way. The *only* way!" He got up and approached the East Wall, where a long Carrera marble plaque was illuminated by elaborate track lighting. He contemplated the tall words chiseled in the brilliant white stone. "CORPORATIONS HAVE AUTHORITY OVER SOCIETY," he read slowly, with pride and reverence. "If we weren't here to provide structure for society, why, the world would degenerate into the blackness of utter chaos. Doesn't he know we're fighting for the common good?"

"He doesn't think so," threw out young Arthur Hayes, who was there at the pleasure of his uncle. "By the way, could someone open a window?"

"Nope," the Chairman continued, eyeing this upstart relative. "Had them hermetically sealed for security purposes. Tell me, Arthur m'boy, what's wrong with *our* order? We represent freedom, justice and economic advantage. Hell, Gerrard's wealthy enough. He could have been one of us, realizing the good life. I think he's gotta screw loose, that's what I think."

The Chairman's chairphone beeped. He pressed a button, "now what?"

"ENN is satelcasting their report right now."

The Chairman moved his finger ever so slightly and switched the monitor to ENN. The words 'SPECIAL REPORT' ballooned across the expansive screen, dissolving into the gargantuan image of the ENN anchor.

"Buenas días. This is Magdalena Severeide at the Earth News Network studio in New York. About an hour ago, a global phenomenon occurred which has governments, scientists, theologians and philosophers in a tailspin looking for an explanation. What we know so far is that an atmospheric disruption took place on the Temple Mount in the Old City of Jerusalem. It temporarily interrupted all satellite transmissions, telephone communications and electronic devices planet wide. And, while it had enough force to disintegrate large stone blocks, miraculously, no one was hurt. Three American women captured the whole event on their digicam. What you're about to see is their actual, unedited footage."

As the video played, the chairmen looked at each other and frowned. "We have to do something fast," Morris Reynolds wheezed, as he lit up another cigarette. "We can't let people think they see this."

"No problem," the Chairman responded. "We have our own copy of the footage, so we can just make a few modifications before we broadcast the story on our network. We're still bigger than he is."

The ENN anchor came back on the screen. "And now we go live to Jerusalem, where Dorit Dahled and our ENN mobile unit are standing by."

"Thanks Maggie. As you can see, after centuries of being sealed shut by limestone blocks, the Golden Gate is now open. The stones have disappeared, but the Gate itself has been left intact." The camera panned to a wide shot of people crowding into the plaza near the Gate. "As of yet we have no explanation for the phenomenon. Whatever it is or was, it's drawing people from all parts of Jerusalem. Every major road surrounding the Old City is blocked by people trying to approach the area. Each of the eight gates leading into the Temple Mount is completely jammed, and hundreds of cars have been abandoned along the roadsides."

The camera focused in on her again.

"Perhaps the most remarkable thing is the feeling of goodwill that has somehow permeated this place." She shook her head in astonishment. "There are *thousands* of people gathered here, in Jerusalem, and no reported hostilities or injuries."

A young Israeli man joined her on camera. "This is one of the many people who witnessed the event first hand. Please, tell our viewers what you saw."

"I was standing over there, and suddenly a blazing light surrounded the whole Gate. I heard a very loud noise and then for an instant, a woman appeared and was, in the middle of the light! A few seconds later, she disappeared with it. And the Gate is open!" he said, as if he could barely believe his own words.

"Thank you, sir. And what about you two," she asked a young couple, who started speaking rapidly and simultaneously in German. "Please, one at a time, in English."

"A circle of light surrounded the Gate," the woman said excitedly, tracing a large circle with her outstretched arms. "It grew more intense. Then a wave, no a ring, of energy radiated from its center, where I could see a human form."

"I saw it too," her companion interjected. "And I heard a loud, ringing sound." He pointed off camera and added breathlessly, "the stones just disappeared!"

The reporter turned to a Canadian tourist in her late sixties. "And what did you see, ma'am?"

"I was standing right about here with my tour group, listening to our guide tell us about the Gate, when all of a sudden a brilliant light appeared around it, and around *me*. In another second, I could make out a figure in the center of the light. I know how this sounds, but I think it was Jesus Christ! He looked just like I always imagined," her voice wavered a little and her eyes filled with tears. "He's come back."

"Oh, Christ," the Chairman hissed, shifting uncomfortably in his chair. "We've got to diffuse this one immediately."

The reporter thanked the woman and turned to a Muslim

cleric. "Excuse me, sir, what did you see here today?"

"A new beginning," he replied, with a wide smile and weepy eyes.

"What do you mean?"

"Allah has removed a wall which has separated all of us for too long," he gently touched her arm. Dorit, an Israeli, was so stunned by his gesture she was speechless, despite the fact she was still on the air.

The camera cut back to Magdalena in New York. "Thank you Dorit, we'll be checking in with you periodically. At this point, we have nothing further to report. Since our station's policy is to avoid excessive speculation in the absence of facts, we return you now to MarsLive, where you can ride along with Sojourner II as she surveys the Martian Fossil Beds. When we have more facts, you'll get them – here on ENN."

"Cut that shit off!" the Chairman bellowed in disgust. "I'll tell you the facts. The Mars Rover is a bunch of shit. What's it good for? Scientific exploration. Big deal. My Goddamn Republicans promised to can those NASA missions and revive the Star Wars program. My company could have built them something they could really be proud of."

"We've got bigger problems right now," Morris Reynolds blurted out, coughing uncontrollably.

"We have to come up with a different version of the story," DowPont added rather deviously. "It should neatly explain the phenomenon and completely eliminate any unpredictable consequences which might affect The Margin. We need to get control over this immediately."

"I think it should be a bomb," the Chairman mused. "Bombs are exciting, they get people's adrenaline flowing. We haven't had a bombing in Jerusalem for at least a year.... How about a new technology? One which creates an im-plosion instead of an ex-plosion. An ultra-smart bomb – that doesn't leave a mess!"

"Does anything like that exist?" asked young Arthur Hayes.

"If we say so, it exists."

"So we'll take the guy out of the video," Burdock thought aloud, "and maybe cut that light effect by about 90%. A bomb flash should be short and sweet."

A low, sustained wheezing sound signaled Morris Reynolds was about to speak again. "That'd make it seem a little snappier!"

"I'll call an emergency meeting of the network minions and instruct them what to do," Burdock declared.

"Wait a minute," Arthur interjected. "It seems like something extraordinary has happened here, and we're going to explain it away with the same old bomb theory? Shouldn't we try to figure out what that was before we manipulate it?"

"It doesn't matter what it was," the Chairman retorted. "We control reality around here. Besides, our explanation is marginally plausible, and for all we know, the guy was dubbed in. In fact, I like that angle. Ruther, tell your servants to claim this radical left wing ENN propaganda machine invented the whole thing about the guy in the light. While you're at it, round up some eyewitnesses. Say it's an ENN media hoax designed to increase their Nielson ratings. With a little luck, maybe we can improve The Margin *and* destroy Gerrard's ENN, once and for all."

"Here, here!" came the response from around the table.

"And Hayes," the Chairman continued, pointing a cragged finger at Arthur, "watch it. We don't need any leftist sympathizers in our organization. I can throw you outta here like that," he snapped his fingers. He slowly swiveled his mammoth chair away from the table, and at the touch of another button, was hydraulically elevated up and out to a standing position. He lumbered over to the solid gold shrine on the other side of the room, where the original CHAOS Articles of Incorporation glowed green under protective glass. The Chairman thrust his index finger toward the sacred charter. "Keep your mind focused on what is important, Arthur. Remember Article I, Section I: Thou Shalt Protect The Margin!"

"Mr. Chairman?" an official voice barked from one of the

many speakers wired into the room.

"What is it now?"

"The three eyewitnesses who recorded the video have gone to the American Embassy in Jerusalem. We've also retrieved a Yale University file and intercepted two e-mail transmissions from Greece. You might find them interesting."

"I'll decide if it's interesting," he bellowed back. "Those antiterrorist surveillance chips we developed for the old leadership are really coming in handy. A real boon to business too. Ahh, those were the good old days, when we had 'em all in our back pockets." He patted his fat rump. "We better move on these stories fast before that commie sympathizer fag of a President starts believing Gerrard and those blasted women."

The CHAOS board room sprung into action. Computer screens and telephones emerged from secret compartments in the mahogany table, and instructions went up the satelcom link and down and out over fiber optic cable.

———

In the Oval Office, the President of the United States and several of his top advisors were discussing the upcoming United Nations Millennium Summit in New York City.

The new Administration had settled right in after their unexpected rise to power just eleven months ago. The Great Scandal of '98 had so damaged the integrity of both the Democrats and Republicans, that Americans had completely lost faith in the two-party system. The Coalition of Progressive Third Parties swept the 1998 congressional elections, took over the House, and forced the President and Vice President to resign in disgrace. The new Speaker of the House, elected to his congressional seat just two months before, assumed the highest office in the land.

A voice interrupted the conversation from some hidden speaker, "Mr. President?"

"Go ahead Bernie," the President responded casually in mid-sentence.

"The Secretary of State has an urgent call."

"Put it through."

The Secretary pulled out his pocketphone and flicked it open.

"Yes?"

"Mr. Secretary, this is Ambassador Goldstein in Jerusalem. Something extraordinary has occurred here and I felt you should know immediately."

"Yes, go on."

"About an hour ago, an incident took place on the Temple Mount in the Old City of Jerusalem. A burst of light surrounded the Golden Gate, and somehow disintegrated the stone blocks which had been sealing it for centuries. It lasted less than a minute, and as incredible as this may sound, a human figure appeared and remained briefly inside the light before disappearing with it. Hundreds witnessed the event, and many more felt a strange sensation, which has been described as a warm electrical surge."

"How do you know this?" the Secretary asked, without betraying his surprise.

"I myself experienced it, as did the entire staff. Also, we have three American tourists here at the Embassy who captured the whole thing on video disc. I've just seen it and it's truly astounding. They gave a copy to ENN and I suspect it will be broadcast shortly." He paused for a moment and then exhaled audibly, "also, CHAOS has attempted to obtain the disc."

"Did they get it?"

"Not that we know of."

"Send it to the White House immediately."

"Yes, sir."

The Secretary flicked his phone closed and approached the President.

"Excuse me, Mr. President, I just received a call from Ambassador Goldstein in Israel. He has informed me of a most unusual event."

The President looked up at his good and trusted friend who calmly relayed what he had just heard.

"What!" The President practically jumped out of his chair.

"Do you hear what you're saying?"

"That's not all. Three eyewitnesses captured the whole thing on video disc and gave a copy to ENN. They'll be broadcasting it shortly if CHAOS doesn't get their hands on it first. They've already made one attempt."

A little buzzer sounded.

"Yes?" answered the President.

"I'm putting Ambassador Goldstein's datafile through now," Bernie said, selecting the Presidential AV icon on the communications control panel.

The lights dimmed and two bookshelves retracted, revealing a large television monitor. They watched in silent astonishment. When it was over, they all turned toward the President who was now on his feet, leaning halfway over the desk.

"This could be the most profound event in 2,000 years! If it's real."

"It doesn't matter if it's real or not," his Communications Director said bluntly. "If that gets out and people think it's real, we've got big problems on our hands."

"Of course it matters whether or not it's real," rebuked the Secretary of State. "But I agree, this could create pandemonium. The potential for political and religious fallout is enormous."

"Maybe we should contact ENN and try to buy some time," suggested the Communications Director.

"No!" interjected the U.N. Ambassador emphatically. "The people have a right to a free press. Furthermore, we shouldn't give the public any reason to think we're trying to cover it up."

The Secretary narrowed his eyes, "we can count on CHAOS to pull some clever stunt."

The President shook his head in disgust. These private hierarchical tyrannies no longer had any regulatory restraints. They continued to pursue their empire building with reckless disregard for the social and environmental damage they caused, then manipulated the public's perceptions with propaganda and diversion. Since becoming President, he had introduced legislation aimed at meaningful corporate reform, but thusfar, the CHAOS-controlled Senate had successfully blocked it. "We need more information, fast. Let's find out what ENN knows before they broadcast."

"That's if they haven't already beamed it around the globe," chimed in the Communications Director.

The President grabbed the remote control. He got to ENN just in time to catch the tail end of Shayda's video before it cut to the eyewitness commentary. LIVE FROM THE TEMPLE MOUNT IN JERUSALEM rolled across the bottom of the screen.

"Oh my God!" The President pressed his intercom button. "Bernie, please get me Ambassador Goldstein on the phone immediately!" He turned to the Communications Director. "Contact the networks and ENN. Find out everything you can." Then he addressed his Chief of Staff. "We better get the Vice President, Secretary of Defense, the CIA Director and the rest of the Cabinet in here." He looked back to the Secretary of State. "I'd like to talk to the Prime Minister of Israel, the President of Palestine and the Pope for starters."

The advisors pulled out their phones and started madly pushing buttons.

The President's phone beeped. "Yes?"

"Goldstein here, sir."

"We've seen the video. Extraordinary situation, Reuben. Do you have any more information?"

"Yes. I just found out the eyewitnesses stopped at the AmEx office and downloaded the datafile to their home e-mailboxes, before they realized they were being followed. You can bet CHAOS has the file by now."

"You've confirmed CHAOS' involvement?"

"A well-known lackey tried to intercept them before they got to ENN, presumably to steal the disc. The woman from New York belted him a good one," the Ambassador laughed, "and they got away. They were also followed from ENN to the Embassy without incident."

"Reuben, you said everybody felt this phenomenon. What was it like?"

"Like – an energy wave which slowly passed through me. I suddenly felt very warm and peaceful. We also had an Embassy-wide power surge and all electronic systems were affected."

"You know, we had a blackout a little while ago, and I thought I felt something too. What about the eyewitnesses? Are they okay?"

"Just fine. I'd even say ecstatic."

"Good. Thanks, Reuben. Keep us informed."

"Of course. Goodbye, sir."

The President flicked his phone closed and turned toward his colleagues. "It's a good bet CHAOS has the datafile. The eyewitnesses downloaded it at an AmEx office on their way to ENN. What do you think CHAOS will do?"

"They'll try to discredit it," the Communications Director responded. "There's too much at stake for them to let the truth come out, if in fact what we have seen is the truth."

"Have you reached the networks?"

"Yes, ENN will be running the footage repeatedly throughout the day. However, the big five declined to comment. They said they'll be breaking their stories soon."

The President's phone beeped. "Yes?"

"Mr. President, CIA here. I've just received a report of a potentially volatile situation in the Middle East."

"If you're talking about the incident on the Temple Mount, we've already seen a video of it. Christ, ENN has already shown the world!"

"Well, I have preliminary confirmation that something unusual has indeed happened at the Golden Gate. Several agents witnessed a suspicious phenomenon. They also report CHAOS was in the vicinity."

"Are they responsible?"

"We don't have that information yet."

"What were they doing in the area?"

"Same thing we were doing, gathering information on religious fundamentalists."

"Have you spoken with NATO intelligence?"

"Not yet, sir. I wanted to discuss it with you first."

"Very well then, contact them and get over here as soon as possible."

The President closed his phone, but before he could set it down, it was beeping again. "Yes?"

"Mr. President, this is the Secretary of Defense. We have confirmed that two powerful electromagnetic disruptions have occurred in the eastern Mediterranean region. At first we thought it was a system-wide glitch, but we are now picking up intelligence reports confirming the readings. One event was centered near Jerusalem, the other on the island of Crete. Both lasted 52 seconds and were powerful enough to temporarily affect our entire power and communications grid. We haven't determined the cause yet."

"Crete? What part of Crete?"

"Heraklion. It has minimal military significance."

"What was it?"

"We don't know. Only a nuclear bomb or a volcanic explosion could cause the levels of disturbance we detected, yet there is no atmospheric clouding at present. In fact, current radar and satellite images show it to be," he paused, grimacing, "clear and sunny."

"Are there any unusual movements of troops or machinery in the region?"

"No."

"I'd like you to join us here at the White House."

"I'll be there promptly, sir."

"Mr. President," picked up the Secretary of State, "the Israeli Prime Minister is on AV line one. I suggest we request a joint scientific inquiry into the phenomenon."

The President nodded at the good idea. "Put him through. In the meantime, I need you to contact our Ambassador to Greece and find out what she knows about a similar event in Heraklion."

The Israeli leader popped on the screen.

"Mr. Prime Minister, my good friend, how are you?" the President said, looking toward the microcam which just happened to be imbedded in the Minister's right nostril.

"Well, to tell you the truth, Mr. President, we are baffled and concerned. This unexplained phenomenon is drawing thousands of people from throughout the region. I have spoken with the President of Palestine and we are in constant communication. We have deployed the Special Israeli Palestinian Community Guard to keep the peace. So far there has been no violence, but we are very concerned."

"The United States would like to help. I suggest we form a joint scientific team to study the site. We can provide the technology to analyze whatever evidence has been left behind."

"Excellent. I'll discuss it with the Palestinian President."

"Perhaps we can both approach him via the Peace Line?"

"I will try him now."

The monitor went black for a few minutes, then the two men reappeared on a split screen.

"Hello Mr. President," the President began.

"Mr. President."

"A most incredible event wouldn't you say?"

"Indeed."

"At this point, we all need more information, and we need it fast. I propose we create a cooperative scientific partnership to investigate the phenomenon. The United States would be delighted to send a team of scientists to work with your people."

"I am agreeable to your proposition," he replied, his expression never seeming to waver. "As long as we all share equally in the information your wonderful technology makes possible."

"Of course. I suggest we move quickly on this. My aides will contact your representatives and make the arrangements. By the way, did you see the broadcast on ENN?"

They looked surprised.

"Three Americans recorded the entire phenomenon and ENN has already transmitted it over their network."

"Very well then," replied the Israeli. "We must act with haste. When will your team arrive?"

"They will be in Jerusalem late tonight. Gentlemen, I want to thank you for your willingness to let the United States participate in this historic event. This collaborative effort will help us determine exactly what has happened and reaffirm the unity of the region." They exchanged a few more pleasantries and signed off.

The President then addressed his Chief of Staff. "Contact our Science Advisor and ask her to put together two top teams – one for Jerusalem and one for Crete."

"I'll call her immediately."

"Well, anything on Crete yet?" The President asked the Secretary of State.

"Yes. The Greek government contacted our Embassy to report the disappearance of an American archeologist. Apparently, she vanished into some sort of energy vortex while excavating a cave on the island."

"This is incredible. Are reports coming in from anywhere else? Were there more of these phenomena?"

"Not that we know of. I suggest we contact the Prime Minister of Greece immediately and offer our assistance."

"Right." The President pushed a button on his desk console. "Bernie, please get me the Prime Minister of Greece, on the AV if possible."

"Right away."

The President rested his elbow on the shiny desk and cupped his chin in his palm. He stared at his reflection, and swore he could see the left and right hemispheres of his brain discussing the situation. The logical, rational left making every level headed, scientific explanation it could think of. And the right, trying to tune out the chatter and become one with the universe.

Over the years he had learned to trust his intuition, and he sensed something was happening. Something big. And he knew he would play some part in it. He finally looked up. "What's taking so long?"

"You have to account for Greek time," said the Secretary of State, enjoying the moment of levity.

Bernie's voice broke in from yet another part of the room.

"Mr. President, I have the Prime Minister of Greece."

"On screen."

The Greek leader appeared on the monitor. "Hello, Mr. President."

"Good day, Mr. Prime Minister. We understand an unexplained phenomenon has taken place near Heraklion, and an American archeologist has disappeared."

"That is correct. Eyewitnesses report she vanished in a brilliant flash of light. We have no explanation. We have seen the ENN report, showing a human figure in the Jerusalem flash. Perhaps the two events are related?"

"Perhaps they are. In fact, that's part of the reason I called. The Israeli and Palestinian governments have agreed to form a joint scientific team to study the phenomenon. The United States is providing the technology and covering the costs of the investigation. We agreed to share any and all information. I propose a similar arrangement with your government."

"Perhaps you can also share with us your findings from Jerusalem?"

"Of course."

"Then we will agree to work with you. When can you send your people and technology?"

"We're assembling a team now; they'll be on their way shortly."

"Very well. We will make arrangements."

"Thank you, Mr. Prime Minister."

"Para kalo," he answered, cracking the smallest of smiles.

The President disconnected the channel and looked at his Chief of Staff.

"I'm on it, sir. The Science Advisor has been contacted and she's assembling the teams."

"Excellent. Mr. Secretary, I think its time to talk with the Pope."

"We've got a call in to him now."

"Looks like you're one step ahead of me. Good job. Maybe you can also tell me what the *hell* is happening here?"

"Mr. President?"

"Go ahead, Bernie."

"Pope's on the AV."

"Thanks."

The all-white Pope appeared larger than life on the big screen.

"Your Holiness, I'm sorry to interrupt you."

"It is no trouble, Mr. President," the aged Pope replied.

"Have you learned of the events in Jerusalem and Crete?"

The Pope looked surprised. "Crete? No, I have heard nothing of an event in Crete. However, I am aware of the occurrence in Jerusalem. My Cardinals and I are discussing the matter at this very moment."

"As are we. What do you make of it?"

"It is too soon to say. Tell me what you know of the event in Crete."

"An American archeologist disappeared in some sort of energy surge. That's all we know at the moment. I've sent scientific teams to Crete and Jerusalem to assist in both investigations."

"I see. I must discuss this new information with my aides. I will contact you shortly."

"Very well. I'll be waiting to hear from you."

The Pope switched off the desktop videophone and leaned back in his gilded throne. His attention momentarily drifted upward, to the Raphael masterpiece painted on the vaulted ceiling. Seven little, pink cherubs rose up off their billowing clouds, floated gently down and whispered something into the Pontiff's ear. He smiled as they twirled around his head and returned to their lofty perch. He then turned his attention to the junior members of the Curia, who were seated quietly along the back wall. "We need information about a second phenomenon in Crete."

The underlings got up, filed by the Pontiff's desk, kissed his hand and silently left the room.

The Pope faced his two most trusted Cardinals, Opudias and Ignatious, who were seated in high backed chairs across the ornate, 16th century marble desk. Cardinal Opudias had been a member of the Old Curia for over 60 years. He was now serving as the Pope's Prefect of the Sacred Congregation of the Holy Office, and as such, had control of the Vatican's internal affairs. Cardinal Ignatious ascended to the Vatican with Pope John in the 1960s. He had served as Prefect of the Sacred Congregation of the Council of One Heart, part of the New Curia, for over 30 years.

"Ah, Ignatious, my dear beloved advisor whose wisdom has never failed me. What do you make of the strange events taking place today?"

"Your Holiness, today's unexplained occurrences have the potential to impact the world greatly. We have already spoken with people in many countries, and have found anxious and excited souls who are hopeful that something wonderful has happened. People are believing what we have seen and heard on ENN. It is fantastic fiction."

Ignatious paused for dramatic effect, and also to gauge the Pope's mood.

"Or is it fiction? This is the central question. Has Christ, our Savior and King come again through the Golden Gate into the Holy City, in all His glory, to judge the living and the dead, whose Kingdom shall have no end? Or, has a massive hoax been perpetrated on an unsuspecting and vulnerable public?"

He paused again to let the Pontiff think.

"Your Holiness, we have known each other a long time. You have never known me to base my opinions on groundless or frivolous assertions, and I must be candid with you. My instincts tell me that Christ has returned. My heart has been touched and I feel alive with hopefulness. About the time the phenomenon took place I had a *physical* sensation – a surge of light and energy passed through me. I believe it was the hand of God, and I sense we may be on the verge of a spiritual reawakening!"

"I see," replied the Pope neutrally, as he turned to Cardinal Opudias. "And what say you my other sensible friend and advisor whose keen and analytical mind has kept me squarely focused on the realities of our present day society?"

Cardinal Opudias lowered his head slightly in deference. "Your Vicar-ness, my brother has accurately described our dilemma, but he chooses a path wrought with dangers his kind heart will not allow him to see. Moreover, his optimism has him believing he physically experienced this phenomenon, which took place hundreds of miles away. I do not wish to sound cynical or skeptical of the possibility of a miracle, but I say to you we must not lose our faculties based on a few frantic phone calls and a television broadcast. In fact, it is far more likely this is a mighty hoax. It has effectively provoked widespread hysteria, but is clearly in the realm of fiction. And now there is *another* phenomenon? What better way for a new network to get publicity? I predict as time passes we will learn these *phenomena* are nothing more than a Madison Avenue fabrication. We should not overreact. I urge patience, your Holiness. The patience of your years is needed now – do not act in haste."

"But Opudias, what about my flock? They will be looking for spiritual guidance. What do I tell them? To disregard their hope? To disbelieve this fraud? To pray? To wait and be patient?"

"Yes, your Holiness. To wait and be patient, and God will let them know the Truth when He is ready."

"What is your recommendation, Cardinal Ignatious?"

"Caution is always prudent, but please do not let it stop you from acting once you know the truth in your heart. Truth is the most important consideration. Opudias can ignore it if he wishes, but I felt that energy wave. You did too, your Holiness, didn't you?"

"I must admit I did." He paused to consider the sensation. "You felt nothing Cardinal Opudias?"

"Nothing," he lied with the straightest of faces.

The Pope leaned back in his regal chair. "Thank you both for your counsel, upon which I so depend."

They bowed their heads solemnly.

The Pope motioned for the Cardinal Secretary of State, Prefect of the Sacred Congregation of the Secretariat of State to step forward and state his view.

"Your Holiness, I must tell you the political ramifications would be great should you endorse this matter in any way. I understand your concern for the spiritual well-being of your flock, but we must remember, one of these phenomena occurred on the Temple Mount in Jerusalem, a place of highly conflicting and fervent religious beliefs. The Jewish and Islamic people will not accept the Christian world claiming ownership over this phenomenon, or, fraud. We should not make any strong statements initially. Opudias is right. You should proceed very cautiously."

The Pope gave a hearty "harrumphh" and, noticing it was time for the top of the hour news updates, aimed his remote control at the tall 12th century cabinet containing his multimedia center. Once again, ENN was showing Shayda's video. When it was over, they cut to Jonathan KenCairn's interview with Shayda, Regina and Simone.

The Pope listened carefully to their account before tuning into the other American networks. He was startled to see slick graphics with the words JERUSALEM BOMBING and BOMB ON THE MOUNT twirling across the screen. Clone-like anchors reported the ultra-smart bomb version of the story, highlighting the probability that it was developed by a new underground Muslim fundamentalist organization. Each station had a video which showed a brief flash of light, but the pulsating energy oval and human figure were gone. He watched with bewilderment as the networks accused ENN of perpetrating a cruel joke and making a mockery out of a terrorist act.

When the reports were over, the Pope was visibly confused and upset. He switched to the EuroNet, which showed news commentators analyzing the ENN stories, but they made no mention of a bomb. He switched back to ENN.

"We have just received reports of a second phenomenon occurring on the island of Crete in Greece," Magdalena Severeide announced. "This oval of light appeared near the ruins of Knossos about the same time as the phenomenon occurred in Jerusalem. However, several eyewitnesses saw an American archeologist *disappear* in this energy pulse. At present, we do not have any footage, but an ENN crew is on its way to the scene and we'll be satelcasting live on location within a couple of hours. I repeat, a second phenomenon has taken place on the island of Crete. We will continue to provide you with more information as it becomes available."

The Pope shut off the TV.

"What in Heaven's Name is going on? If there was a bomb, why haven't we heard about it? And why didn't the President of the United States say anything about it? If a bomb exploded on the Temple Mount, hundreds of people would have been injured."

"Your Holiness," interjected Cardinal Opudias, "bombs don't always cause casualties. But they do cause flashes of light. If this were a deception, then the bomb could be part of it. Think about it. ENN needs some real event to get everyone's attention, like a blinding flash of light in a prominent location. Then they invent a fantastic video showing the Second Coming and explain it as a miracle. When the world realizes the video is a fake, ENN can simply scapegoat the three Americans who supposedly recorded the 'phenomenon.' The major networks all report a bombing has occurred. It seems likely ENN is attempting to pull a publicity stunt."

The Cardinal Secretary stepped forward again. "Your Holiness, what about the Golden Gate? Surely, our people in Jerusalem can tell us if the Gate has been blown apart by a bomb, or miraculously opened as in the ENN video."

"Your Holiness," Cardinal Ignatious interjected. "I have spoken with Cardinal Vincent of Jerusalem. His reports were very clear. His top aides have visited the Gate and they have seen it with their own eyes. The stone blocks have disappeared."

"What about those stones, Opudias?" The Pontiff questioned. "How could a bomb have done that?"

"I'm not certain your Holiness. I do not know what kind of technology could accomplish what Cardinal Vincent has reported, yet, that does not mean the technology doesn't exist; nor can we be certain Cardinal Vincent's report is completely accurate. He too could have already been swept up in the hysteria," he glared at Ignatious, "which seems to be spreading."

"Granted, Opudias, hysteria can twist reality. However, Cardinal Vincent is not one to get caught up in the moment. He is a conservative soul, and I have never known him to cast his rational mind aside. No, something unusual has occurred. What you call hysteria Cardinal Ignatious calls spiritual reawakening."

The Cardinal Secretary stepped forward again. "Your Grace, I have an idea. You want to show your leadership at a time when the world is full of hope, yet you don't want to leave yourself vulnerable should this hope turn to despair. The ultimate truth is not known at present, and I believe the best course of action is to determine what it is. However, we must be extremely careful not to alienate other governments and religious leaders. The political consequences are potentially enormous because of the fundamental religious issues at the heart of these, phenomena. It is clear there will be a significant global impact regardless of the ultimate explanation.

"The American President is acting quickly to forge cooperative alliances in an attempt to uncover the truth. You can advocate for expanding the cooperative effort. The United Nations Millennium Summit is three days away. I believe it would be an excellent forum for the nations of the world to work together, and try to achieve some common understanding about what has occurred.

"Your participation would demonstrate your leadership and your belief in international cooperation. If, in the end, you believe it is the Second Coming, you can still exercise your spiritual authority. I recommend you contact the President and suggest it."

"Ignatious, what do you think?"

"It is an excellent idea. I would further recommend you personally attend the Summit."

"Opudias?"

"I think it is too bold a step without more information. I continue to urge caution."

The Pontiff let his eyes drift across the room, to his favorite Michelangelo nativity scene displayed on the baroque wall, where his friends once again came to life.

"I think you should listen to Opudias," said Melchior, leaning on his staff. "It's all a hoax."

"It's all a hoax," Balthazar and Gaspar agreed in unison.

The sheep started bleating and the donkey brayed.

Mary got up, put her hands on her hips and rebuked them all. "Now wait just a minute, you know as well as I do that was no hoax!" She looked at the Pope. "Your Holiness, you know the truth in your heart."

Joseph agreed. "Just be careful, your Holiness."

The Pontiff then looked to the baby Jesus, who pulled himself up in his straw crib and whispered a message across the room.

The Pope nodded. "I must be cautious, but I see no reason to refute it yet. The masses are weary from 2,000 years of waiting for a sign which has never come, and real or not, this event has stirred my flock to consider the Second Coming. There are many souls who would welcome such news amidst the apocalyptic predictions with which they are inundated. The promise of the Second Coming brings with it a sense of hope which so many have forsaken. Yes, the people need to hear this message of hope. Please contact the American President on the video telephone."

The Pope looked into his monitor and the President's image appeared. "Mr. President, I have been watching your American television networks. There are some very contradictory and confusing reports about the incident in Jerusalem. Do you believe it was a bomb, and that ENN has somehow perpetrated an ingenious deception?"

"Your Holiness, as I indicated, I am sending teams to conduct investigations of both sites. I'd prefer not to speculate until we have reliable information. We can expect a report by tomorrow."

"You will keep me informed?"

"Of course."

"Mr. President, I'm sure you are aware of the potential impact of this event, both political and spiritual. We need a quick, unified response or we risk chaos. The upcoming United Nations Millennium Summit would provide the perfect opportunity to address the event in a cooperative setting, and to provide guidance to the world. I suggest we both encourage political leaders to expand their delegations to include the religious and scientific communities. Let us come together in New York to discuss these phenomena from every perspective. I have decided to attend myself and I urge you to do the same."

"A splendid idea. I will issue a statement to that effect. Hopefully, we'll learn the truth about the phenomena and, perhaps, learn something about our common humanity."

The Pontiff smiled. "I look forward to seeing you in New York."

"Until then."

The President returned his attention to the growing entourage in the oval office. The Vice President, Secretary of Defense, CIA Director and other Cabinet members had arrived.

"Mr. President," CIA began, "I have received the NATO intelligence reports you requested. They confirm a tremendous energy surge surrounded the Golden Gate. It lasted 52 seconds, and a human form appeared inside it for 22 seconds. The light and the figure disappeared in a flash, and so did the stones which had been blocking the gate for centuries. There were many eyewitnesses. Thousands of people are flocking to the site from all over the Middle East region, Europe and even Africa. A similar effect is being observed in Crete. The commercial airlines are already diverting flights to meet some of the demand."

"I see. That essentially confirms the ENN version. Have you got anything else?"

"Yes. I've run comprehensive profiles on the three American women who recorded the phenomenon. Shayda Farzoneh has a Ph.D. in comparative mythology and is a full professor at the University of Michigan, Ann Arbor. She and her family emigrated to the U.S. from Iran in 1979, though two of her uncles still live in Jordan. We don't know much about them, but we do know Dr. Farzoneh had been visiting them just prior to her arrival in Jerusalem, yesterday.

"Simone Blumenthal, alias Simone Bloome, is an actress living in New York City. She has a twin sister in Crown Heights, Brooklyn who's part of that ultra orthodox sect, the Hasidim; they have known ties to the Likud party. Ms. Blumenthal spent the last six months on an Israeli kibbutz prior to her arrival in Jerusalem, also yesterday."

"What about the third one?"

"Regina Highland. She's an organic farmer and peace activist who lives on a commune outside of Eugene, Oregon. She's been arrested several times for civil disobedience, but the only suspicious thing we could find was that she also arrived in Jerusalem yesterday. However, as far as we can tell, the three of them have had no previous contact.

"We've also been monitoring CHAOS' communication systems. We've confirmed they intercepted the eyewitness' datafile from the Jerusalem AmEx office, doctored the video and instructed the networks to run it. They're clearly trying to prevent the story from getting out."

"Just as we suspected," the President affirmed, turning his attention to the Secretary of Defense – the one cabinet member he hadn't appointed. When the President assumed office, he realized that with the two-headed monster Republicrat nearly dead, the military might have felt threatened enough to launch a coup and impose martial law. He believed it was in the best interests of the country to allow the previous defense secretary to retain his position. This action appeased them for a while, however, tension had recently flared over significant cuts in the military budget. "Mr. Secretary, do you have anything to report?"

"We have still not detected any troop movement in either region, nor have we received any reports of casualties. The Israeli Palestinian Joint Security, I mean *Community*, Force has been dispatched, and that operation is going smoothly. Israel has activated their National Guard because of the increased security risks. They may need reinforcements if people continue to flock to the Temple Mount at the rate we are currently seeing.

"I have a similar concern for Crete. The Greek government sent their Special Security Force to reinforce the Heraklion Police Department. They will be able to handle the initial influx of people, but once again, if they keep coming, both governments are going to need help.

"Additionally, I believe this phenomenon represents a significant threat to the stability of the world, and therefore, to our national security. We should be nearby and remain on alert. Specifically, I recommend we deploy our two Mediterranean aircraft carriers currently stationed in Sicily. The Enterprise should move in to the Eastern Mediterranean, just off the Israeli coast, and the Voyager should be assigned to monitor Heraklion Harbor and the Cretan coast. Both should be reinforced by small contingency forces. We will be able to monitor all traffic and gather more information while offshore."

"Hold off on that. I'd like to consult with the Congressional leadership before making any deployments."

The Defense Secretary exhaled loudly.

"Please invite the Speaker of the House and the heads of the appropriate committees to join me for a meeting," the President asked the Chief of Staff. "And have the Press Secretary do a news conference for the White House Press Corps. Notify them we're investigating the phenomena, and sending scientific teams who will work cooperatively with the Israeli, Palestinian and Greek governments. Inform them I will be attending the Millennium Summit and that we're also encouraging political, scientific and religious leaders to attend, so we can all discuss the phenomena in a collaborative forum. Did I forget anything?"

"No, I don't think so," replied the Secretary of State.

"Okay. Let's get on the horn and convince the world to come to New York."

CHAPTER FOUR
SEEK AND YE SHALL FIND

Up the eastern seaboard on the crazy concrete island of Manhattan, Ben Gerrard and Angela Wright were analyzing CHAOS broadcasts from inside the ENN brain center. They stood on the central control mound, encircled by a wall of monitors, computers and blissed out engineers directing electronic information at light speed. From his terminal on the mound, Gerrard could access every commercial satellite signal from around the globe, and sounds and images from his extensive digital archive. Billions and billions of photons, carrying megamegs of information, shot through them from all directions.

"The bomb theory again!" Ben shook his head in disgust. "Have they no shame? There's nothing to suggest a bomb. And look how they've manipulated the footage. Rogues! We need to get back on the Net with this as soon as possible. What more do we know at this point?" he asked the station's Science Editor.

"They were some kind of electrical atmospheric disturbances, but I've never heard of anything like them. A pulse emanated from their epicenters and surrounded the planet, like ripples shimmering on the surface of a gigantic pond. All electronic activity was temporarily affected, but there wasn't any measurable long term disruption or any apparent residual effects. We detected a minor increase in solar flare activity, but otherwise, nothing unusual. The international scientific community is abuzz and the Nets are jammed. I've instructed our science staff to investigate further."

"Good work. What have you got Ange?"

"People felt it all *over* the planet. They're describing the sensation as an energy surge, a sustained vibration or fluid wave. They feel uplifted, even euphoric. And, where the waves overlapped, they say it was *really* intense. I think they've felt the beat of the Drum."

Ben flashed back to their trip to Africa, and the Yoruba drum ceremony. Orishas danced wildly around the burning red fire, in flowing colors and magical masks....

"Jonathan is on his way to Crete with a crew," she continued. "They'll establish a feed and hopefully get some footage. Right now, all we have is a local news clip and it doesn't show much."

Ben turned to Master Engineer Reginald Quinton Lee. "Let's start researching Knossos, Reg. I want every bit of information you can get me."

Reggie spun around to his console, his long fast fingers gliding over the controls.

Gerrard looked back at monitor 111, which froze the surreal human image inside the Jerusalem light phenomenon. "And who is *that*? There's no way that figure could have been dubbed in, right Reg?"

"Nope. It's seamless as baby skin."

"Well, who is it then? Could it be the archeologist?"

"Could be."

"Could it be Christ?" Ben looked at Angela.

"I wonder if it just might be," she replied, raising her eyebrows high. "Whatta ya say we interview some religious folks?"

"Excellent idea."

"Comin' in," Reggie announced in his smooth, tenor voice. "Unscheduled White House press conference starting in ten minutes."

"Good. We'll cover it live and run the video again as a lead-in. When it's over, interview the science staff. Then we'll air the religious reactions."

Angela sat down at another station. "Hey Reggie, patch me through to the studio, willya?"

"You got it."

Within seconds, she was connected and prepping Magdalena for her White House intro.

Reggie swiveled around in his chair and said nonchalantly, "CHAOS is trying to jam our signals again, but I saw it comin' a mile away. It won't be a problem."

Ben patted him on the shoulder. "You're amazing Reg."

"Wanna go with the new graphics?"

"Definitely."

Reggie touched a few keys on his pad and the On-Net screen went black. Space. Out there, in the realm of the galaxies. Stars begin rushing by. We approach our solar system, sailing silently by Saturn, Jupiter and Mars, through the asteroid belt to our fragile blue pearl adrift on the cosmic sea. We rush through the white puffy clouds, and the Mediterranean rotates into view. Out of the corner of the screen, like a blazing comet, a point of light splits and explodes in the two locations, before filling the screen and burning off to reveal the anchor.

"Great day! Maggie Severeide reporting once again from ENN Central in New York City. We've just received word the White House will momentarily be holding a special press conference to discuss the unexplained events occurring today. Just in case you haven't seen it yet, this is the unedited video of the Jerusalem Event."

The flash dissolved into the White House press room, where the Press Secretary was about to begin. Angela, Reggie and Ben scrutinized his every word, trying to glean hints about what the Administration really knew. However, the Secretary was pretty tight lipped. He confirmed the existence of the two phenomena, but he gave no indication as to any possible explanation. He also reported the formation of the science teams and the President's plan to attend the Millennium Summit, but declined to answer any questions at this time.

"They're keeping an open mind!" Ben exclaimed. "Hey Reg, would you mind patchin' me through to Jonathan?"

"No problem, their chopper should be flyin' high in the Mediterranean sky by now," Reggie replied, as he made instantaneous audio contact via the air phone. "You're connected."

"Hi Jonathan! It's Ben. Where are you?"

"Hi Ben! Getting close to Crete. We should be there shortly."

"Good. The White House just held a press conference; they're sending international science teams to both sites and the President is urging world leaders to attend the Millennium Summit."

"When will the scientists be here?"

"First thing in the morning."

"Got it. Any other news from Heraklion?"

"Nope. It's all we've got."

"Okay. Talk to you soon."

Jonathan clicked off and looked back out the window of the helicopter. He'd shed his suit for a sweater and jeans and was psyched to be on assignment. Below, he could see the purple-blue mountains of Crete thrusting upward from the deep blue Mediterranean Sea. As they got closer to the shoreline, the old Venetian port and its arching stone pier came into view. Boats and buildings caught his attention at first, but then he noticed the mass of people flowing toward and around the ruins, just a few miles away. "Look at that!" he exclaimed to the crew. "Start recording! Can we fly over the site?"

"Sure," the ENN pilot replied. "But we only have permission to land at the airport."

"Great! Get as close as you can."

Moments later, they swooped over the ruins at Knossos, bringing a bird's eye view to the TV world. Masses of people surrounded the site, spilling out onto the hillsides and into the road.

The pilot circled twice around, then brought them in for landing at the Heraklion airport. Security had been tightened and the place was crawling with Greek special forces. A lieutenant greeted them as they got out of the copter, and after he was satisfied they were who they were supposed to be, took them to a waiting vehicle. The crew loaded up the slick, white four-wheel drive with equipment and headed to Knossos.

The streets were packed, but at least traffic kept moving. They slowly wound their way around the outskirts of the city and up the hill toward the ruins. Tour coaches lined the old Royal Road like a colossal metallic caterpillar, and people and cars were everywhere. They parked as close as they could, grabbed their equipment and set off.

The four of them meandered through the morass of parked vehicles, which after about twenty minutes, finally gave way to the grove around the entrance. A line of excited, chattering people led up to the gate. Jonathan and the crew cut to the front, flashed their new press passes and the guard waved them on.

They made their way through the crowded path to the old stone plaza. Three gleaming red and black pillars rose above the buried bricks and rubble, and more partial rooms and walls beckoned from across the courtyard. Jonathan felt the pull of the Minos legends, but he knew his exploration of the Minotaur's Maze would have to wait. He found another security guard who directed them toward the dig.

They walked down the hill, through thousands of people milling about in the afterglow of the light phenomenon. Groups of people sat together, excitedly exchanging their accounts. Some were singing and chanting. Others were kneeling on partially exposed limestone blocks peeking out of the dusty ground, praying quietly to themselves. Many lit candles and brought flowers and garlands to decorate the grounds. Still more were just wandering around, trying to make sense of it all.

Jonathan lucked out and found an open spot under a tree, not too far from the cave entrance. "Okay, let's set up the link here," he said to the other three crew members. "I'll go talk to the archeologists."

As he inched his way up to the front, he could see local police officers posted all along a yellow tape, encircling the dig site. He kept squishing through until he was right up against it. He could see a few workers continuing to clear rocks and dirt out of the hole, but the cave entrance was not yet exposed. A few men were taking a break over near a worktent, but he didn't see the archeologists. For now he'd just have to wait, so he struck up a conversation with the elderly man standing next to him.

"Hello, sir. Did you see the phenomenon?"

"Yes I did," the old man replied in his heavy accent. "I saw it from the taverna. It was a glorious circle of light, and Vasilios says it happened right there," he pointed, "five feet, no, ten feet from the new tent. The old one went up in flames!"

What do you think it was?"

"I think it *is* a sign."

"A sign of what?"

"Of good things to come."

Just then, two figures emerged from the tent.

"There's Vasilios!" the older man shouted. "Vasilios, ella!"

Jonathan's heart raced.

The other man, probably Dr. Adalat, disappeared into the hole, but Vasilios came over to them. "Tikannes, Nikos!"

Jonathan observed the two while they talked excitedly in Greek. When Vasilios was about to walk away, Jonathan spoke up.

"Excuse me, Mr. Koulouris, my name is Jonathan KenCairn.

I'm with ENN, the Earth News Network." He pulled out his photo ID. "We're going to be broadcasting an international report from here, and I'd really like the chance to do a live interview with the archeologists. Do you think it could be arranged?"

Vasilios took the identification and compared the picture to Jonathan's face. He handed it back and replied curtly, "I'll see what I can do."

Vasilios climbed down the rope ladder, and ducked through the widening cave entrance. They'd set up portable lights in the antechamber, but didn't want to risk damaging the frescoes, so the stairway and inner chamber were dim. He found Nizam standing two inches away from the cave wall, inspecting a minute portion of the fresco with his high-powered magnifying glass.

"Nizam, ENN is here and they want to talk to us. Do we give them an interview?"

"I think we should, Vasilios." He backed away from the painting and put down the lens. "As we discussed earlier, we cannot hide from the media, but we should not volunteer too much information yet either. I think we must be very, very careful what we say. I suggest we brief them on the nature of the excavation and describe what we witnessed. However, I do not believe we should mention the tablet or the translation until it has been secured."

"In other words, we'll be vague and buy more time."

"Precisely!"

"Agreed. I'll go get the reporter."

"I'll be right there."

Vasilios climbed out of the cave to find Jonathan waiting with Abe, the camera operator.

"Mr. ENN, are you ready?"

"Whenever you are."

The police officers lifted the tape and motioned for them to come inside.

"Thank you for agreeing to meet with us, Mr. Koulouris."

"Para kalo."

Nizam emerged from the hole, and a crew member very carefully passed up one of the glass lamps they'd found in the inner chamber. The crowd oohed and ahhed as the artifact was removed from its ancient resting place.

"Mr. ENN, this is Dr. Nizam Adalat."

"Hello Dr. Adalat. I'm Jonathan KenCairn. We really appreciate your willingness to do a live interview. This is a most extraordinary event and we're anxious to bring news of it to the people. I'd like to include Dr. Deegan in the report if she's available."

"She wasn't feeling well after all the excitement," Nizam lied quickly, "so she went back to her room for a rest."

"Oh. I, hope she feels better."

"Thank you. Now, may we proceed?"

"The ENN anchor is just finishing a news update, and we should be ready to go any minute. Would it be possible to do the interview inside the cave?"

"No, I'm afraid not. We must finish securing the cave and removing the rubble from the entrance."

"I see. How 'bout on the rim of the excavation, then? So we can look down inside?"

"That would be acceptable."

Abe set up the opening shot as Magdalena's voice came over Jonathan's headset. "...and now we go live to Crete where Jonathan KenCairn is standing by."

"Thank you Maggie! Behind me are thousands of people who have gathered outside a newly discovered cave near the ancient Minoan ruins of Knossos."

The crowd cheered and waved into the camera, which followed Jonathan over to the site of the phenomenon.

"Several hours ago, on this spot, American archeologist Dr. Zoee Nikitas disappeared in an unexplained atmospheric phenomenon." He approached the dig. "With me now are two members of the archeological team, Dr. Nizam Adalat and Mr. Vasilios Koulouris. First of all gentlemen, can you tell us what happened to your colleague, Dr. Nikitas?"

"I'm afraid not," replied Nizam sadly. "We have no rational explanation. She was inside the tent when a surge of light and energy engulfed her. The tent disintegrated, and after about a minute, she and the light disappeared in a tremendous flash."

"I saw it too. The light was miraculous, but our poor Zoee. She has vanished!"

"Did you feel or hear anything?"

"Yes. The light emitted waves of energy which passed through our bodies, and I heard a harmonic ringing sound."

"Like crystal angels." Vasilios clasped his hands.

"Was there any damage besides the tent?"

"No. Except for the disappearance of our colleague, everything is just as it was before the phenomenon."

"I tell you, it is a miracle!"

"What are you working on here?"

"We are excavating an ancient cave which has been hidden beneath this hillside for at least three thousand years. Dr. Nikitas discovered it three months ago using sophisticated X-ray imaging technology. You can look into the excavation pit and see the narrow entrance."

Abe peered the camera over the edge and down into the hole. Two crew members waved and pointed toward the opening.

"We began excavating yesterday in search of Minoan artifacts."

"Who are the Minoans?"

"They were an advanced civilization which flourished on this island from roughly 3000 to 1450 b.c.e."

"What did you find?"

"So far, we've found five oil lamps like this one." Nizam held it up and Abe zoomed in. "It is made of rock crystal. This shallow well was filled with olive oil, and the wick was placed here, in this groove on the rim."

Abe zoomed back out.

"What else did you find?"

"The cave walls themselves are painted with the finest Minoan frescoes found to date. It is an extraordinary discovery. When the cave has been secured, we will be delighted to invite you in to see them."

Jonathan took the cue and wrapped it up. "Well, thank you Dr. Adalat and Mr. Koulouris! Good luck with this exciting find. We'll be checking in with you over the next few days, and we look forward to seeing those frescoes!" He looked into the camera. "That's all from Crete for now. Back to you in New York."

Abe shut off the camera, and Jonathan removed his headset. "Can you tell me anything more about this phenomenon, off the record?"

"No. I'm sorry, but we have no more information."

"I'll be covering this story and if I find out anything else, I'll let you know."

"Thank you."

"Oh, by the way, could either of you recommend a good place nearby, to get a bite to eat?"

"My old friend Tasso has the best food around." Vasilios pointed off in the distance. "His taverna is just up the road."

Jonathan thanked them again, and he and Abe rejoined the crew.

"Something isn't right," Jonathan said to the others.

"What do you mean?" Abe wondered.

"Where's the other archeologist?"

"He said she went back to her room."

Jonathan leveled an unconvinced look at the other crew members. "They make an *extraordinary* find, their colleague disappears in a bizarre atmospheric distortion and she needs to take a nap? I find that incredibly unlikely. But why would she leave, and where would she go?

"I think I should follow up with Vasilios' old friend Tasso down at the taverna, and while I'm there, I'll pick up some local Greek take out. No doubt we could all use a bite. I'll be back as soon as I can. Tape as many eyewitness accounts as possible and find some film or video of the phenomenon. With all of these tourists, somebody had to get at least part of it."

When he arrived at Tasso's, several locals were gossiping briskly in their emphatic Cretan dialect. They paused ever so slightly when Jonathan walked in, but quickly resumed. He had a seat and tried to glean something from what they were saying. Tasso soon appeared with a basket of crusty bread, bellowing a hearty greeting. "Kali spehda! What can I get for you?"

"What do you have?"

"Whatever you want. I recommend a nice piece of spanikopita. It's right out of the oven, nice and crispy, with a little tsatsiki and a horiatiki salata on the side."

He hadn't heard of any of them. "Sounds great!"

"Very good!" Tasso poured him a glass of retsina before disappearing into the back.

Jonathan sipped the strong, resinated wine and tried to observe the villagers without being too conspicuous. Unfortunately, most of the conversation was in Greek, and he couldn't make much of it. However, a few minutes later, and much to his delight, Nikos came in. He quickly got up and approached the older man.

"Hello sir, remember me? We had a nice visit this afternoon."

"Of course I remember!"

"Would you care to join me?"

"Why not? But let me first say hello to my friends." He had a brief exchange with the locals, then joined Jonathan at his table.

"They sure seem excited about something."

"They are always excited about something."

"What's got them going today?"

"The Miracle of course! They are debating what it means. Mostly they are arguing about whether or not it was the work of God."

"Are they reaching any conclusions?"

"Some say yes, some say no. But they all think they have the answer."

"What do you think the answer is?"

"Time will tell."

"Your friend Vasilios and Dr. Adalat gave a good interview today. I'm only sorry the other archeologist, Dr. Deegan, wasn't feeling well. I would've liked to talk with her too."

"She didn't look sick when she lugged that crate into Vasilios' jeep this afternoon."

"Oh?" Jonathan asked, trying to sound disinterested.

"I heard they went up the Mt. Juktas road."

Just then one of the locals, an old woman who had evidently been eavesdropping, turned and added something in Greek. Nikos responded, and a few of the others chimed in with their comments. Finally, Nikos turned back to Jonathan.

"Poletimi says that Vasilios' yai ya lives up that way, in a small mountain village called Varvari."

"His *yai ya*?"

"His grandmother."

If Tasso hadn't appeared with the food just then, Jonathan might have bolted out of the taverna. But he knew he had to eat sometime and the food looked delicious. "Thanks. I'd like some of this to go for three of my friends too."

Nikos got up. "I leave you to your dinner, and to your business."

Jonathan swallowed a large bite and stood up. "I have enjoyed talking with you."

"Me too. Goodbye."

"Goodbye, sir."

He scarfed down the food and hurried back to the site. As the crew ate their dinner, they relayed what they'd learned. Sure enough, several tourists had seen Fiona leave with Vasilios shortly after the event, though nobody knew where she went. The crew had also interviewed numerous eyewitnesses and found footage of the phenomenon.

"Excellent work. Let's take a look at that video."

Abe pushed a few buttons on the portable monitor and played the clip. It cut in about halfway through, but clearly showed Zoe disappearing.

"Amazing. It's just like the phenomenon in Jerusalem! Okay, send that footage and the eyewitness shots to New York immediately. We have to find that archeologist and whatever it is she took from the site. I think I know where she is, but I'd better go alone. So I'll see you later – oh, remember, we need to be prepared first thing tomorrow when that science team arrives."

As Jonathan walked through the crowd again, his mind was alive with ideas, swirling about, interlacing into tenuous form. He sensed their connection, but couldn't quite bring them together into a coherent picture. He finally found the vehicle, and before he took off, climbed on top to take a look around. Layers of hills and purple ridgelines rose in the distance, and a crystal blue sky arched overhead. People and cars flowed toward the ruins, glowing gold in the afternoon sun.

After a few minutes, he jumped down, got in, and slowly maneuvered his way out of the jumble of cars. Once he turned onto the Mt. Juktas road, the traffic clog vanished. He grabbed his cellphone and pressed the auto dialer. "Hi Angela, it's Jonathan."

"Hey, Jonathan! Great job so far. We got Abe's footage and are getting ready to run it. What else've you got?"

"Well, I've stumbled onto another mystery, and it might be important. The other archeologist, Dr. Fiona Deegan, was seen leaving the area shortly after the event with a crate of what may have been artifacts. I think she's in a village about an hour away from here. I'm en route now to try and find her."

"Check it out, but we need you back at the site by sunrise tomorrow."

"I'll be there."

"Good luck!"

As he drove into the village of Varvari, the sun was setting behind Mt. Ida, which appeared indigo against the pink and orange sherbet sky. He came to a small grocery, and once again, found a few locals inside shooting the breeze. They took note of him as he walked around the store, trying to decide what the most appropriate gift would be. He finally selected a bottle of red wine and approached the counter. "Do you speak English?" he asked the shopkeeper.

The man shook his head no, but pointed to one of the customers.

"I'm the village schoolteacher," the woman said, "and yes, I speak English. How can I help you?"

"I'm a friend of Vasilios Koulouris. I was just passing through and thought I'd say hello to his yai ya. Could you tell me where I might find her?"

"Vasilios!" the shopkeeper said excitedly, adding some unintelligible commentary.

"Apparently, you're the second guest she's received today. I was just leaving, I'll show you where she lives."

Jonathan paid for the wine and followed the schoolteacher out the door.

"How do you know Vasilios?" she asked, as they walked down the street.

"I'm an amateur archeologist and I've been visiting Knossos," Jonathan exaggerated, feeling a little guilty. "Vasilios is currently working on a dig there. I mentioned I was heading to Mt. Dikti, and he told me his grandmother lived in a village right along the way. So I thought I'd stop and say a quick hello."

"We heard about what happened at Knossos. Is Vasilios okay?"

"Yes. He's fine."

He told her what he knew as they went up a hill, past several whitewashed houses. Soon they came to a small fence, which turned up a narrow alley and to a gate. The teacher rang the goat bell hanging on an overgrown orange tree, and Panayota called from inside the simple little house. A few seconds later, a hunched, white-haired woman dressed entirely in black emerged from behind a wooden door. She was speaking loudly and enthusiastically to the teacher, who explained who Jonathan was and why he was here.

She took Jonathan's hand. She didn't have a clue who he was, but she didn't care, she liked visitors. "Yanni!"

"It is your name in Greek," the teacher explained.

He gave Panayota the bottle of wine and she invited them inside. He ducked through the low doorway and she directed them into her small living room, where a tall red-headed woman in her late thirties sat plucking a bazoukia. He smiled and sat down on the other end of the antique davenport.

With the teacher's help, Panayota explained that Fiona was also Vasilios' friend. Jonathan thought he detected a sudden tenseness coming from Fiona, but she quickly recovered and said hello with the utmost composure.

Suddenly, the old woman whirled around and disappeared into her tiny kitchen. Seconds later she reappeared with a large loaf of bread tucked under her arm. She snapped a red checkered cloth in the air and placed it on top of the old wooden table, then made an announcement, thumped the bread down and spun back into the kitchen. Jonathan and Fiona looked at the teacher.

"She's going to prepare eggs for dinner."

Jonathan tried to steer the conversation away from Vasilios and the dig. He babbled on about this being his first trip to Greece, and how he likes to travel. Did they like to travel? Where are some other nice places to visit in Crete? He was looking for an opening to say something to Fiona, and a couple minutes later he got it. Panayota shouted something to the teacher who shouted something back, then got up and went into the kitchen.

The moment she was out of sight, he turned to Fiona. "I'm really here to see you."

She looked at him squarely, without betraying how concerned she actually was.

"But don't worry," Jonathan said, looking earnestly into her eyes. "I'm a reporter with ENN and we are committed to reporting the truth about your find. Something extraordinary happened at that site today, and I think you have a clue. I think it's somehow related to the Jerusalem Event, but I don't know how. Please hear me out. I'll be leaving shortly after dinner. Will you meet me at the ouzeria?"

Fiona leveled a steady gaze at him but said nothing.

Panayota broke the brief silence when she rematerialized with a plate of fresh, olive oil saturated fried eggs, pepperonchinis, feta cheese, kalamata olives and orange slices. She made another announcement and Fiona and Jonathan didn't need a translator to figure out they were being summoned to the table for supper.

The teacher hadn't dared leave without nibbling on a little food; yai yas do not easily take no for an answer. But she really needed to get going. So she ate a bit of everything and tried to start wrapping it up – a process she knew could take a while. After a few false starts, she was finally able to find a suitable opening and say her thank yous and goodbyes to Panayota. She got up from the table and extended her hand to Jonathan and Fiona. "A pleasure to meet you. Have a nice stay in Greece."

Jonathan saw this as his opportunity as well. "Before you go, please thank Panayota for the delicious dinner." *I am so full.* "And tell her how much I enjoyed meeting her, and her grandson Vasilios, then I think I'll be going too."

Panayota was watching Jonathan as she heard his translated message. Without warning, she reached up, pinched his left cheek really hard, spun around and headed out the door. Before he left, he gave Fiona one last please trust me, please meet me look, but her expression gave him no hint of what to expect.

After a few more pearls of Cretan wisdom, they were finally on their way. The teacher took the first left and waved goodbye as she hurried off down the narrow street. Jonathan continued on to the ouzeria in the center of town.

Like many ouzerias, this one had a covered outdoor patio with tables occupied by men playing backgammon and sipping ouzo. Jonathan found a seat up front near the sidewalk, so he could keep an eye out for Fiona. He ordered an ouzo and tried to relax. After 15 or 20 minutes he had to remind himself it wasn't that easy to escape Panayota, and it might take a while for her to get here. He was just starting to formulate a Plan B when the archeologist emerged out of the darkness. He stood up to greet her.

"Thank you for coming Dr. Deegan." He offered her a chair.

"Vasilios would never have told you where to find me. How did you know where I was?"

"Maybe you haven't noticed, but these people are very open. They like to exchange news and speculate about what's going on. Tasso's taverna is abuzz with news of today's events. They're all talking about the energy wave, the disappearance of your colleague and," he leaned over the table and lowered his voice, "the artifacts you smuggled out of there." He sat back in his chair. "All of Heraklion probably knows where you are by now."

She was not pleased to hear this, because even if he was exaggerating, the tablet was not secure. She maintained an emotionless face and said, "you've found me, so what do you want?"

"I want to know how those artifacts fit in to what's going on here, and everywhere." He started to sound more enthusiastic as he recounted the events. "Something incredible happened this morning. At precisely the same time, a tremendous atmospheric disruption of unknown origin occurred at Knossos and in Jerusalem. Why those two places? What's the connection? I think those artifacts you're hiding are a clue and that's why you're hiding them. I want you to tell me, and the world, what you've discovered."

She looked at him hard, trying to analyze his pheromones. She detected no ill vibes, but could he really be trusted? She wanted to believe him but she had to be cautious. "Don't you people carry ID?"

"Absolutely." He took it out of his pocket and gave it to her.

As she was handing it back, a black Mercedes sedan careened around the corner and came to a sudden stop at the curb, just a few feet away. Two burly men got out and approached their table.

"I think you better come with us," one of them said in a heavy English.

"What makes you think I'll do that?" Fiona stood up and demanded.

The other man revealed a gun concealed in his coat. "We'd like you to be our guests for dinner."

"I've already eaten two dinners tonight," Jonathan said, slowly rising from the table, "so I think we'll have to have a miss. But thanks anyway."

"I don't think so."

Just then, Panayota appeared behind the men, madly shaking a gigantic pink rose and yelling in Greek. She belted one of them and shook her flower at the other. Within seconds, the fourteen men in the ouzeria were yelling epithets and converging on the two strangers.

As the locals closed in, Fiona and Jonathan slipped out of the crowd and broke into a dead run back to the house. Panayota's pandemonium had saved them. At least temporarily.

Fiona ran inside the gate and Jonathan was right behind her. She abruptly turned around, looked him squarely in his periwinkle blue eyes and grabbed him by both shoulders. "Now I have no choice but to trust you. You had better be telling me the truth."

"I am, I promise. Look, those guys freaked me out too. We have to get out of here! My rig is parked at the corner grocery. Where are the artifacts?"

"Inside. Get your *rig* and bring it here."

"Okay. I'll be right back."

Jonathan ran to the vehicle, jumped inside and zipped back to Panayota's. He backed in the little alley alongside the gate, pulled up as close as he could and popped the hatch.

Fiona came out carrying a wooden crate. "Do you mind grabbing my bag and the blankets, they're inside the door."

"Not at all."

Fiona carefully loaded the crate in the back, and packed the blankets around it. Then she hopped into the passenger's seat. "Go!"

"Where to?"

"Keep going up the mountain, I know of a spot that's way out in the back of beyond. We'll hide it there."

"Okay!" As he drove out of the alley, he said softly, "thank you Panayota, for everything."

"I'll say," Fiona agreed.

They passed by two cross streets. "See anything?"

"Nothing suspicious."

As he turned up the main road, he asked again, "anything?"

She looked back over the headrest. "All right so far."

They passed through a large olive grove, which sent them on their way up the dark mountain road. Fiona remained completely turned around, watching for any sign of unwelcome headlights, and Jonathan kept glancing in the rear view mirror.

"I don't think we're being followed," he finally said.

"Jaysus, and who were they!?"

"I suspect they're with the same bunch as the guy who tried to prevent us from getting the Jerusalem disc. I've had some inkling about who they are for a long time, but I haven't quite made the link."

"I take it the 'Jerusalem disc' is somehow related to the Jerusalem Event?"

"Yes. Three American tourists recorded the entire phenomenon on video, and were en route to ENN when a man threatened them with a gun. They escaped and gave us the disc."

"Did you see the phenomenon?"

"No, but I felt it. I was at my office in the New City, and all of a sudden, we felt a wonderful, mystical, thing, and the equipment in the control room went berserk."

"What do you think it was?"

"I have no idea, yet. But maybe, with your help, we can both figure it out. Will you tell me what you've discovered?"

"I really can't. I have to go through this with my colleagues first. We believe the artifact is a very important discovery, and I don't want to see it sensationalized."

"Then, why not tell the world about it? We have a global mystery on our hands and you are the only one who has a clue right now. Share it with the rest of us, so we can work together to solve it."

"I'm not prepared to do that right now. My immediate priority is to ensure the safety of this artifact. Otherwise, it won't be any good to anyone. I appreciate your help, but I'm afraid I have to ask you to be patient."

"I understand and I won't pressure you. I just want you to know I will do everything in my power to get to the truth without sensationalizing your find."

"I appreciate that."

"So, tell me about the Minoans."

"Now there's something I can talk about! The Minoans were an elegant, sophisticated people who were magnificent artists and architects. They lived in a highly egalitarian society, and in fact, may have been the people of Atlantis."

She got real quiet for a minute and her eyes misted over.

"Are you okay?"

"I was just thinkin' about a conversation we had last night."

"You and Dr. Nikitas?"

"What in heaven could have happened to her?"

They were silent for a little while.

"Let's focus on the Minoans. What more can you tell me about them?"

She nodded, wiping away a stray tear. "They were the last of the Goddess cultures."

"A matriarchy?"

"No. Neither sex dominated. Their society was based on partnership and mutual respect between women and men. The most remarkable thing about the Minoans is how they were able to maintain their traditions long after everyone around them had been conquered."

They came to a fork in the road. "Which way?"

"To the left, up the Mt. Dikti road. We still have a few more miles to go."

The road soon became more of a dusty, bumpy two-track, which eventually wound around the southwest flank of the mountain. It just seemed to be getting darker and darker.

"So where are we going?" Jonathan wondered.

"A little cave I know of."

"I noticed quite a few caves on my map of Crete."

"Yes. There are over 2,000 scattered around the island. In fact, one of the most famous, the Diktean Cave, is not too far from here. According to legend, that's the cave where Zeus was born."

"He was born here? Will you tell me the story?"

"Sure. Zeus was the youngest child born to Rhea and Kronos, but don't you know, he was the only one left. Kronos actually ate the rest of his sisters and brothers, because poor, old paranoid Kronos was afraid one of his children would kill him and take away his power. Anyhow, Rhea didn't want Zeus to be Kronos' next meal, so she bore him in a cave on Mt. Dikti and left him safely there with his grandmother, Gaia. Well, didn't Rhea fool old Kronos, because what did she do, only wrapped up an old stone in babies' blankets and served it up for dinner! Kronos ate up the rock, smacked his lips and went about his business. All the while, isn't Zeus growing up to be a fine young lad plotting how to do his father in, and sure didn't he end up being king of the castle."

"I *have* heard that story, but never told so well!"

She pretended to ignore his flattery. "We're getting close now, so look for a huge, old olive tree on the right. There." She pointed out the windshield. "Just after we pass it, veer off the road to the right and keep going straight for a few hundred feet."

He cut the wheel to the right, then immediately swerved to miss a good-sized boulder. "You could have warned me about that!"

"And I'm supposed to remember every bloody rock? Just go as straight as you can, it's not much further. Okay, you can stop right here." She retrieved a flashlight from the bag and got out. "Follow me."

They walked a few feet along the edge of the hill, until they came to a dense gob of underbrush. She carefully pulled a little aside, revealing a small cave. "This is a very ancient, sacred spot," she whispered. "When the Minoans entered a cave, they were entering the womb of Mother Earth, seeking their connection with the universe."

Jonathan stared into the grotto. "What should I do?" he whispered back.

"Enter slowly, and with respect."

They carefully moved the rest of the brush, and crept inside. There was enough room to stand but the whole cave itself wasn't more than about five by seven feet. It had a damp, mossy smell, and they could hear little droplets of water.

She walked toward the back wall and shined the light on a carving.

"What is it?"

"A labrys. It's known as the double axe."

"A weapon."

"No! A sacred symbol used in Minoan religious rituals. See how it resembles a butterfly?"

"Yeah?"

"That stylization invokes the idea of rebirth. Like the butterfly emerges from a cocoon, so does new life emerge from death. Many cultures have known this symbol."

"How old is it?"

"Four thousand years, give or take a few hundred."

"Wow!" is all he could manage to say. He gently traced his fingers over the inscription. "Don't you wonder about the person who carved it?"

"Yes. I do."

"What else is in here?"

"This is the only Minoan artifact, though some male figurines, probably votives to Zeus, were also found in here. But you must remember, the myth of Zeus arose almost a thousand years after the Minoans lived. The Classical Greeks, like so many other dominator cultures, simply usurped the sacred places of the people they conquered. That's why Zeus was born in a Cretan cave – to establish the link, which then enables them to co-opt the stories."

"And now, this cave will once again protect a Minoan artifact. It comes full circle."

Fiona looked into his eyes. "Yes, it does. Well, I suppose we'd better bring it in then."

After placing the crate safely inside the cave, she recovered the entrance with brush.

"What now?" Jonathan asked. "Do we head back down the mountain?"

"I'd just as soon hang on awhile; I want to make sure we're not being followed. I know another road, which'll take us down a different ridge, and we can still get back to Knossos before sunrise."

She retrieved the micro computer from her bag and started to log on.

"What are you doing?"

"I'm going to e-mail Nizam and Vasilios. At least I can let them know the artifact is safe for the moment."

"Um, that's probably not a good idea. You see, on my way to Varvari, I used my cellphone to call New York, and that *might* be how those men found us. I don't think we should risk it."

"Oh great, that was your doin'?" she said, cracking a smile.

"I suppose it was, but don't worry, we'll be back in a few hours, and I really don't think we've been followed. So let's try to relax. We'll leave when you think it's safe."

"Okay. That's a good idea. I'll get the blankets so we can have a rest."

They stretched out under the stars, burning brightly by the

billions in the dark, clear sky.

"There's Orion, the Hunter," Jonathan pointed.

"Uh huh. Though you know, some people believe Orion is actually a messenger, not a hunter."

"A messenger of what?"

"I'm not sure."

Just then, a brilliant green meteorite blasted through the atmosphere, leaving a glowing gold trail blazing across the sky.

CHAPTER FIVE
A VOICE FROM THE PAST

As Fiona and Jonathan drove down from Mt. Dikti, a fuchsia sun peeked through the stillness of the sea. Along the horizon, thin bands of clouds took on colors of dawn, and the mountains yawned out of night. Off in the distance, the early rays kissed a golden Knossos good morning.

Soon they were walking down the road. People were just waking up, slowly emerging from cars and tour busses parked everywhere around them. As they got closer to the entrance, they encountered clusters of tents and the remnants of smoldering fires. They passed by an old man, who was softly blowing on glowing embers, trying to revive his flame. He reached for the long slender handle of his briki, and tapped a healthy teaspoon of dark, finely ground coffee into it. Then he placed the small copper pot on the fire. He added a little sugar to the mix and waited for the froth to rise.

When they reached the forested area outside the gate, they heard a gentle cooing in the branches above their heads. High up in a tree, a young, long-haired American man sang, "I hear the Muses, they're coming! I see the Muses, they're here!"

Jonathan and Fiona looked at each other. "Well," she said smiling, "who's to say he can't see them?"

"Not me!"

The lines at the gate had grown, though people were still patiently waiting their turn to enter. They tried not to call too much attention to themselves, as they cut to the front and breezed through the gate. Once inside, they had to step around and hop over acres of people carpeting the grounds around the ruins and down to the cave site. When Vasilios saw them coming, he called Nizam out of the worktent.

"Everything is safe and I'm all right," Fiona said, slipping under the yellow tape. "Have you seen Zoee?"

"No," Vasilios replied anxiously. "What happened to you?! We heard you had some trouble and we've been worried."

"Jonathan found me in the village, and two big hulks in a black Mercedes tried to kidnap us, but we managed to escape, thanks to Panayota. She was wonderful, Vasilios, I'll tell you about it later. We hid the artifact in a cave near Arkothanes. It's safe for the moment, but we need to retrieve it as soon as possible."

"I'm going to check in with my crew," Jonathan interjected, "and I promise to keep everything in confidence until you give the word, Fiona. I'll be back shortly."

"I appreciate that, Jonathan. Thanks for your help last night."

Vasilios took note of the impish grins they exchanged.

"Does he know about the tablet?" Nizam asked, as soon as Jonathan was out of ear shot.

"No. He only knows it's an artifact; I didn't give him any details."

"The Greek and American governments are sending a science team and they'll be here shortly."

"I know, and maybe they can help us. We're going to have to tell them about the tablet anyway; it's not something we can keep a secret. I think we're going to have to trust the government."

"I think we can trust them," Vasilios said reassuringly. "I know one of the Greek scientists. He is an honorable man."

"It doesn't appear we have a choice," Nizam said flatly. "Once the tablet is secure, we can inform the press."

"So we agree on that, then." Fiona concluded.

Within an hour, an international, five-member team arrived by military helicopter. The team consisted of three independent university scientists, and scientists from both the American and

Greek governments. Along with them came improved site security and high tech scientific equipment. Despite a slight case of red eye, they were nonetheless ready to investigate. They wasted no time convening around the worktent table.

After the introductions, Nizam provided a brief overview of the dig and Dr. Nikitas' work, then Fiona picked it up from there.

"We began digging two days ago and entered the inner chamber yesterday morning. The cave is lined with breathtaking Minoan frescoes and five rock crystal lamps have been recovered. However, the most significant artifact is a gemstone marble chest, which contained an exquisite marble tablet with a Linear A inscription. Dr. Nikitas was analyzing this tablet when she was surrounded by the light phenomenon. She disappeared, but the tablet remained and was undamaged. When people started converging on the site, our immediate reaction was to secure it, so I took it to the home of Mr. Koulouris' grandmother, in a small village about an hour from here. Last night I was attacked at gunpoint by two men who were after it. I escaped with the help of an ENN reporter, and we took it to a cave on Mt. Dikti. Now we need your help to retrieve and secure it as soon as possible."

"Is the cave accessible by helicopter?" asked the Greek scientist.

"Yes, I believe it is."

"I suggest we retrieve the artifact by helicopter and take it to the Heraklion Archeological Museum. We can secure that location."

"Excellent idea," responded the American scientist. "I would like to join you and Dr. Deegan. I would also suggest one of our three university colleagues accompany us as well. The other two can remain and conduct the site tests."

"Vasilios and I will assist here," Nizam offered.

"Very well," the Greek scientist agreed. "We can leave immediately. We will notify you when the tablet has been secured."

Before leaving, Fiona was able to meet briefly with Jonathan to tell him the plan.

"What can I say about the artifact at this point?"

"I'd prefer you didn't say a word until it's secure. Once it's at the museum and we've had the chance to run some tests, we'll do a press conference."

"Okay, I'll meet you at the museum." He gently touched her arm, noticing the green green of her eyes for the first time. "Please be careful."

"I'll see you in a few hours. Don't worry, I'll be grand."

Fiona and the three other scientists boarded the helicopter. She indicated the location on the pilot's topographical map and they lifted off. Her heart fluttered as they quickly rose, up and over the ruins. The island's coastline came into view, soon becoming an etching in the cobalt blue Cretan Sea. Green, red and orange farmlands collapsed into a patchwork landscape, speckled with little white villages.

Fiona watched for landmarks as they flew up Mt. Dikti's ridgeline. "Okay, follow that dirt road. Now, take us in a little closer. There!" She pointed to the big old olive tree.

The pilot landed as close as he could, and they jumped out and ran to the cave. Fiona removed the brush from the entrance and shined her light inside. She was greatly relieved to see the crate, but she wasn't going to be completely at ease until that tablet was under guard in the museum.

As she reemerged from the cave, the pilot came running toward her. "I have just been informed that we're being followed."

"Shyte!"

They hurried the artifact on board and lifted off, just as another helicopter appeared from behind a huge rockface in front of them. The pilot swerved up and successfully maneuvered around it, but the other pilot did a sharp loop, and in a flash was right on their tail. A series of loud popping noises erupted over the cadence of the propeller, and the pilot swore emphatically in Greek.

"Bloody hell, they're shooting at us!" Fiona yelled in astonishment.

"Hold on!" the pilot warned, as he threw the copter into a dive and then pulled back hard. He took evasive action and the other helicopter couldn't get a fix.

Fiona held the chest tightly, "who in God's name are they?"

Before anyone could respond, they fell into a particularly impressive ninety degree turn and the pilot released a smoke screen. He now had the room he needed to beeline toward the airport. Realizing the intercept effort was now futile, the other chopper pilot swerved to the right and headed out across the sea.

"Bravo!" exclaimed the Greek. "Very well done."

The pilot shrugged. "It was nothing," he said, as he brought the helicopter in for a soft landing.

A police escort was waiting for them and the rest of the trip

went smoothly, save for a few brief traffic jams.
When the tablet was finally safe in the lab, Fiona was finally able to breathe. She carefully unpacked it and placed it on the felt-covered table. The other scientists were visibly vibrating with anticipation, as were the four museum staff who'd joined them. The team gathered around it, in awe.
Fiona let them look at the tablet for a few minutes, then she loaded the decryption data into the lab computer. "Excuse me, but I really think you should look at this, too."
They came around the screen.
"I'm terribly sorry I didn't mention this before, but we really felt it was important to secure the tablet before we let anyone know what else happened. When Dr. Nikitas disappeared, she was in the process of translating this tablet."
Several scientists began to object.
"I know, I know. Linear A has never been deciphered. Until now. I believe Dr. Nikitas' program does correctly interpret the inscription on the tablet. After she vanished in the light phenomenon, we found this message on her computer screen." She called it up. "Now, I honestly think it's up to us to verify it, by analyzing the tablet and the decryption key." She surveyed the shocked expressions of her counterparts and pointed back to the computer screen. "Well, there you have it. Let's try to disprove it."
Meanwhile, outside the museum, a very relieved Jonathan was ready with a live uplink.
"This is Jonathan KenCairn reporting live from the Heraklion Archeological Museum. We have just confirmed that an artifact from the Knossos Cave has been transported here, and it is now being analyzed by two members of the government science team, several museum staff and Dr. Fiona Deegan, a member of Dr. Nikitas' archeological team. Other scientists are still conducting tests at the site of the light phenomenon, and there will be a press conference as soon as they've completed their investigations. We will be here live, so stay tuned."

The Israeli/Palestinian/American science team had arrived at the Golden Gate at the break of dawn, and had somehow been able to work amidst the masses of people who continued to gather in and around the Old City. The team was now prepared to make a statement from the Institute for International Peace and Justice, and representatives from the entire world press were waiting. The scientists entered the press room and took their places behind a fiber optic bouquet of logo emblazoned microphones. The Israeli representative read their jointly prepared statement.

"We have completed our preliminary inquiry into the phenomenon which took place yesterday at the Golden Gate, and we have made the following joint findings. We have confirmed that some kind of sustained atmospheric disruption did occur. Space Station instruments and military satellites clearly recorded it. We have investigated the site and taken numerous measurements, and two facts stand out. First, we have analyzed dust particles discovered at the Golden Gate. They are clearly the remains of the stone blocks used to seal the Gate in the seventh century, though they have somehow retained a substantial electrical charge. We do not yet have an explanation. Second, we have detected an electromagnetic signal of unknown origin, which continues to permeate the site.

"In addition, there were hundreds of eyewitness reports, essentially describing two different accounts of what happened. Many claim they saw a man, or a woman, inside an enormous oval of light, which surrounded the Gate and disintegrated the stones. Some claim a bomb exploded, however the evidence does not support this explanation.

"We have analyzed the original video recording of the phenomenon and have found no evidence of tampering or editing. It appears to be authentic. Also, numerous eyewitnesses have subsequently submitted video footage corroborating the light oval theory. We will now take questions."

The press corps went into a frenzy as the Israeli Science Minister calmly selected the reporters whose questions would be answered.

"How were you able to determine the age of the dust?"

"We used accelerated radio carbon dating techniques, and compared them to samples taken prior to this incident. It was a match, save for the unexplained electrical charge."

"Couldn't the ultra-smart bomb have charged those dust particles?"

"No. We know of no bomb capable of causing the residual effects we have detected. A bomb would also have left behind some evidence of its detonation. We have searched the area and have found no such evidence. I repeat, we do not think this was caused by a bomb."

"Have any terrorist organizations assumed responsibility for the destruction of the Golden Gate?"

"First of all, the Golden Gate was not damaged. The Gate is intact; only the blockade was destroyed. And no, no one has assumed responsibility."

"What about a natural phenomenon like lightning, have you ruled that out?"

"No, not completely. A powerful lightning bolt can leave an electromagnetic trace behind, but as a rule, it doesn't linger."

"How long was the disruption as recorded by the military satellites?"

"52 seconds."

"How could lightning last that long?"

"We're not saying it did, but it hasn't been completely ruled out. It is safe to say we have never seen anything like this before."

"If there was no evidence of tampering of the video disc, are you saying that the video shows what happened?"

"No, only that we have found no evidence of tampering at the present time."

"Is this related to the event in Crete?"

"That team has not yet concluded its investigation."

The Jerusalem press conference lasted about an hour as reporters speculated madly about the phenomenon. The science team urged restraint, refusing to speculate at all.

ENN followed up the press conference with a panel discussion, featuring prominent physicists and meteorologists. They agreed the evidence thus far clearly ruled out the possibility of a bomb or lightning. Instead, they debated other theories, like microscopic white holes and cracks in the space-time continuum – ideas usually in the realm of science fiction.

In the realm of virtual reality, the CHAOS media machine cranked out a superabundance of their own scientists. When the ultra-smart bomb theory bombed, they switched to the lightning bolt theory with a vengeance. Their lightning experts attested to the awesome power of lightning, and how it could have easily disintegrated the stone blocks. They claimed the government's "unusual E-M pattern" was a common lightning bolt signature, which could account for the not-so-unusual electrical charge in the soil. More experts suggested the satellite readings were caused by other natural phenomena, like meteorites, aurora borealis and geothermal activity. They heavily edited the press conference to support their position, and employed scads of eyewitnesses to describe the fantastic, killer lightning bolt.

The battle for the hearts and minds of the world was beginning to pick up steam. Regular broadcasts were now preempted on all networks, and television viewers around the globe flicked from channel to channel to channel and back to ENN, trying to figure out what was going on.

CHAOS was determined to discredit ENN, so they expanded the scale of their attacks. They branded Gerrard an Orson Welles copycat and claimed he was trying to recreate the hysteria of the 1938 invasion from Mars. They rebroadcast the "War of the Worlds" in its entirety, complete with soundbites of terrified listeners old and new.

By the time the Heraklion Press Conference began, most of the world was completely confused.

Jonathan was ready when Angela's voice came over his headset. "Okay Jonathan, three, two, one..."

"This is Jonathan KenCairn, reporting live from the Heraklion Archeological Museum, where the international scientific team will soon be convening its press conference. There's a lot of excitement and anticipation here as we wait to hear the report. Eleven different scientists from all over the world have been analyzing data at the event site, and here at the museum. In addition to the five scientists on the Greek/American team, two members of the original archeological expedition and four museum staff are looking at the evidence and trying to figure out what happened. Here they come now."

The door opened and a herd of scientists entered the room. The Greek and American representatives approached the podium and the others formed a semicircle behind them.

"Welcome ladies and gentlemen," the Greek began. "Our team has just concluded its preliminary investigation into the Knossos Event and the artifacts found in a cave nearby. We have analyzed and compared the data, and have been able to confirm a sustained, atmospheric disturbance identical to the Jerusalem Event occurred at Knossos at precisely the same time yesterday.

"Also yesterday morning, in a cave near the Palace at Knossos, Dr. Zoee Nikitas and her archeological team discovered a 3,600 year old tablet, inscribed in Linear A. The marble tablet contained eleven new symbols, which enabled Dr. Nikitas to decipher the language, and translate the ancient text. We have carefully analyzed Dr. Nikitas' data and are in agreement that it is indeed what it purports to be – a translation of the Linear A tablet! The translation is as follows:

> *"We are the people of Keftea. We record our way of life*
> *so our descendants may know how we lived.*
> *We are the island communities of Keftea, Kalliste, Lesvos,*
> *Nexos and Cypri.*
> *We are the people of Gaia, a fragile world adrift*
> *on the cosmic sea,*
> *blessed with the rare and precious gift of Life.*
> *Where Mother Earth and Father Sky live in love and peace*
> *as do we, in honor of their Sacred Marriage.*
>
> *But now the world is changing.*
> *The Gods of thunder and war have darkened*
> *the hearts and minds of many men.*
> *They will transform the world,*
> *and there will be much death and destruction*
> *as the Evils roam the Earth.*
> *Hope will be imprisoned, but she will not be lost forever.*
>
> *It will take many generations, but one day,*
> *Hope will be set free*
> *and our way of life will reemerge.*
> *When the time comes, we know our descendants*
> *will bring back the light and pierce the veil*
> *of darkness which has descended upon us.*
> *We send this message to the future,*
> *when the world is ready to transform again.*

"Additionally, we have determined that *at the very moment* Dr. Nikitas was translating this message, the light phenomenon reportedly engulfed her. There is no evidence she was harmed, in fact, we can find no trace of her at all. Copies of the text are also available. We will now take questions."

The press corps went nuts as they tried to process the information. Jonathan was given the first few questions because he'd been so helpful to the scientific team.

"Do you think Dr. Nikitas is still alive?"

"We don't know and we don't want to speculate."

"How are the Jerusalem and Knossos Events connected?"

"We don't know, but based on the timing of the phenomena, eyewitness descriptions, and scientific data we have collected to date, we believe they are related."

"What is Linear A?"

"A Bronze Age script, which until yesterday, had never been translated."

The other press surged forward for a turn in the spotlight. A feisty old Network clone named Chara Moanin was selected to ask the next few questions.

"What about lightning? Could this event be nothing more than lightning, as several of the eyewitnesses reported?"

"We cannot definitively rule that out. Lightning does cause an electromagnetic disturbance, however we've never seen patterns like this before. Also, because the event lasted 52 seconds and emanated waves of energy, we believe it is highly improbable that lightning was the cause."

"Have you conducted polygraph examinations of the other scientists?"

"No, we didn't feel that was necessary."

"Isn't it possible that this is all nothing but a hoax, and you've allowed yourself to get caught up in the hysteria?"

The scientist frowned and took a deep breath, trying to keep his annoyance in check. "We have applied the scientific method to all of the findings we've reported today. We do not make unwarranted speculations and we certainly do not fall prey to hysteria."

CHAOS networks were now broadcasting on a 60-second delay, so they could effectively manipulate the official responses. When the scientist hesitated, it gave them the perfect opportunity to dub in the right answer. "Yes, it is possible this is all a hoax."

The EuroNet correspondent got the next question.

"What can you tell us about the Minoans?"

"They were a seafaring agrarian people, who built sophisticated palaces on Crete fifteen hundred years before the Classical Greek civilization emerged. They are known for their elaborate artwork, fine sculpture, pottery making and peaceful way of life."

For another hour, reporters deluged the team with questions. As soon as it ended, Jonathan did a quick wrap and grabbed a copy of the Message. He walked outside, sat on the museum steps and read and reread the text. He tuned into the last sentence of the translation. *We send this message to the future, when the world is ready to transform again....* The words reverberated in his mind.

"Excuse me, Jonathan, but would you mind awfully if I joined you?"

The sound of Fiona's voice resonated through him, and for a second, brought back the energy wave sensation. He was still tingling as he looked up and into her emerald green eyes. "I wish you would."

As she sat down, a long, red curl fell forward into her face. He gently lifted it up and placed it out of the way.

"Well," she patted him on the knee, "what do you make of the Message?"

"It's fantastic! Is it really true?"

"Yes. It's really truly true. Zoee's Linear A research is right on – all of her hard work has finally paid off. It really is too bad isn't it, that she's not here to enjoy it."

"It must be hard to accept her disappearance."

"Oh it is, yet, I'm not sad. Part of me has this idea in my head that she must be alive, I just have this feeling, ya' know?"

"Maybe she *could* be alive somehow! You should trust that feeling, Fiona."

"Even if it goes beyond the bounds of all rational explanation?"

"Absolutely. For too long we've been taught to believe our emotions get in the way of judgment and reason. But I've always believed intuition, our gut feelings, are the very foundation of our rational mind. We should trust them – and right now, I'm feeling things I've never felt before. Change is happening; it's all around us," he paused, allowing everything to gel for a minute. Then it clicked. "Could these phenomena be the spark for a transformation in human society?"

"Maybe they could. You know, I've always believed there was a time when we lived in partnership with each other and with nature, you know what I mean? Maybe this Message confirms it, I mean who's to say if one radical transformation already took place, even if it was for the worse, who's to say we can't have another one, for the better this time?"

"Maybe it's already happening. Look at the masses of people coexisting peacefully in Jerusalem – a place which has been holding on to extreme hatred and hostility for over 4,000 years."

"And I suppose if it can happen there, it can happen anywhere."

"What choice do we have anyway? If the human species doesn't radically change its priorities, we are either going to poison our natural environment and die, burn off our planet's atmosphere from overuse of fossil fuels and die, or annihilate ourselves with nuclear weapons, and die. Eventually, we *will* destroy ourselves unless we change. The question now is what can *I* do to help bring about this change?"

"Well, you know, maybe the world just needs to know more about the Minoans. Most people know very little about them, if they've even heard of them at all. This museum is loaded with art and artifacts which speaks volumes about who these people were, and what their Message means. Maybe it's time for a special report?"

"Excellent idea!" He abruptly leaned over and kissed her on the cheek, but then lingered in close for a moment.

She cupped his face softly and kissed him back, this time going right for the lips. After a good long one, she pulled away and slowly got up, smiling. "I'm going back to the lab. See ya later, so!"

"Thanks, Fiona," he whispered, coming out of his trance. He reread the Message one more time, and tried to collect his thoughts. When he had them together the best he could, he dialed up his cellphone.

"Jonathan!" Angela answered enthusiastically. "Fantastic press conference! What's up?"

"I have an idea for a special report. Is Ben around? I'd like to bounce it offa both of you."

"Yeah, hang on."

"Oh, by the way, thanks for sending me on this assignment."

"The universe gives you what you need, when you need it."

The line beeped once and Ben joined the conversation. "Hi Jonathan. Great job on the story so far!"

"Thanks! I've got an idea for a special report."

"On the tablet?"

"Yes."

"Excellent. What's your angle?"

"I think we should focus on the transformation idea."

"Go on."

"Since I've been here in Greece, I've learned a little about the Minoans – they were the last of the partnership societies, flourishing for millennia before the warrior races imposed a dramatically different social order of domination and aggression. The Minoan Message confirms that transformation occurred long ago, and it also speaks of a time when the world will be ready to transform again.

"This tablet remains buried for 3,600 years, then, at the precise moment it's translated, the light effects occur? Impossible to be unrelated. Somehow, the Minoans sent that Message to us and my gut tells me we're on the verge. I think we're finally coming full circle."

Ben and Angela were both quiet for a few seconds.

"What you're describing is a bifurcation point," Ben finally responded. "In any chaotic system, be it a weather pattern or a human society, there are countless random forces at work, each potentially influencing which way the system will go. At certain times, just the right set of circumstances exist and the system is hurled off in one direction or another. These times, these brief instances, are bifurcation points – moments of possibility, when anything can happen.

"Think of it this way, when atmospheric conditions are just right, a tornado forms. The tornado is self-organized. It spontaneously emerges from the disorder surrounding it. If one or two random factors, like temperature or barometric pressure are off by the slightest amount, all you have is wind.

"Maybe the phenomenon is that factor which somehow makes radical change possible. The closer we get to the year 2000, the more anxiety we've generated about our future. On the one hand, we have the doomsdayers – Armageddon, Judgment Day are upon us! On the other, we have those who are entering the new age with cautious hope and optimism. Our human system is in a state of extreme flux, and we could go either way – we'll either destroy ourselves or we'll turn it around. If enough people choose the latter, a radical transformation in thought and reality is possible. And, we're at a unique point in time. For the last thousand years, we've been focusing our collective attention on the year 2000. We've taken this arbitrary point in time and given it a life of its own. In essence, we've created a bifurcation point for ourselves. Something is going to happen, and we are all playing a part in it."

"So, Jonathan," Angela interjected, "you put everything you've got into that special report, because *you* are going to help make the transformation happen!"

"We'll air it early tomorrow," Ben said. "Good luck!"

"Thanks Ben, Angela."

Jonathan rang off, and hurried into the museum to find the crew and get to work.

As day two came to an end, the waiting, watching world tried to make sense of it all. Had two miraculous events really taken place, or were they all schmucks caught up in some tremendous hoax? It was clear someone was manipulating the information, but the masses couldn't decide who to blame. People's hearts and curious minds wanted to believe in ENN, but their skepticism and fear still told them it was all a scam.

The Minoan Message sent new ripples around the globe, and began to seep into the world's consciousness.

CHAPTER SIX
HOPE FINALLY ESCAPES FROM THE BOX

In the preceding two days, CHAOS had done their best to play down the story, to obscure it, discredit it, vilify it. You name it, they tried it. When the lightning bolt theory played no better than the ultra-smart bomb theory, they stepped up the grand hoax theory, while simultaneously intensifying their anti-government campaign.

CHAOS accused the Administration of wasting taxpayer dollars and botching yet another important investigation. They called for more privatization and less government influence in our lives, reminding the people they mistrusted the government and hated regulation. But people had had enough. More and more, they were just plain tired of scapegoating the government for all the woes of the world; and some even started to remember *they* were responsible for their *own* government.

When the phony science and government bashing didn't work, CHAOS resorted to what they do best – character assassination. They called Zoee Nikitas an opportunist and an exploiter of a long dead culture. They questioned the legality of the current dig, and suggested she was not in good standing in her profession. They accused her of plagiarism when she was in college, and claimed she was largely responsible for the hoax ENN was perpetrating on the world. Worst of all, they accused her of smoking pot.

Regina, Shayda and Simone were labeled feminist frauds, whose involvement in this scam was a mockery to the religious people of the world. In the past, that assertion alone would have been enough to spur fundamentalists to call for their deaths. But no one did. To the contrary, they were the "Star Eyewitnesses," who already had 42 radio and TV talk show offers, and who were invited by the President to be part of the U.S. Delegation to the Millennium Summit.

CHAOS showed even less restraint when they aired their libelous exposés on Ben Gerrard. They dismissed the event as pure fabrication, and accused him of masterminding an elaborate and sinister plot to raise his Nielson ratings and save his failing network. They called him "The Trickster," whose favorite pastimes were manipulating the public and practicing black magic.

They somehow found pictures of Ben at Woodstock, half-naked, with long, tangled hair and a Rasta sized spleef in his hand. They splashed the image across the tabloids – *The Daily Star*, *Newsweek*, the *Washington Post* and the *New York Times* – all of 'em ran front page stories. Hired psychiatrists questioned his sanity and diagnosed him with a plethora of DSM-IV disorders. They branded him a homosexual who was trying to bring about the downfall of organized religion, and alleged he personally paid for thousands of abortions. Yet none of it was sticking. It was as if Ronald Reagan's teflon armor pulled itself out of mothballs, switched ideologies and attached itself snugly to Ben Gerrard.

The men of CHAOS were fit to be tied. Once again, they convened in the penthouse board room to brace for the Special Report.

"Get in here, Hayes," the Chairman bellowed out into the hallway. "The God damn Special Report is about to start." He swiveled around in his big puffy chair. "God damn Gerrard. He's smarter than we thought. Those God damn Nielson ratings are soaring, and we *own* Nielson. What the hell is going on?"

"Our minions are deserting us," Morris Reynolds explained weakly, gasping for air.

"Then fire 'em and get new minions. We're here to figure out how we're going to respond to Gerrard's God damn report – he's ruthless and no doubt capable of anything. Now shut up and listen."

"Buenas días! This is Magdalena Severeide, reporting from ENN Center in New York. It's the morning of day three of the Energy Wave, and we'll continue to cover it from around the globe, throughout the day and night. Coming up, Jonathan KenCairn with a Special Report from Crete. But first, we check in with our Middle Eastern correspondent, Dorit Dahled."

The video cut to Dorit, standing in front of the gleaming Dome of the Rock.

"Good day from Jerusalem! And it is a beautiful day here on the Temple Mount, where the crowd is continuing to grow by the minute. An estimated 2.3 million people are now peacefully congregating within and around the walls of the Old City. Most are patiently waiting their turn to walk through the Golden Gate.

"Since the event, people from all religious faiths and nationalities have been coming here, to cross over the newly revealed threshold. Many pause to kiss the Gate as they pass through, leaving flowers, candles, coins and pictures wherever they can find room. Though everyone has a different interpretation of what they saw, a shared sense of wonder and expectancy has permeated the area.

"And it's evolving into a regional call for action. Presidents, prime ministers, ayatollahs and kings are all making preparations to attend the Millennium Summit tomorrow in New York City. Even the nomadic Basseri tribe is sending a delegate! We'll continue to bring you the latest from Jerusalem, but now, it's back to you in New York."

"Thank you, Dorit. This Summit is shaping up to be an unprecedented event in human history. Individuals and organizations around the globe are flooding the phonelines and jamming the Nets, calling for action and calling for change. Leaders from virtually everywhere are making plans to attend, and so are we. So stay active, stay vocal and stay tuned for an amazing journey into the world of the ancient Minoans. Thank *you* for being part of the Earth News Network."

"God dammit. This Summit could be trouble."

The video faded out, then back in on Jonathan, sitting comfortably in a darkened room.

"This is Jonathan KenCairn, reporting from the Heraklion Museum on the island of Crete. In the next half hour we'll take a close look at the events of the last couple days, and try to unravel the mystery of the Energy Wave which has swept around the globe and into the human consciousness.

"Day before yesterday, the Golden Gate in Old Jerusalem and the archeological site of Knossos experienced a powerful, concentrated, light/energy disruption. The phenomena seemed to be centered in these two places, but the effect has been felt planetwide. Scientists have confirmed a connection between the two incidents, but they're at a loss as to what it could be.

"In Jerusalem, a human figure appeared in the eruption of light, which emitted a euphoric energy wave and disintegrated a stone barricade. At Knossos, an archeologist *dis*appeared in an identical light phenomenon while translating an ancient text, discovered only an hour before.

"How are these two places connected? Who is the figure in the Jerusalem flash, and what happened to Dr. Nikitas? Does the Linear A tablet provide a clue? Who are these people who left this Message so long ago; what are they trying to tell us? Right now, its all a mystery. Let's look at the clues by starting in the past.

"Tradition tells us that two thousand years ago, Christ first entered Jerusalem through the Golden Gate, where he received his palm-waving welcome. After his death, Christian believers maintained he would return in the future, passing through the Gate once again. For millennia, Jewish believers have held that their Messiah would also come to Jerusalem through the Golden Gate. For countless generations, millions of people have been focusing their hopes and dreams for a better future on this spot.

"In the seventh century, an Islamic ruler tried to prevent both comings by sealing the Gate with sturdy stone blocks. But now, 1,300 years later, the seal has been broken by an unexplained light/energy phenomenon, with a human figure inside it! Depending upon which eyewitness you talk to, this figure has been described as Jesus, the Jewish Messiah, Mohammed, Inanna, Isis, Hera, Krishna and Buddha, among a dozen others. Could it be one, or *all*, of them?"

"In my wildest nightmare," the Chairman snarled.

"Our Cretan clue takes us back further, into the distant past. Four thousand years ago, a sophisticated, artistic culture flourished here on Crete and throughout the Mediterranean. But until the turn of the 20th century, little was known about these remarkable people.

The video cut to old black and white film footage of the original dig.

"In 1903, the British archeologist Sir Arthur Evans excavated the great palace at Knossos and brought the wonders of this civilization to light. He uncovered an elaborate, complex maze of a structure, with 1,500 rooms, chambers and catacombs. He was certain he'd found the labyrinth of the King Minos myth, so he dubbed the people who lived there 'Minoan.'

"As the story goes, King Minos lived in a great palace and ruled the Mediterranean region with powerful seafaring armies.

But according to the historical record, the Minos legend was born *after* the Indo-European conquest of the civilization who wrote the Message.

"According to the archeological record, the Minoans were a peaceful, seafaring people who traded extensively throughout Africa, Egypt, the Middle East and Europe. Their culture was centered in Crete, but it spanned the Mediterranean, linking with the other great Centers of the Agrarian Period.

"They were accomplished artisans and architects, who constructed futuristic, multi-story houses and buildings, decorated with magnificent art."

The lights went up and the camera zoomed out to reveal the stunning frescoes on display in the museum's Great Hall. Colorful, life-sized paintings of priestesses and cup bearers in elaborate processions, women and men leaping over horned bulls, bluebirds, lilies, dolphins, monkeys and other graceful depictions of nature covered the walls of the vaulted hall.

"What you're seeing are the *restorations* of frescoes discovered here at Knossos."

The camera zoomed in a little closer.

"As you can see, only a few fragments of the original frescoes have withstood the eons. Fortunately, enough survived to enable archeologist-artists to restore the original images, and give us a glimpse of an elegant and sophisticated people who had a deep connection with nature.

"In addition to these marvelous frescoes, numerous Minoan artifacts have been discovered all over the island. This museum contains gallery after gallery of pottery, jewelry and statuary created by these mysterious people who lived so long ago. Here is a very small sampling."

The video cut to a montage of various artifacts: an exquisite, v-shaped rock crystal cup displayed in a gold stand; a black steatite bull's head, with gilded horns and eyes of glittering rock crystal; a bright red and blue Kamares Ware pitcher, with coils and rosettes painted on the eggshell thin clay; a display case of gold and silver necklaces, earrings and pins, inlaid with precious and semi-precious stones. The final image was a 14" statue of a woman wearing a long, bell-shaped skirt and open breasted bodice laced at the waist. She wore a tall tiara with a snake resting high on top. It wound down around the headdress, interlacing with another snake, which wrapped around her body and rested its head at her waist. In her right hand, she held the head of a third snake coiling up her arm, around her shoulder and down and around to her left hand, where she held its tail.

"And this is the famous Snake Goddess figurine, found here at Knossos. In ancient cultures, the snake was a divine symbol. With each shedding of its skin, the snake is reborn – a cycle which mirrors, and embodies, the great cycle of life, death and rebirth."

The video cut back to Jonathan.

"Thousands of different artifacts revealing a complex and rich religious tradition have been discovered in temples and caves throughout the Mediterranean. In fact, caves have been used as sites of worship for thousands and thousands of years. In Crete alone, numerous ancient cave sanctuaries have been discovered, each providing important clues about who these distant ancestors were and how they lived.

"Thanks to British tourist John Lukas, we can see Dr. Zoee Nikitas and her colleagues excavating the Knossos Cave just two days ago. Dr. Nikitas was born in Chicago in 1961. She is the granddaughter of Greek immigrants who came to the States from Crete around the turn of the century. After receiving her masters in linguistics from the University of Chicago and her doctorate in archeology from Yale, she returned to Crete to study her great love and fascination, the Minoan civilization. That was over ten years ago and she's been uncovering artifacts and making new discoveries ever since.

"Though only a few hundred yards from the great temple at Knossos, this cave site had gone unnoticed for millennia. Sometime in antiquity, a strong earthquake completely buried it until three months ago, when Dr. Nikitas rediscovered it, using sophisticated X-ray imaging technology. The day before yesterday, she and her colleagues opened its door, and stepped through a time portal 3,600 years into the past."

Jonathan got up and walked off camera. The video cut to the cave site and he walked back into the frame and over to Nizam, who was standing by the cave's exposed opening.

"This is Dr. Nizam Adalat, one of the three original archeological team members investigating this site. Well, Doctor, this site has sure transformed from that hole in the ground we saw two days ago!"

"Yes, as you can see, Mr. Koulouris' crew has done a fine job of clearing away the rest of the debris from the mouth of the cave. It has been surveyed, and we can now safely go in and see where the tablet was found. Please, follow me."

Jonathan flashed an adventurous look at the viewers before following him into the large antechamber and down the passageway. Nizam described the cave as he descended the greenstone staircase.

"Consider this panorama of nature," he raised both of his arms. "These frescoes reflect what the Minoans held most dear, the love of life and the appreciation of natural beauty."

The camera slowly panned the cave wall.

"What does the inscription say?"

Nizam cracked a smile and energetically pointed. "The first part of the inscription, which goes down the passageway and toward the inner chamber says, 'Here we collect our mind, body and spirit.'" He practically whirled around. "And here, on the other side, leading back out of the cave it continues, 'To set sail on the sea of time.'"

"What do you think it means?"

"These frescoes are the finest we have encountered to date, and the artifacts we've uncovered here represent the best examples of Minoan artistry I've ever seen. I believe the Minoans were trying to capture the essence of themselves, here, in this cave." He emphatically gestured toward the inscription, "'Here we collect our mind, body and spirit...'"

"For what purpose?"

"Like many ancient cultures, the Minoans believed caves were passageways, tunnels, which linked the people to the Cosmos through the Earth. I believe they were intentionally trying to funnel their collective energy through this cave, and into the future." He swept his arms upward. "'To set sail on the sea of time!'"

Jonathan looked into the camera and his eyes got really big.

They slowly continued down into the inner chamber, where the two golden bulls faithfully stood in attendance. Nizam gently touched the gemstone marble chest. "And this is where the Minoan Message was found."

They zoomed in on the glistening butterfly lid. Nizam removed it and the camera peeked inside before fading out.

It faded back in on the tablet inside the museum lab.

"The tablet contained eleven new Linear A symbols, which led Dr. Nikitas to her incredible breakthrough, the decipherment of Linear A. And, at the *very moment* she deciphered this tablet, the energy vortex appeared, then disappeared, taking her with it. A very lucky John Lukas captured it on video. Thanks again, Yanni."

They ran the clip and cut back to Jonathan, shaking his head in renewed amazement.

"Extraordinary! There's no evidence she died and no indication of her possible whereabouts. She just vanished into the light, like the figure in the Jerusalem flash."

The video cut to a split screen freeze-frame of both figures inside the light.

"What happened to Dr. Nikitas? Is that her, somehow reappearing for an instant, hundreds of miles away? Or is that someone or something else? If so, who? or *what*? The only other clue we have is the Message itself.

"The Minoans saw their way of life coming to an end, but they weren't willing to allow their culture and their values to die with them. They believed the time would come again when people would choose to live in partnership and peace, and they went to great lengths to make sure their Message would be heard. Like the Golden Gate, the Knossos Cave was the focal point of their collective hopes, dreams and thoughts for the future – *when the world is ready to transform again.*

"Could there be something to this idea of the power of collective thought? Are we on the verge of the global transformation the Minoans predicted so long ago? Are they speaking to us? Have we somehow opened a door to the possibility of a new future, a new reality?

"At ENN, we're searching for the truth behind the phenomena. We're not lying to you or trying to manipulate you. We're seeking, just like everyone else. We're able to bring you the footage, the press conferences, analyses and special reports, but we don't have all the answers – we're still trying to figure out the questions!

"Here's a question you might want to consider: Perhaps our thoughts and beliefs *do* influence the physical world around us. If so, what kind of world do you want to live in? As you look at these newly released Space Station images, think about what the Minoans said."

The video cut to an image of our fragile, blue Earth, surrounded by a warm halo of golden light, slowly dissipating into the endless blackness of space.

"*We are the people of Gaia, a fragile world, adrift on the cosmic sea....* Are you willing to think about the possibility of global transformation, of radical change toward a more equal, more just global community? Can't we do better? If enough of us think so, and *act*, anything is possible.

"We'll continue to bring you all the information we have. We urge you to call, write, fax or e-mail us – and the politicians – with your thoughts and comments."

Earth News NETsite, address, phone and fax numbers appeared at the bottom of the screen.

"Together, we'll search for the truth and if we act now, maybe, just maybe, we *can* create a better future for ourselves. Think about it, and keep hope alive! This is Jonathan KenCairn, reporting from Crete."

The Chairman ripped the remote control out of his chair and hurled it at the impressive screen. "God damn it! Global awareness was only supposed to be a marketing tool – they weren't supposed to take it to heart. Gerrard is jeopardizing everything. Who the hell does he think he is, talking revolution like that. We can't afford a revolution!" He pounded his fat fists on the mahogany table. "We have got to come up with a plan to regain control of this situation. We've got to, upstage the bastard. Yeah, that's it. We'll create our own, bigger, better phenomenon!"

He pressed another button on his control chair, the venetian blinds went up and the panorama of the Manhattan skyline appeared on the other side of tinted floor-to-ceiling windows. "And ours will take place right here, in our own back yard, at the Millennium Summit in New York City."

"We've developed some pretty impressive holographic projection technology, which might just do the trick," Ruther Burdock suggested.

The Chairman's smug look returned as he retrieved a cigar from its golden case. He lit up, swiveling around to face the northern window. Off in the distance, the ENN Tower rose like a gleaming pillar from the glass and concrete landscape. The Chairman exhaled a thick cloud of smoke and snarled, "you're goin' down Gerrard! If it's the last God damn thing I do!"

When the Special Report aired, the Pope was half way across the Atlantic in his private papal jet. He switched off the set and folded his hands in his lap. He closed his eyes a moment, then looked out the window and into the open sky. He remained motionless for a long time, watching the angels play in the white, puffy clouds below. Finally, he turned to his trusted cardinals and spoke.

"How can that ancient culture be linked to our Most Holy

City of Jerusalem?"

"Your Holiness," Ignatious replied graciously. "As you know, in Biblical times, Crete was called Caphtor. There are only a few references to it in the Bible. The most descriptive passage occurs in Jeremiah, Chapter 47, where we learn of the prophecy against the people of Caphtor. It proclaims: 'The Lord caused the waters to rise up and overflow the land, and the noise of His thundering horses and rumbling chariots was so fierce, fathers could not look back to their children for feebleness of hands.' But I know of nothing in the Most Holy Scriptures which foretells these phenomena, or in any other way links Crete with Jerusalem.

"However, let us consider the ancient Linear A text. Its message is one of love, and peace – the cornerstones of Christ's teachings. Perhaps that's the link. Perhaps God is sending Christ's message to the world through the words of this ancient civilization. We can no longer seriously doubt the events in Jerusalem and Crete are the work of God. It is nothing short of a Miracle."

"Your Most Holy Holiness," interjected Opudias sharply. "Once again I urge caution and restraint. The hysteria is spreading and Cardinal Ignatious is almost completely lost to it. We most certainly *can* continue to doubt these events are the work of God. I am more convinced than ever this is one of Ben Gerrard's publicity stunts. I must admit, I underestimated the extent of the deception and the resulting impact, but nevertheless, it simply must be a fraud. If God were responsible, surely He would leave no room for doubt."

"I am not so sure," mused the Pope. "We have always told others that they must have faith. Well, perhaps now, we must have faith. These phenomena cannot be explained by our finest minds. To me, this suggests the presence of a finer mind, the Mind of God. I like Cardinal Ignatious' interpretation of the Linear A tablet. I believe the Minoan message could be interpreted as being consistent with Christ's teachings."

"I beg your most Excellent pardon, but I do not believe that tablet is consistent with the Bible *or* Christ's teachings. Those barbarians worshipped the *Goddess*. The Abomination! And they were punished for their beliefs." He glared at Ignatious and hissed. "Cardinal Ignatious puts a colorful glow on the Prophecy against the people of 'Caphtor,' as he so euphemistically puts it. Your Holiness, the people of Caphtor are known to us as the *Philistines*!

"Once again, Goliath rises from the grave. You must act to defeat this specter of our barbarous past! You must now champion the cause of King David who, in his noble bravery, rose to slay the Philistine of Gath. Please, follow now in the footsteps of David. Take now a stone, and sling it, and smite the Philistine in his forehead, that the stone sink into his forehead; and he fall again upon his face to the earth! Your Holiness, don't you see, this message threatens the authority and order ordained by God? It threatens the very foundation of your Church!"

"I disagree, fair Opudias," the Pope said kindly. "Our beloved Church has seen her way through many difficult times. I trust in her strength and endurance. We must not be afraid to ask difficult questions. Please try not to get so upset Opudias, I worry about your high blood pressure." The Pontiff was quiet a moment, then continued. "While I do believe the message is not inconsistent with our beliefs, I am still hesitant to associate the tablet too closely with Christ."

"I have a suggestion," announced the Cardinal Secretary. "Take the position the Minoan message is consistent with Christian, Jewish and Islamic belief. Let the mystery of the phenomena remain a mystery attributable to God, the one being in whom all three faiths believe."

The Pope breathed a sigh of relief and returned his attention out the window.

In the Oval Office, the President and several key aides had taken a break from Summit speech writing to watch the Special Report.

"A global transformation," the President thought out loud.

"An interesting idea," confirmed the Secretary of State. "The millennium does bring with it a unique opportunity for reflection."

"Yes. How rare indeed to witness the passing of a millennium." The President stood up, walked around the front of his desk and leaned on the edge. "And look how far we've come since the last one. A thousand years ago, we were in the midst of the Dark Ages. We saw the fanaticism and cruelty of the Crusades. Powerful religious hierarchies vied for domination, brutally executing those who dared question their divine authority. Fear prevailed for centuries, until something remarkable happened.

"Old stories from old cultures resurfaced, and people began questioning the status quo. The Renaissance re-awakened the human mind, and the Enlightenment brought dramatic societal change. Once again, after so many centuries, reason came to light and began to triumph over superstition. Democracy was resurrected out of the distant past. New ideas flourished and we launched ourselves into the industrial age – an age which has brought incredible innovation."

He walked over to a beautiful globe mounted on an exquisite cherry stand, and gave it a spin. "Now, we face the new, post-industrial challenges – finally bringing democracy's promise of freedom and equal representation to women, and to people of all colors and creeds. Creating a more just economic system, which uses and shares the resources responsibly. Doing away with poverty." He watched the globe come to a slow stop. "Cultural transformation is always taking place, but like everything else, it seems to be accelerating. Despite the hardliners' dearest wishes, we do not live in a static, homogeneous society."

The Secretary of Defense cringed.

"In fact, we live in an exciting, dynamic system. Perhaps we've been building toward something like this for a long time. Maybe we *are* on the verge of radical social transformation."

The Defense Secretary puffed out his chest. "Personally, sir, I believe our strategic military planning will determine whether or not radical change is likely. We need to send a strong message to the world that we will continue to lead from a position of military strength. People need to be reassured that as they enter the new millennium, they can feel safe. Too much change can lead to chaos. We do not want to encourage too much change."

"I disagree," countered the U.N. Ambassador. "This is an historic opportunity. We don't want to enter the new millennium with a message which reinforces the status quo. We want to express optimism and confidence in our ability to overcome humanity's problems. I think you should embrace this idea of global transformation in your speech. Challenge ourselves to higher heights. Commit ourselves to resolving the social ills of our world, and finding unity amongst nations, cultures, religions and people."

"I agree," said the Communications Director. "This is the message ENN is sending out and it's creating an unprecedented response. The Earth News Net has brought this story to hundreds of towns and villages throughout the Americas, Asia, Africa, Australia. People are speaking up, on-line and in the streets, interacting like never before, calling for change. Politically speaking, it's definitely what people want to hear."

"I think I should talk about global transformation – maybe even make it the main focus. I only wish we knew more about the phenomena."

"Maybe it's okay if they remain a mystery," suggested the U.N. Ambassador. "After all, it's the mystery which has caused such a stir. If we could explain it, there'd be no mystery. It seems to me the important thing is not that we solve it, but rather that we utilize it for positive ends."

"Yes," added the Secretary of State, "but we should at least incorporate the science teams' latest findings."

"Good idea," agreed the President, turning to the Chief of Staff. "What is the latest?"

"All of the evidence continues to substantiate what we've seen on ENN, and there's no question the two events are related.

As for the Linear A translation, the team is certain about the authenticity of the tablet and the accuracy of the decryption code. In fact, they're deciphering other Linear A fragments, and a 4,000 year old civilization is opening up to them for the first time."

"Mr. President," the Secretary of State said abruptly, "what about CHAOS? This may also be an opportunity to expose them to the world. The people suspect the major networks are skewing the images, but they don't have anybody to blame. They could eventually start believing CHAOS' government bashing propaganda or turn on Gerrard and ENN. I think we seriously need to consider exposing CHAOS as the master manipulators they are. We may not get another opportunity."

The Defense Secretary stepped forward. "That would not be a good idea, *sir*."

"I don't know if we need to," interrupted the Communications Director. "They're presently doing an excellent job of self-destructing. They've become so zealous in their attacks on ENN they're rapidly losing any credibility they have left. I'm getting reports that some of the more ethical network types are quitting, refusing to participate in such blatant deception. CHAOS' tactics have backfired yet they continue to use them."

"Don't underestimate the effectiveness of old tactics," retorted the Defense Secretary, sounding a little more threatening.

The President took note, but ignored him.

"Once exposed," continued the Secretary of State, "the Senate will be forced to pass legislation that will start to bring these transnational corporations under control. We may never again have the opportunity."

The Communications Director agreed. "The public is insisting on change. White House phone banks are jammed, our e-mail system crashed from the deluge of correspondence, faxes are on a five-hour delay and mail is pouring in. I'm happy to report however, the U.S. Mail is keeping up with the increased demand."

"Well," the President finally said, "I am merely a representative of the people of this country, and when they speak, I am duty bound to listen and represent their interests to the best of my ability. If change is what they want, then change is what they'll get." He looked every aide in the eye. "It's time to reveal the face of Oz."

"No!" the Secretary of Defense pleaded, having recently learned he didn't have the key support for his planned military coup.

"I've made up my mind. If there's going to be a global transformation, CHAOS' old world order must be exposed."

By now, people were starting to form an opinion. Some were still skeptical about whether or not the ENN story was real, but for most, it didn't seem to matter. It excited their imagination, made them feel optimistic. The phenomena had broken through the iron curtain of fear and suspicion which had controlled them for so long, and they began to believe in the potential of a brighter future. The doom and gloom of four thousand years was finally giving way to the hope of a new reality for the 21st century.

As the People of Earth slept that night, their consciousness coalesced, bringing the energy of the Cosmos into a collective focus so awesome, so powerful, the seemingly impossible would become possible....

CHAPTER SEVEN
FIRE ON THE MOUNTAIN

In the wee hours of Solstice Morn,' Sun started cookin' up some fresh, supercharged particles in preparation for the day. They streamed forth at light speed, sailing high on the energized solar wind. As they approached the Earth, some of them careened off course, whirling into the powerful electromagnetic eddies surrounding our planet. Trillions of them funneled downward, swirling into the North and South Poles, where the Sisters Aurora were waiting.

They collected the golden beads of light, and gently blew upon them. All at once, they began to glow, and then to move and shimmer, dancing in their shifting forms in emerald, silver and crimson. Down below, the Earthlings watched and wondered....

They gathered at the ancient observatories and sacred spots of Chaco Canyon, Haleakala, Machu Picchu, Borobudur, the Great Pyramid, Delphi and Stonehenge to experience the Solstice Moment – that moment when the Sun reaches its furthest point south and begins its slow return back north. The moment the old year has died and the new year is yet to be born. At that instant, we pass through a thin membrane between the past and the future, between death and rebirth, perched on the threshold of oblivion.

Every Winter Solstice for the last five thousand years or so, people have been gathering in Ireland, at a place called New Grange – a huge dome mound covered with brilliant white quartz. A place where Earth and Sky are joined in Sacred Marriage to conceive another year. Many hundreds of generations have come and gone, yet people still appear, to celebrate the completion of one cycle and invoke the beginning of the next. Today, thousands came to establish their link with the universe, the past and the future.

As Sun's long, low rays rolled up over the Irish hillside, they caressed the smooth curves of the eggshell mound, bringing out its subtle glow. They climbed to a small roof box, paused a moment, then gently slid down a long stone passage and into a vaulted chamber, illuminating a triple spiral carved many moons ago. For 17 minutes, the rays bathed the sacred symbol with life giving energy, before passing out of the window again....

Gatherings took place at other centers of worship as well, but today people met with an openness and trust many had thought long dead. Large interfaith services were being held in Northern Ireland, the Balkans and the Middle East. The good will spread to the African continent, where tribal conflict eased and militants laid down their weapons. Indigenous peoples and new age spiritualists performed healing ceremonies together in the desecrated lands of Earth – the Brazilian Rainforest, the Nevada Test Site and toxic waste dumps around the globe.

Spontaneous demonstrations were occurring in cities, towns

and villages everywhere. Hundreds of thousands rallied in San Francisco, Paris, Rio, Beijing. They carried signs, banners and Earth flags, calling for unity and calling for action at the Millennium Summit.

ENN brought these images to the world, and by now, an estimated 74% of the planet's population was tuned in. But people weren't just stuck with their own little nuclear families in front of their own little TV sets. They were seeking out others to share the event. They met in coffee houses and pubs, community halls and village centers. Local leaders and civic groups put televisions in parks, schools, libraries and municipal buildings. Superdomes and stadiums were filled to capacity. Ben Gerrard made sure all the Planet Earth Co-ops and Net sites had large outdoor screens so the people could participate together.

On the Indonesian island of Gili Air, sarong vendors, basket weavers, woodworkers and backpackers met at Gili IndoExport to watch and connect with the wider world. They contacted governments and international organizations, calling for democracy and demanding trade reform.

Himalayan EcoTreks in Pokhara, Nepal drew villagers out of the mountains and trekkers from far and wide. They called for a United Nations Constitutional Convention and championed the abolition of the U.N. Security Council.

Native Hawaiians and activists went to the Big Island, to a place called Puna, an organic farm and center for nonviolent action nestled in Pele's lowland tropical rainforest. They lobbied the world's governments to go beyond START I and II and the Comprehensive Nuclear Test Ban Treaty, and eliminate nuclear weapons once and for all!

In the village of Manzanilla, Costa Rica, descendants of banana plantation slaves rallied with Bri Bris and Ticos at Flores Pura Vida. This Co-op member grew exotic flowers, and harvested sustainable rainforest products for international sale. Members poured messages into the Net, urging other nations to disband their militaries as Costa Rica had done in 1978.

As people's thoughts crisscrossed the Earth, zipping faster and faster, each of them spun a special thread, and wove it into our electronic web. Round and round and round they went – interlacing the fibers of human consciousness, creating planetary mind.

Sun's rays glided gracefully over the waters of the Atlantic Ocean, until they reached a platform rising from the Sea. They slinked up over the broad stone base, glistening the dew dropped grass and tickling Lady Liberty's copper toes. She shook the shackles looser, then flung them high up in the air. They crashed down through the glassy water, and sank into the depths. The energy was rising, as it surged up toward her breast. She felt Her heartbeat strong again, and thrust Her torch up high. The golden flame burst forth anew and light once again filled the sky.

As the first of the glittering stardust sprinkled down over Manhattan, Shayda lay dreaming, fast asleep in a government safe house in Greenwich Village. Somewhere in the depths of Mind she stood, holding a small beeswax candle. In front of her appeared a dark-haired woman with golden eyes, and a living snake coiling round her tall headdress. The Goddess looked at the candle and it burst into flame, and as she faded into rising mist, she whispered, "thank you, Shayda." Shayda looked into the light, feeling the warmth, absorbing the energy.... When she opened her eyes, the dream slipped away, replaced by the morning rays just peeking in through her window.

The smell of coffee pulled her out of bed, and she threw on a sweatshirt and jeans. She followed the scent down the hall and into the kitchen, where she found Simone rummaging through the cupboards.

"Good morning, Simone. What's for breakfast?"

Simone wrinkled her nose. "An assortment of unidentifiable, processed lunch meat and white bread."

"You're kidding. That's all they've got for us?"

"That's it. I've searched every cabinet."

A sleepy-eyed Regina came shuffling in. "I'll have a tall latte, please. No. Make it a double!"

"Dream on, Regina," Simone laughed. "I'm afraid it's expired Folgers and bologna sandwiches."

"Yuk! That's cruel, Simone!"

"I'm serious. That's all the government has for us."

"Maybe one of the security guards will get us something else."

"I've got a better idea," Simone grinned. "Balducci's is right around the corner. It's a *great* market. Maybe we can sneak out and go get some *real* food. Besides, this is my neighborhood! I'm dying to see how people are reacting to everything."

"Me too," agreed Regina. "I appreciate what Uncle Sam has done for us, but I want out of the cloister." She walked over to the barred window and looked out. "These bars were made for fat, old men. We could easily slide on through, and climb right down that sycamore tree. Whatta ya say, Shayda? Are you with us?"

"Hell, yeah! We've still got two hours before the limo leaves!"

They opened the window and each of them slipped through and climbed down, but they didn't even make it a block before they were recognized.

A large man in a white tee-shirt was leaning out his third floor window, and when he spotted them, he started hollering and waving profusely. "Welcome home, Simone! Welcome home! Hey Harry," he shouted to the man next door, "it's the Star Eyewitnesses. Get Loretta, fast!"

Within seconds, more and more people appeared at their windows, and started gathering in the street. Soon, the three of them were totally surrounded by well-wishers asking for autographs, and shaking their hands. They slowly kept moving, and the growing crowd made way to let them pass.

"This is marvelous," Simone beamed. "I feel like a nominee for best actress!"

"No doubt it's just a dry run," Shayda egged her on.

They stepped inside the old-world market, with half of New York in tow. Simone navigated the crowded maze with ease, stuffing her basket with a nice selection of delectables, while Shayda dodged the hanging garlic and tried to keep up. They lost Regina at the cheese samples, but when Simone looped back around to get the Neufchatel, she picked her up again. They somehow made it through the fawning throng and up to the checkout line, and to Simone's visible shock and amazement, were given cuts to the front.

"It *must've* been a miracle," Simone whispered.

When they got to the counter, Simone's friend Ralph was waiting. "I always knew you'd be famous," he said, shaking her hand. "So, I spose this means my favorite customer won't be shopping at Balducci's anymore, ey Simone?"

"You can't get rid of me that easily, Ralph. Besides, where else can I find this selection, in such an atmosphere? Tell me, did you see the ENN broadcast?"

"Mama mia! How could I *not* see it? Everybody is talking about it. I even saw you being interviewed by a handsome young man." He winked at her. "I almost flipped! Did you really see the Miracle, Simone?"

"Yes. I did."

"What was it like? How did you feel?"

"It was absolutely amazing, but I'm sorry, Ralph. I don't have time to talk right now. We've been invited to the Millennium Summit and we're running late."

"Ahh, Simone. Always running late."

Just then, two secret service agents burst through the door, and ploughed their way through the crowd to the checkout counter.

"Oh, good." Simone smiled. "You're just in time to pick up the tab."

One of the agents pulled out a credit card, but Ralph held up his hand. "From you, I only take cash."

By nine o'clock in the morning, the island had metamorphosed into a street fair 100 blocks deep. The United Nations Plaza was completely surrounded. Thousands formed human corridors along the motorcade route, cheering as the delegates drove by. The limos paraded past the flags of the world, around the shooting fountain and on to the General Assembly Hall. A steady stream of diplomats had been arriving since the break of day.

When Simone, Shayda and Regina stepped out of their car, the crowd went wild, clapping and shouting their names. The cameras exploded like fireworks as they sailed past ecstatic onlookers, who were cheering and trying to touch them. Simone stopped suddenly when she saw her twin sister Celeste, reaching out from the other side of the rope.

Simone cautiously approached her, then ran into her arms, hugging her tightly. "I've missed you so much Celeste," she said, choking back the tears.

"Me too, Simone. I don't know exactly what's happening, but I'm going to do what our sweet Bubbie used to tell us – trust in my heart. I don't want to be apart anymore."

Simone squeezed her again. "Call me tonight, okay?"

"Okay."

Their escorts whisked them inside the Great Hall, and the huge auditorium was virtually humming with charged excitement. Delegates, leaders and citizens from around the globe were anxiously awaiting the Summit to begin.

They were seated in the VIP boxes, right up front. "Hey, look," Shayda pointed to the other side of the stage. "There are the archeologists from Crete."

They looked over just as Vasilios was pointing them out to Fiona and Nizam. They all tentatively waved at each other.

"And there's Jonathan KenCairn," Simone said, pointing to the press box.

Jonathan had already spotted the Star Eyewitnesses and waved back.

The lights flashed, a spotlight illuminated the main stage and a hush fell over the crowd. One by one, the speakers emerged from the wings, crossed the stage and took their seats amidst enthusiastic applause. The Secretary General of the United Nations. The President of the United States of America. The Prime Ministers of Greece and Israel. The Presidents of Palestine, Russia and South Africa. The Pope, the Dali Lama, and a host of other religious leaders. As the last of them took their seats, a Cherokee Elder, dressed in a white beaded ceremonial cloak, gracefully crossed the stage and approached the podium. She was the President of the United Federation of Indigenous People.

"Good morning delegates, world leaders and members of our global community. I am honored to welcome you to the first-ever United Nations Millennium Summit."

Applause erupted from the audience.

"We have convened this conference to discuss the serious issues facing our planetary community as we prepare to enter the new millennium. We have also come to ponder a great mystery, and hopefully, achieve some common understanding. This is a time of great opportunity, and of great hope.

"As today is the Solstice, and because we are seeing the dawn of a new period in our global history, I honor our human spirit with a story of my ancestors.

"Long ago, during the time of the Great Darkness, there was no Light in the world of the animal people. After many years of relentless night, they began to grow weary of stumbling around, bumping into each other in the dark. They began to say, 'We need Light! We need Light!' Everyone agreed, so they gathered together in the forest to figure out how to find it. Right away, wise old Owl came forward. 'I believe the Light lives on the other side of the world!' he said.

"'But who will go?' everyone cried. Then they began to argue about who was more cunning and quick. Finally, bushy-tailed Possum stepped forward and announced he would go steal the Light and bring it to the Darkness. After many days he finally reached it. He crawled toward the brilliant Light on his belly, trying to hide from its powerful rays. Poor old Possum was partially blinded, but he would not give up. He backed up close to the Light and scooped up as much as he could with his big bushy tail. Sadly, it was too bright for him to carry and by the time he returned to the Darkness, it had burned off his tail fur and disappeared.

"The creatures of Earth were very disappointed in poor burnt Possum, but then Buzzard stepped forward, raising their hopes again. 'Let me go,' he said. 'I can bring the Light back, *safely*.' So, off Buzzard went, soaring high in the sky, far above the Light, so he would not be seen. He swooped down into it, swiping as much as he could carry. He placed it on his head and flew as fast as he could, back to his home to the Darkness. Sadly, the Light was also too bright for Buzzard, and by the time he returned, it had burned his head bald and disappeared. The creatures of the Dark Earth were beginning to give up hope, until Grandmother Spider spoke up.

"'I will go to the land of Light and ask if I may have a small amount,' she said, 'but first I must collect some earth and water, and make a special bowl.' She formed the bowl with love and care, then took it with her to the East. As she made her way, she spun a long thread behind her, to mark the way back home. When she arrived, she bowed respectfully to the Light, and asked permission to have a small amount. She reached out with her long, delicate arms, carefully lifted a little Light and placed it gently in her bowl. She bowed once again, thanked the Light, then followed her thread back home. As she came back West, the beautiful Light came with her, spreading over the Darkness.

"The creatures of the Earth were elated. 'Thank you for bringing us the Light!' they sang to her. 'You will always hold a place most honored.'"

The Elder paused for a moment before concluding. "People of Planet Earth, I formally open the United Nations Millennium Summit." Just then, before the crowd had a chance to react, a diamond of light appeared above the podium. As the Elder took a few steps backward, it exploded into a brilliantly radiating oval with two human figures inside. A few people jumped to their feet, but most were too stunned to move.

The cameras zoomed in, and the Chairman of the Chairmen swore, "it's not time yet!"

CHAPTER EIGHT
KEFTEA

    Suddenly Zoee was aware of her self again, slowing down, flowing out of the rushing stream and into a tranquil pond. As pulsating light swirls dissipated in the endless glow, structure began to form around her. Something was emerging. She leaned a little forward, squinted, and tried to make it out. A figure took shape, and she realized it was another person, a man, standing right in front of her. They blinked through the glare, trying to bring each other into focus. As they made eye contact, the light collapsed into a pulsating ball suspended between them. Then it popped out of existence.
    "Who are you?" Her voice quivered.
    His beauty brown eyes only smiled.
    She looked over his shoulder and saw the Knossos Cave, resting under the thick, broad branches of an old oak tree. Red poppy clusters sprang from the rocks and wild thyme decorated the low, arching entrance. They were at the edge of a dense green forest.

She half expected it all to disappear and return to normal, but then an old woman appeared at her side.

"Welcome to Keftea," the elder said, pinching her cheek and pulling her in for a hug. "Welcome to you too," she said to the man, likewise reeling him in.

"Keftea?" Zoee echoed, analyzing the woman's attire. Several colorful fabrics wound around and around her graying head. She wore a short sleeved blouse, a flounced skirt made of layers of colorful overlapping linens, and sandals. Her wise old eyes and impish grin were somehow reassuring, but Zoee's heart was still racing.

"And you are just in time," the woman added, patting her cheek before darting away.

"In time for what?" Zoee called back. "Wait!" But it was no use, the woman had already disappeared into the woods. She looked back at the man. "Who was that?"

"I do not know," he replied, looking as though he were trying to place himself. He glanced upward and saw a large building rising above the forest canopy. "What's that?"

She turned around, following his outstretched arm.

"Jesus Christ! It's Knossos!" She wobbled down to the thick, mossy grass and placed her hands on the Earth. "But in the past. Somehow the ruins of Knossos have been transformed." Long rows of red and black pillars supported multiple floors and terraces, some rising five stories high. Even from this distance, she could clearly make out the unmistakable bullhorn frieze adorning the highest floors. She blinked hard, but the massive stone and wood structure remained. "What's happening here?"

As he sat down beside her, a lock of wavy dark hair fell over his shoulder. "I really do not know," he said softly. "I've been, elsewhere. I can see faint images of other places, but they're, different." He smiled weakly and gave her an apologetic look.

"Different than what?" She checked out his off-white, knee length tunic and matching pants. "Maybe you've been in India?"

"I'm sorry, but at this moment, I cannot tell you anything

more."

She took a few deep breaths, trying to pull her own thoughts together. "The university computer ran the application, sent the translation to my laptop, and then that light appeared. I only caught a glimpse of the translation." She looked off to some unseen point, "it said, 'We are the people of Keftea....'" Her mind was suddenly on fire with the idea she'd somehow traveled through time. "I wonder if it's in there." She looked over at the cave, then stood up. "I need to see."

"May I come too?"

"Sure."

She again asked permission to enter, then cautiously ducked through the natural limestone archway. He followed her in, gently touching the portal as he passed underneath.

"They haven't sealed the inner chamber," she said from the back of the cave. "And I can smell the plaster. The frescoes have recently been painted!"

They slowly approached the lamp lit stairs, and as his foot touched the first greenstone step, she felt a ripple in the space around her. "That weird feeling again," she whispered. "Did you feel that?!"

"Most definitely."

He took another step and she could somehow sense him absorbing an energy from the cave.

"These are some of the most beautiful paintings I have ever seen. What does the inscription say?"

"I don't know. I vanished before I had the chance to decipher it."

"Is this what you're looking for?"

"Only part of it. We also found a tablet down there, this morning."

"Then, let us look further."

They descended into the inner chamber, where tall red and white lilies swayed in the flickering lamp light and the two golden bulls stood waiting.

"It's not here yet."

"No. It is not complete."

She looked again into his endless eyes. "Who *are* you?"

He searched the distance of his mind. "My name is, Joshua; and you are called?"

"Zoee."

They emerged from the cave to see Knossos gleaming above the forest. "I have to go up there," Zoee decided.

"Perhaps this stone path will lead us."

Oak, plane and cedar trees thrust upward from clover mounds of Earth, arching their moss-laden limbs into a dense canopy 150 feet above. Light beams shot through like spotlights, illuminating fluorescent green ferns, fanning high overhead. Red and yellow mushrooms and giant white lilies sprung from the plush forest floor, and a pair of turquoise dragonflies hummed by. Garlands of purple and yellow orchids draped around a creaky old knobby oak tree, and a hare darted across their path.

"Listen. There!" he whispered, pointing to a troop of monkeys, way up in the trees. They pointed back, and started to cackle.

"They're waving," she laughed, waving back.

Joshua waved and laughed with her.

They continued up the winding path, meandering by a creek, and past a small waterfall nestled in a lush bed of ferns. They stopped for a moment on a wooden footbridge. As the clear water rushed over red and green rocks, the song of the stream rose. Somewhere, far in the distance, she thought she heard an echo of the Dove.

Further on, they came to a mammoth red cedar. Four immense tentacle roots arched over the path, anchoring its tremendous trunk around the shadow of a long forgotten nurse log. They followed the mighty column up, up, soaring skyward, shooting past the other treetops, disappearing into the heavens. Zoee patted the rugged bark as they walked through the Titan in awe.

Before long, they encountered another, wider stone walkway.

"A crossroads," Joshua said, breaking the silence. "It seems to go around the hill."

"I think we should keep going straight up."

He nodded and started off.

Their path led them to a magnificent greenstone stairway, rising out of the cool, dark forest and into blue sky and brilliant sunlight. Zoee put her hand on the polished bronze railing, grasped it tightly and closed her eyes.

"Are you all right?" he asked, concerned.

"This is all so bizarre. I feel like I've stepped through the looking glass."

"You'll become accustomed to it."

"What's that supposed to mean?"

He smiled a little more confidently and walked up the stairs.

They emerged onto a broad stone plaza adjoining the magnificent temple, towering over their heads. Several hundred people were strolling through terraced gardens, sitting under shady maples and coconut palms, and splashing in an immense round fountain. Many of them had the long, dark curly hair and almond shaped eyes so characteristically Keftean. But there were also quite a few fair-haired people and some with much darker skin. Most of the men were clean shaven and wore short skirts, dyed or woven with chevrons, meanders and zig zags. The women were dressed in longer, layered skirts and colorful sheer blouses. Everyone wore exquisite jewelry – earrings, bracelets, pins and anklets of gemstones, silver and gold.

"Many of these people resemble you," Joshua whispered.

"If I'm not mistaken, they're my ancestors. This island is called Crete, and this complex is what I would call Knossos, a major center of the Minoan, I mean Keftean, civilization. This is probably the second of the 'Early Palaces.' It was built after the original was destroyed by a massive earthquake. I'd say its about 1650 b.c.e."

"What is 'b-c-e'?"

"It generally means before the current era, or before the Christian era. It's how we measure time where I come from."

"I see. How do you know about this place?"

"I'm an archeologist. I've studied this culture all of my professional life."

"Please, go on."

"Knossos is an incredibly sophisticated work of art and architecture, covering an area of almost five acres. We've estimated the complex consists of 1,500 roofed areas, including apartments, storerooms and workshops. Many archeologists stubbornly maintain it was a palace, though there is no evidence a monarchy existed in this culture until it was absorbed by the Myceneans in the 14th century b.c.e. The archeological record indicates the Kefteans were," she struggled with the tense, "*are* a highly egalitarian society, one in which the wealth and resources are more or less equally distributed amongst the people. And unlike almost all major Bronze Age cities, Knossos had no military fortifications; these people were not warriors."

"Remarkable."

Quite a few people passed by, talking and laughing with friends, when a man noticed them and came over to greet them. "Welcome to Keftea, brother," he said, embracing Joshua warmly. "And to you, sister," also embracing Zoee. "I hope this day finds you both well."

She instantly felt the love and sincerity radiating from him. Though she wanted to ask a million questions, the emotion of the moment washed them all away and she couldn't think of a thing to say. She let them go and allowed the feeling in.

He gently pulled away. "Enjoy your visit," he added, walking away.

"What a lovely way to greet people!" Joshua said.

"It's wonderful! I wish more people practiced that custom," Zoee agreed, watching the stranger as he walked over by the elaborate fountain in the center of the plaza. "Can you believe that fountain?!"

"Would you like to go see it?"

"Sure, why not?"

Five bright blue dolphins leapt from the center of the pool, spraying water high out of their blow holes. Green spirals and red octopi decorated the basin, and blue monkeys and flowers were painted around the wide stone bench.

"Shall we sit?" Joshua suggested.

"Actually, I'd rather try to go inside Knossos."

"All right. Lead the way."

"That must be an entrance over there." She started walking toward a twenty-foot wooden column in front of a tall, open doorway. As they approached it, she could see double axes carved all the way up to the top. Some were large and elaborate, and others were small and delicate, just barely scratching the surface at all.

"What is this symbol?" Joshua asked, tracing his finger over one of them.

"The labrys – one of the Keftean's most sacred symbols. It appears on walls and pillars throughout the complex, and it's the reason Knossos came to be known as the Labyrinth, which means the Dwelling of the Double Axe."

"What does it represent?"

"There are a number of interpretations, but I believe it expresses their awareness of the double-edged nature of technology. In this case, bronze. I think they knew that bronze could either be used to enhance their society, or to destroy it."

"I understand. He who lives by the sword, dies by the sword."

"Exactly."

She turned around and unexpectedly came face to face with one of her favorites, painted in red ochre and sky blue. "The Bull Leaping fresco! Unbleevable!"

"What are these people doing?"

"We think this was some sort of ritual, or possibly a sport, in which participants perform acrobatics over a bull. See," she pointed to the central figure, "the male acrobat is handspringing over the bull's back, while the two women are waiting their turn."

"We may see this during our visit."

Zoee eyed him intently, "what's that supposed to mean? Do you know something more?"

"Do not underestimate your own knowledge."

"I'll try not to, but that doesn't answer my question."

"I know a few things. However, at this moment, you know more about where we are than I do."

"But I think you know how we got here."

He gently touched her shoulder. "Each is on her own journey. If you continue to search, you will find answers. Of course," he laughed, "the answers always lead to new questions."

"Isn't that the truth. All right, I apologize for accusing you. It just seems like you're keeping things from me."

"I cannot keep from you what you already know inside. Relax."

"I'm trying to relax. But put yourself in my shoes."

"I've been in your shoes."

"This is all a dream. That's it. Any second now, I'm going to wake up in my little bed. I haven't even been in the cave yet. We never found the tablet and I never deciphered Linear A. It's all been a dream, a figment of my imagination."

"Maybe it is," he shrugged. "In many ways, my existence seems like a tapestry of dreams, woven together by the energy of the cosmos."

The energy of the cosmos...his words echoed in her mind, as she momentarily flashed to the light effect. The colored lights returned, swirling past her, picking up speed, sending her off again...till the sound of his voice brought her back.

"You know this place as Crete?"

"Yes," she said, trying to snap out of it, "apparently, though, the people who live here call it Keftea. That makes sense."

"What do you mean?"

"Because 'Keftea' sounds a lot like 'Keftiu,' which is how it was known to the ancient Egyptians. It's also been known as Kaphtor."

"Caphtor?"

"You know that name?"

"Yes, I suddenly remember a story. It was an island."

"What else do you recall?"

"The old ones told of a fantastic civilization overcome by a flood so fierce, their island sank to the bottom of the sea. Others said God caused the waters to rise, as punishment for a hedonistic, pagan people."

"So you know about the Bible."

"The Bible? No, that is not familiar."

"All right then, who are the old ones?"

He thought about it for a minute. "I'm sorry, but I cannot remember."

"Maybe it'll come to you. Let's keep going."

She tip toed into the passageway and looked around for someone who might protest their entrance. "Many archeologists presumed a sentry was posted here – looks like they were mistaken. Come on!"

They entered a long hallway, decorated with larger-than-life images of women and men in elaborate robes, carrying chalices, rhytons and lyres, painted in vivid colors.

"The Procession fresco," she said, placing her hand on her heart, "in its original form! Only fragments have survived the millennia into my time, and archeologist-artists have had to extrapolate the images from tiny bits and pieces. The restorations are on display at the Heraklion Museum, which will be built just down the road, in about 3,600 years."

They followed the long mural down the corridor, around a corner, and into sunlight at an inner entrance way. Two magnificent stone arches framed the Grand Staircase directly in front of them. They paused before passing through, then slowly ascended the elegant gypsum stairs to the central open-air courtyard. It was surrounded on all sides by multiple layers of rooms and verandahs, spilling over with flowers and ivy. They looked up and around the huge enclosed area. Red and black pillars supported doorways and awnings, and people were milling about on every floor. It was more splendid than she had imagined.

"Please, tell me more about this place."

"We think the living quarters are over there, on the east side. And the rituals take place here, on the west. Magnificent artifacts have been recovered from this part of Knossos – let's see if we can go in."

As they approached the entrance, they were stopped by a woman who stepped out of the doorway and into their path. "Sister, brother, welcome to Knossis!" She greeted them both with a warm embrace. "We're glad you've come to visit us. Our home is your home, and you may come and go as you please. You should know though, that these are our most sacred rooms. If you feel prepared to enter, then you are welcome to do so."

"Thank you, but I'd prefer to become acquainted with the community first," Joshua replied, looking at Zoee.

Before she had to respond, she noticed the old woman waving at the other end of the courtyard. Zoee only got a glimpse of her before she slipped outside.

"Thank you very much, but come to think of it, I'm no where near ready to go in there. I think I really need to speak with that elder first. Let's try to find her, Joshua."

They hurried across the courtyard and down a long, narrow stone ramp to the North Plaza. They rounded the corner to find her poking around in a flower garden, obviously waiting for them.

"It's about time you got here," she chuckled.

"Excuse me? We're the ones who've been chasing *you* all over town. And before you take off again, we'd like to ask you some questions, if you wouldn't mind."

"I bet you would. But first, let me ask you one. Are you hungry?"

"No!"

"Yes ma'am," Joshua piped up. "And we're also a little tired." He glanced at Zoee. "We've traveled far today. Is there an inn where we might find accommodations?"

"Nope. No room." She eyed them closely. "But you can come

to my house in the village. I'll fix you a little something and you can have a rest. Then, you can look around a little. Get to know us. We're a very hospitable people, and we love to share our good life, with *peaceful* travelers."

"I assure you ma'am, we are peaceful. Our only wish is to visit and learn of your ways. We're new to this place and have many questions. I'm Joshua, and this is Zoee. We are very grateful for your kindness and generosity."

"Yes, thank you," Zoee said, a little embarrassed.

"Wonderful!" She grabbed their cheeks and hugged them enthusiastically. "First, I want to show you something. Come with me."

They followed her to a walkway, which wound through a thick grove of oaks. Zoee watched the ease with which Joshua interacted with her. He had a very appealing gracefulness, and he was so calm.

"Relax," she said to herself. "Just relax."

They came out of the grove, onto a beautifully tiled patio overlooking the countryside. They could see the long stretch of the Royal Road, winding through more lush forest to a village nestled amongst the trees. The shiny road continued on to the sea, and along the shoreline in both directions. Pastures, vineyards and many layers of terraced orchards stretched out into the distance.

"This is incredible. I can hardly believe my eyes."

"Oh, believe them, dear," said the old woman, looking directly into her soul. "They will not lie to you. Keftea is a beautiful place. See it with your eyes and with your heart." She looked out across the cobalt blue sea. "You can see Kalliste today."

"The volcano!" Zoee gasped, feeling weak in the knees again. She stared at the black cone-shaped mountain rising above the sea, far off on the horizon. "I always wondered what it would have looked like from here."

"Come, we must go to the market now," the woman said.

"May I know your name?" Joshua asked, following her.

"I am Iseas."

Zoee had to pull herself away from the view and run to catch up.

They followed Iseas down several staircases to another walkway, which hooked up with the Royal Road. Overgrown oak trees formed a shady tunnel over the busy avenue. Zoee was shocked to see wooden pedal cars of all shapes and sizes, weaving in between the brightly dressed pedestrians. Other wheeled vehicles carried grains, olives and fruit from the surrounding fields.

As they approached the village center, the buildings became more dense. Two and three story structures were built in and around the oak forest, and connected by a complex system of walkways and patios. Windows and doorways were decorated with elaborately painted flowerboxes and pots, brimming over with fire red geraniums and bright blue azaleas. A group of people were sitting on a large verandah, surrounded by rose covered trellises. Several waved to Iseas as they passed by.

They entered the round open-air courtyard in the center of the bustling village. Whitewashed buildings painted with blue, red and yellow trim encircled them. Tall pillars supported broad awnings, providing people with shady areas to congregate, practice their arts and trade. In the very center, a huge sailing ship fountain bubbled and squirted water high into the air. Blue dolphins jumped across its bow and sea birds flew over the mast. Iseas headed straight for the market area, while Zoee and Joshua gawked and tried to keep up.

The market was a cornucopia of people and pithoi with products for trade. Olives, figs, quinces and grapes, lettuce, asparagus, carob and dates. Nuts and seeds, barley and peas, and hundreds of things she could just barely see. Thyme, basil, oregano, sage, cumin, mint, marjoram, tisane. Cheeses and oils and fresh, crusty breads – all whirling and twirling inside her head!

Zoee suddenly felt dizzy, disconnected from her surroundings. She was afraid if she blinked, it might all disappear, and she didn't want it to. She leaned up against a sturdy pillar, took a deep breath and watched.

Iseas chose a large smoked fish, two loaves of bread, some figs, a large jar of juicy olives, a basket of assorted vegetables and a big hunk of cheese. "I'm going to need a little extra," she said to her friend. "I've got guests." She finished selecting her goods, handed each of them a few things to carry and scooted off down one of the five main streets leading out of the central courtyard. The sounds of windchimes and a lyre gently rolled over the hubbub of the city center.

They turned into a doorway and went up a short flight of stone stairs. Iseas leaned against the door and gave it a shove with her shoulder. "Samos? The travelers are here!"

"Excellent!" her husband of fifty years replied, putting down his latest carving project to help her. The tall elder man stood up and opened his arms wide in greeting. He had graying hair and a neatly trimmed beard, and wore a long silver blue tunic with a gold embroidered belt. "Welcome! Welcome, come in and make yourselves comfortable." He collected the items they were carrying and went into the kitchen with Iseas.

Their hospitality reminded Zoe of her own Greek American family. She stepped inside and looked around the large living room, painted with a landscape of floor-to-ceiling frescoes. Fragile swallows darted in and out of delicate lilies five feet tall. Near the center of the room, a white narcissus and purple orchid blossomed on a low marble table, surrounded by colorful, overstuffed cushions. Down the hall, she could see several more rooms.

She came around the kitchen counter, leaned over and peeked inside to see Iseas rinsing the vegetables under a faucet. "You really do have plumbing!" she blurted out, practically falling over the counter and into the kitchen.

"Yes, dear," Iseas answered. "Everyone in the village does. We have an extensive aqueduct system which serves Knossis and the surrounding villages."

"I knew it! And what are those pipes?" She pointed at two terra cotta tubes climbing up the wall and out of the house.

"They're for the stove exhaust," Samos answered, chuckling.
"Incredible!"

"Please," Samos insisted, trying tactfully to get her off the counter, "you can examine it more closely after dinner, now sit down and make yourself comfortable."

She nodded reluctantly, went back into the living room and sat down on a big cushion next to Joshua.

"So, what do you think of our beloved Keftea?" Samos continued.

"I am most impressed," responded a calm and collected Joshua. "Rarely have I seen a more beautiful and harmonious place."

"This is unlike anything I've ever experienced before," Zoee added. "I can hardly believe it's real."

Samos put down his obsidian knife and leaned over the counter. "Oh my dear," he was noticeably worried, "don't even think it isn't real. Now tell me, did you visit our splendid Knossis?"

"Yes. We were fortunate to see a part of it," Zoee replied, trying to be a little more gracious. "We walked through the beautiful Procession Hall and into the courtyard, though we didn't go further inside."

"So, you have just arrived."

"We got here about an hour ago. At least, I think that's how long it's been."

"Well then, the best part of your visit is yet to come. Until then, you can rest, gather your strength and see how we live."

Out of the corner of her eye, Zoee noticed two little faces peering around the corner of the open door.

Samos saw them too, before they popped out of view. They soon reappeared, peeking around the corner again.

"All right you two, come in," he said gently.

"Hello Pou," a tall, dark-haired girl of about nine said, as she came all the way inside. "We heard you had guests."

"You have guests!" repeated her little brother.

"Yes we do!" Iseas cheerfully confirmed. "Why don't you

come in for a visit."

"My name is Demmi," she said confidently, "and this is my brother Cori."

"I'm five years old," he added proudly.

"Wanna come sit down?" Zoee patted the cushion.

They piled on the pillows in between them.

"Would you like to see my picture?" Demmi asked excitedly.

"We'd love to," Zoee replied.

She pulled a piece of paper from the pouch in her tunic. She carefully unfolded it, and handed it to Zoee. In the middle of the page, she'd painted a small green egg, encircled by a ring of bright blue. The whole image was enveloped by a midnight blue oval, speckled with silver dots.

"What is it?" Zoee asked.

"It's us! Floating in the sea of Night!"

"That's astonishing."

"I went on the sea!" Cori interjected ecstatically. "In a ship!"

"You did!?" Joshua asked. "Where did you go?"

"I only went a little way out into the harbor, but when I'm bigger, I'm going to sail to Kalliste."

"Demmi? Cori?" Samos piped up. "Your old Pou could use some help in here."

The kids jumped up and scrambled into the kitchen.

"I need you both to take a special message to your parents. Would you go invite them for dinner?"

They spun around and bolted out the door, giggling.

"Are they your grandchildren?" Zoee asked.

"Yes. Iseas and I are very fortunate and thankful. We have a wonderful family."

"How many children do you have?" asked Joshua.

"Three. Our son Horeas is the father of those two. Sappho, our oldest, has twins, Inan and Lillith who are now 15. Our youngest daughter, Cybele, is out to sea."

"The twins are currently serving at Knossis," Iseas said proudly.

"Serving there?" Zoee asked.

"Yes, they're studying our central government, and learning the old ways. All of our young people enter training when they're 13."

"How long do they study?"

"It depends on what their interests are. Those who wish to enter public service train for as many as ten years; those who are interested in the arts usually train for three, then seek an apprenticeship."

"What are your grandchildren pursuing?"

"They're in leadership training."

Cori suddenly came tumbling back into the room. "Here's my mom and dad!"

"Horeas, Driana, come in," Samos invited. "You are just in time." He set a big platter of food on the table, and removed the plants to make even more room.

"Good thing we brought an extra rhyton of wine!" Horeas said cheerfully. He went straight to the cupboard, retrieved the glass cups and had the red wine poured in no time.

Iseas brought over a second platter, and sat down with her family. "You look a little pale, dear," she said to Zoee, handing her a plate. "Help yourself. We don't want you to faint from lack of nourishment."

"Thank you, Iseas," Zoee said, selecting a little of everything.

"Samos is right," Iseas went on. "You two need to rest and gather your strength. Why don't you both stay here, as our guests."

"Thank you both so much for your kindness," Joshua responded. "I cannot speak for Zoee, but I would be pleased to stay with you. And perhaps I can offer something in exchange." He smiled sweetly at Samos. "I too enjoy working with wood."

Samos lit up at the prospect of sharing woodworking secrets. He reached over and patted Joshua's arm affectionately.

"I would love to stay with you," Zoee agreed, stuffing a big piece of bread and cheese in her mouth.

After dinner, they said their goodnights and Samos showed them to their rooms.

"Come, Zoee, you may stay in this room; and Joshua, we'll put you across the hall."

"I don't want to put *you* out, Samos," Zoee said, concerned.

"Nor do I," Joshua agreed.

"Don't you worry, dears. We will go to Cybele's and have the whole place to ourselves." Samos went in Zoee's room. "Let me light the lamps for you. There. Now you have a good rest, and we'll see you in the morning." He kissed her on the cheek and went back into the living room.

"Good night, Samos. Thanks for everything."

"Good night, Zoee," Joshua said from his doorway.

"Good night, Joshua." She closed her door and looked around the spacious room. The queen bed was covered with a midnight blue duvet, and a set of four large pillows made a comfortable back rest against the wall. She muushed the corner of the feather stuffed comforter, then lifted it up, finding silky blue sheets, patterned with yellow seahorses and shells. She peeked under the quilted mattress to see a wooden bed frame supporting a firmly woven web of hemp cord. After carefully tucking the sheets back under, she sat down to test it out. *Pretty comfortable.*

High up near the ceiling, a painted band of blue and yellow spirals encircled the room, bringing her eye to a small white figurine resting on a beautifully carved wooden dresser. She got up to take a closer look at the delicate marble harp player, created by some talented Cycladic artisan. She gently touched the smooth coolness of the milky white stone. *This could already be a thousand years old...*

An owl hooted from somewhere outside, calling her to the open window. She leaned out into the moonlit courtyard, where she could see two stone benches resting under a big old olive tree in the center. The other apartment windows were decorated with flowerboxes and hanging pots, and dark green ivy covered the three-story walls. The owl hooted again, then flew up and away, into the night sky. She closed her eyes, breathing in the fragrant air, as the cool night breeze softly patted her cheeks, coaxing her to sleep.

She came back inside and got undressed, then crawled in the cushy bed. As the moonlight filled the room, images flooded her mind. She saw herself, in front of the mirror the day before, dancing under the stars at Tasso's taverna, inside the cave when they first found the tablet, the words on the computer screen, the flash of light, Joshua's dark brown eyes, the Kalliste volcano...then she was standing in an ancient olive grove, and the other images receded like ghosts into the trees. She was alone, waiting for Joshua to come.

A long time passed. The day grew dark and she waited.

A snake appeared, winding its way slowly through the tall grass, up and around the gnarly trunk of the oldest tree. It stretched out onto a thick branch and rested its head in between two budding limbs. In the serpent's eye, she saw the reflection of an apple; then it was in her hand. She took a bite and Joshua appeared. The snake lifted its head and smiled at her, before winding down the tree, spiraling round and round, back into Earth....

She suddenly realized she was seeing the spirals painted on the walls of her room, and the vision slipped away, deep into the well of her psyche.

I've returned to Keftea.

She stretched her arms and long, slender legs, her toes just peeking into daylight from under the comforter. *I was waiting for something.* She laid there a long while, trying to recall it, but she could only sense a vague impression of Joshua.

She finally got up, opened the door and peered out into the hallway; the house was quiet. She tip toed down the hall and slipped into the bathroom to get cleaned up. A blue tiled tub painted with tropical fish rested along the back wall, and sure enough, they had a flush toilet. A round mirror made of polished bronze hung over a built-in basin, and red and yellow tiles decorated the spacious counter. She turned the faucets and cupped the warm water in her hands. Nikos would be pleased, she thought, splashing some on her face.

After she dressed, she took another tour of the house. Joshua's door was open, his bed was made, but he was no where to be found. She walked around the living room, admiring the frescoes and decorative pottery, then went outside. Before heading to the town center, she went for a little detour down the back streets. The stone sidewalk meandered through tall and small archways, up and down staircases and underneath a terrace full of people enjoying their morning meal. Several waved as she passed under, and she returned the greeting.

The short tunnel brought her into a small park, with another fountain. As she approached it, she could see moving parts, soon realizing it was a complex system of gears propelled by a steady stream of flowing water. It had a large, fixed inner ring with twelve symbols, one for each month. Each of those was divided into thirty sections, one for every day. Another gear measured the phases, risings and settings of the moon. A third was inscribed with constellations, several of which she recognized.

"Good morning, sister," said a woman passing by.

"Good morning, sister," Zoee echoed. "Say, I'm new to Keftea and I've never seen anything like this fountain before. What is it?"

"Our observatory – we use it to keep track of Cosmos. Every Circle has one."

"Circle?"

"Our neighborhood. We all use observatories, so we have them in each Circle park."

"That's amazing. Where I come from, most people wouldn't have a clue how to track the Great Cycles."

"More and more people are losing the art, but for now, it still thrives in Keftea."

"So it does," Zoee said, smiling. "You know, I'm not used to the winding streets either, and I'm not sure I could find my way to the village center. Could you point me in the right direction?"

"Yes I can. Go left, just up there by those orange trees; it'll take you right there."

"Thank you."

"You are most welcome, sister."

By the time she got downtown, the place was buzzing with activity. She passed the crowded market, and wandered over to the workshops – immense work areas covered by sturdy wooden roofs.

In the first one she came upon, the artisans were firing copper and tin in huge stone vats, melting the metals down into bronze. One man dipped a large ladle into the molten mixture and carefully poured it into three clay molds. A woman walked by, and picked up two casts which had been poured earlier and were now cooled. Zoee followed her to the workshop next door, where more artisans cracked off the hardened clay with metal hammers, revealing marvelous bronze statuettes, Goddess figurines and double axes.

One man was exceptionally pleased with a miniature Snake Goddess. He cleared away the last of the clay dust with a soft bristle brush, admiring the finished piece. He deferentially picked it up and took it to show the friend who had made the mold. Zoee followed him around three large workbenches, and into the wax making area. The friend was sitting at a marble table, gently working the soft wax into a flying acrobat. He stopped for a moment to appreciate the finished work, and they complemented each other's artistry.

Nearby, a woman applied ochre red clay to a hardened wax bull head. She smoothed the clay carefully and evenly over the sculpture, and when she was satisfied, she took it to the kiln for firing. As the clay hardened, the wax melted, dripping out of small holes in the mold. Beneath the ovens, stone channels funneled it into vats, so it could be used again. Zoee continued on through the mold making area, till she wound up amidst the jewelers.

One of the younger men peered at his creation through a large crystal lens. He sensed Zoee's interest and invited her to observe. She pulled up a chair and watched, as he applied minuscule grains of gold to the hive of a bee pendant. Two bees embraced the honeycomb, their bodies embossed with fine, slim lines, and their eyes inlaid with red cornelian stone. Three small spiral disks hung from their wings, and on their heads, they carried a delicate gold wire globe containing a small gold bead. After a while, she complemented his fine work and thanked him for sharing his craft. She took her time amongst the other jewelers, admiring their exquisite pieces – silver and gold bracelets, necklaces, hairpins and rings, inlaid with lapis lazuli, amethyst and rock crystal.

In one corner, a middle-aged woman was carving a sealstone, using a tubular drill made of copper. She carefully placed the bit on a tiny piece of green jasper, and used an ibex hair bow to rotate the drill. As it spun faster and faster, it cut through the hard rock. She stopped to add more water and sand, then continued to drill. She repeated the process several more times, then removed the stone to inspect the miniature scene. Though it was only the size of a nickel, she had been able to carve a man and a woman dancing under the Tree of Life with birds and butterflies around them. *Amazing.* More stone cutters used larger drills to fashion goblets, chalices, vases and pots in a variety of sizes, shapes and types of stone.

Zoee traveled on, eventually entering into the potters' area, where rhytons, pithoi and terra cotta figurines were crafted. Several women and men were creating new pieces on large potting wheels, as others painted theirs with twisting, swirling, interconnecting patterns. One man was putting the final touches on a red octopus, whose tentacles spread around a large jar, encircling nautiluses, sea weed and fish. Another was applying faience glaze to a delicate cup, which when fired would turn an iridescent, glassy blue.

A rich, nutty smell scented the air, capturing her attention. It lured her around another corner, and carried her into the textile workshops. Garlands of dried wildflowers hung from the ceiling, and huge baskets of seashells, lichens, tree bark and herbs lined the walls. Cauldrons bubbled with the cooking dyes, and long skeins of yarn draped over wooden racks nearby, waiting to be dipped.

A woman came in, carefully hung another skein and disappeared through a small door. Zoee followed her into yet another room, and found dozens of people, chatting and processing fibers – sorting the fleeces, hackling flax and hemp, and combing and carding the wool. Under the voices, she could hear a low, gentle rhythm, but it was almost imperceptible. As she wandered through the bustling workshop, it began to grow louder and louder, drawing her closer in.

It pulled her around the rolag baskets and past the triangular worktables, then toward a wide stone archway. She passed through the arch and the room opened up to a sky-lit vaulted ceiling. Around the circle, the spinners spun, on wheels of every size. The beat of the treadles filled the room, spilling out into the sky. Wheel after whirling wheel, pulling the fibers together, creating the living thread. Spinning, spinning, spinning her back, back to an earlier time....

She grasped the reins of the carousel pony and hung on tight. The pipe organ played and colored lights flashed as she galloped and galloped around. Her sister was riding on a horse out front; she laughed and flashed her a peace sign. She rode by her family, who stood below, waving and taking home movies. She waved back at them grinning, then looked up to see the gold ring over her head. She reached way up, as high as she could, and plucked it from the hook. She held it gently in her hands, feeling the ecstasy.

The ring began to glow, then pulse, and then the light expanded, filling all perceptions. When the wave receded, a golden loom weight rested in her hands. The treadles again resounded, but now the spinners were gone. In their place, the weavers wove, throwing their shuttles briskly, pulling the living threads together, weaving the endless fabric....

Zoee soon found herself following a path of blue and white tiles out of the workshops. The rhythm of the looms still echoed in her mind, and her heart was racing. She slowed her breath as she took each step, focusing on the smooth, blue triangles beneath her feet. When she came to the fountain in the center of the courtyard, she sat down on the stone bench and listened to the water, letting it soothe her, refresh her mind and cleanse her soul anew.

The bubbles carried a song of voices, and a familiar one rose to the top. It was Joshua.

"I have seen no hunger, no poverty," he said.

She came part way around the fountain, just enough to be able to see him.

"Why would people be hungry?" asked a boy of about 17. "There's plenty to eat for everyone."

Joshua smiled sweetly at the boy's grandfather. "You have a remarkable society."

"Yes, we do," he replied softly, as his eyes began to tear.

"Legends of your people have spread far and wide!" Joshua went on. "They have been an inspiration to many."

"They have?" The old man brightened a little.

"Oh, yes! The seeds you have sewn have been carried on favorable winds, to rich and fertile soil."

"Then we will not be forgotten?"

"No!" Joshua looked into his eyes, and into those of the others around him. "Though you feel fear, you must also feel confident and believe in yourselves. Now more than ever." He stood and held out both arms. "We are all part of a larger spirit, a universal heart. Draw strength from it." He touched the man's arm. "Feel the link to it. You are not alone."

The man patted the top of Joshua's hand and nodded, trying to be brave. But he knew what was coming. The boy was too innocent to realize what the old man knew, and what Joshua was just beginning to understand.

Joshua looked into the others' eyes. "None of us are alone!

Come, let us create a circle."

Zoee watched the circle grow as more and more villagers joined. As it widened around the fountain, a small child reached for her hand. Samos appeared and took her other hand. When the circle was complete, the child began to sing,

> *The Earth, the Air, the Fire, the Water,*
> *Return, return, return, return.*
> *The Earth, the Air, the Fire, the Water,*
> *Return, return, return, return...*

Soon the circle was alive in song,

> *I-ay, I-ay, I-ay, I-ay,*
> *I-oh, I-oh, I-oh, I-oh!*
> *The Earth, the Air, the Fire, the Water,*
> *Return, return, return, return,*
> *The Earth, the Air, the Fire, the Water,*
> *Return, return, return, return.*

When the chant trailed off and the circle broke, Samos gave Zoee a great big hug. "Good morning, Zoee, good morning! How are you today?"

"Wonderful, Samos. I've had a delightful morning just wandering around and getting to know the place a little."

"Splendid. And did you have a good night's rest?"

"I slept really well!"

"Excellent, you look rested and good thing too. The Winter Festival is just around the corner and there is plenty of work to be done. Could you spare a hand?"

"I'd love to!"

The next two days whirled by in a flurry of activity. She'd helped out with the chores, worked in the gardens, pressed olives, made wine and baked bread from dawn till dusk. Zoee was not used to this kind of physical work and by the time she got home, at the end of day three, she was ready to collapse.

"Come dear," Iseas said, beckoning her down the hall. "You could use a hot bath before you go to sleep. I'll draw the water. Let's see, what do I have in here?" She rummaged through a small red cupboard next to the sink. "Mmmmm, I'll take a little of this, and a little of this, and yup, here it is. A lit-tle of this." She slowly swirled each small glass bottle, then poured in just the right amount. The flowing water cascaded out of the faucet, and blended the silky liquids into a hot, bubbling bath.

Iseas lit a small candle and blew out the lamp. She took Zoee's hands and brought her face in close. "Bathe, sweet Zoee. Let the fragrances calm your mind and cleanse your spirit – you have a big day tomorrow." She kissed her on both cheeks, then silently left the room and closed the door.

Zoee undressed and slipped into the pool of opal velvet. It wrapped itself around her, pulling the tension from her aching muscles. She felt each one release, until at last, she became one with the tub. She closed her eyes and allowed herself to drift....

Out of the still, peaceful darkness around her, a mist began to rise. Off in the distance, a gentle voice whispered, "Zoee! Zoee!" A single candle pierced the mist, and then it multiplied, creating a circle of fire around a lustral basin. She peered into the shimmering water, and saw her own reflection. But then she saw her mother, and then her mother's mother, and on back through the generations, into her distant past. When the water stilled, returning her to herself, she heard the old voice speaking. "Be at peace, Zoee, for tomorrow you will come full circle."

"Good morning, Zoee. Good morning!" Iseas said from the hall, tapping at her door. "May I come in?"

"Sure." She sat up, a little startled at being zapped out of a sound sleep. "What is it?"

Iseas flung the door open, grabbed her hands and pulled her out of bed.

"The sails of Cybele's ship have just been spotted! They'll be at the port shortly. Get dressed, get dressed! We must all go down to greet her."

Zoee found her clothes, miraculously washed, folded and nicely laid out on the dresser. She quickly dressed and tore out the door, nearly colliding with Joshua in the hallway. She stepped aside, and gestured with her hand, smiling, "after you."

"Thank you, and good morning, Zoee!" He walked past, quickening his step.

"Come on. Come on! Iseas called from the living room. We cannot be late!"

They flew down the stairs and out to the walkway, where family and friends were waiting.

"Let's go, let's go!" Samos boomed, laughing and taking his grandchildren's hands.

Everyone hurried down the winding stone street, shouting "hello!" and "Cybele is coming home!" as they passed their neighbors. An old man called back from his window, "my Yanni is also returning! It is a happy day!" Iseas threw him a kiss as they ambled on down the crowded roadway.

A canopy of thick oak branches arched high overhead, and on either side, small workshops and apartments were tucked amongst the trees. Carts and wagons streamed past them, taking food and wine up to Knossis for the festival. People were bustling about in all directions, and a sense of anticipation was in the air.

"They are very anxious for this day to begin," Joshua said, trying not to fall behind.

"So am I," Zoee agreed.

"I believe today, we will come full circle."

Zoee stopped suddenly, grasping his arm. "That's what the voice said in my dream last night."

"I know," he said, placing his hand on hers. "I heard it too."

"Come on Joshua! Come on Zoee!" little Cori called from up ahead. "We're almost there."

The trees began to thin, and as they approached the harbor, markets sprung up all along the road. Squid and octopus hung along ropes, drying in the sun, and sea sponges spilled over the brims of large baskets. People were scurrying to and fro, loading crates of mussels, clams and crab onto carts, and carrying bundles of fish on long strings. Gulls glided overhead, squawking and diving for bits, and the salty smell of the ocean grew strong.

They continued along the crowded boardwalk until they reached the docks. When they got to the water's edge, Zoee could finally see the magnificent harbor and the thousand-foot stone pier arching out into the brilliant blue Keftean Sea. People were fishing from the pier, as pelicans dove off shore. Colorful boats were tied to painted wooden moorings, though she noticed several being pulled from the water.

The family inched their way up to the front as the *Wind Spirit* approached the pier, and the crowd began to chant,

Ride the current
 on Breath of the Wind
Thank the Stars in the Sky
 for bringing you back, safely to us
Ay-eye. Ay-eye.
Ride the current
 on Breath of the Wind
Thank the Stars in the Sky
 for bringing you back, safely to us
Ay-eye. Ay-eye....

The sailing ship stretched 90 feet, from spiral prow to stern. Its two sturdy masts soared high in the air, and each of the four sky blue sails was embroidered with a golden winged griffin. Hundreds of passengers leaned over the railings, cheering and waving to the people below. As they glided smoothly into a slip, the crew let down the sails and tossed the lines onto the pier.

When Samos saw Cybele in the front of the craft, he jumped

up and called out her name. She waved back excitedly, threw her satchel over her shoulder and disembarked the ship.

"Mother! Father!" she shouted, quickly making her way through the crowd. "Hello everyone!"

Her family showered her with hugs and kisses, and when the flurry died down, Iseas introduced the two travelers.

"I'm happy to meet you, sister," Zoee said, embracing her.

"As am I," Joshua echoed, also offering a Keftean welcome. "Tell me, where has this fine ship taken you?"

"The island of Kalliste, to the north. We evacuated the last of the people."

Zoee felt an intense surge of anxiety.

"Evacuated, why?" Joshua wondered.

"Kalliste is a volcanic island. For months it has shown signs of a major eruption, but everyone is safe now."

Before he had a chance to ask anything further, two young people came flying down the road in a purple pedal car, gliding to a smooth stop a few feet away. They both had long, black curly hair and nearly identical features. Each wore a long crimson robe, and a gold butterfly pendent with amethyst wings.

"Well, if it isn't my dear niece and nephew!" Cybele exclaimed. "What is this, a special greeting from the Asasra and Asakra?"

Lillith and Inan hopped out of their pedal car and hugged her enthusiastically.

"It is Serendipity who brought us here to greet you," said Lillith, grinning.

"Yes," added Inan, turning to the two visitors, "we have also been sent by the Asasra and Asakra to invite Zoee and Joshua to Knossis today. We expected to find them in the village, but for the arrival of your fair ship."

"Yes!" Zoee accidentally blurted out.

"Well then," Cybele said, "we all have good fortune today! You are in for a special treat. I'm happy to have met you."

The twins approached Zoee and Joshua, and Lillith asked

more formally, "would you honor us by accepting the invitation?"

"The honor is ours," replied Joshua, nodding his head deferentially.

"Yes, the honor is ours," Zoee echoed.

"You have been delightful guests," Iseas said, reaching out to take their hands in hers. "Thank you for sharing sweet life with us, Joshua and Zoee. We kiss your eyes and wish you safe travels."

"Now, hop in that jalopy and go with my grandchildren to learn of your fate," Samos added, smiling warmly.

The two of them hugged the elder couple then climbed into the back seats of the car.

"Thank you for coming to collect us," Joshua said, as they rolled off up the road.

"It is our pleasure," replied Lillith. "We are happy to assist the Asasra and the Asakra."

"Who exactly are they?" asked Zoee.

"They are our decision makers – the ones closest in mind to the collective thought of the people."

"We are all given an opportunity to become decision makers when we're young," Inan explained. "Those who reveal true wisdom are selected by the people to lead."

"Do they live inside Knossis?" asked Zoee.

"Yes they do, and so do we at present. It's a splendid place to live. My sister and I hope to be selected to lead someday. It's been a long time since twins were chosen, but there is precedent for it."

"In fact," added Lillith, "twins who serve as Asasra and Asakra have been the wisest decision makers."

"Well, good luck to you both." She turned to Joshua and lowered her voice, abruptly changing the subject. "I know what happens to that volcano. When that thing explodes, it's going to be a hellatious eruption. Like two hundred hydrogen bombs going off at ground zero in the span of a millisecond."

"That sounds *really* bad. When do you think it will erupt?"

"There's no way to know. It could be a few days or a few months. Our best estimate is that the eruption occurred sometime around 1628 b.c.e., but I don't know exactly where we are in time. One thing is certain. When it goes, it's gonna go big. The ash cloud will blacken the sky for hundreds of miles around the volcano, and ultimately encircle the globe. The Aegean islands will experience catastrophic earthquakes, and shores around the Mediterranean will be overwhelmed by massive tidal waves. People will have to flee."

"The Exodus. Yes, now I remember. Refugees will be forced inland, and many will come to, Jerusalem."

"Jerusalem?"

Joshua sat quietly for a moment, and images rushed back to him. "I lived there during a time of great cruelty and sadness. The Romans were brutal to Jews who wouldn't worship their gods – we weren't much more than slaves to them. Many of us resisted, and some were even put to death for challenging the establishment." His eyes teared up. "They were nailed to huge wooden crosses and left to hang in the sun for all to see, slowly starving and dehydrating."

"A crucifixion. That's how Jesus Christ died." She looked for some sign of recognition.

"Who is Jesus Christ?"

"I was hoping you'd heard of him. He lived about 2,000 years before my time, but his legacy continues to have an enormous impact on the world. His teachings are the basis of one of the largest religions, called Christianity. Christians believe Christ was, and is, the son of God, sent from heaven to save humanity. You must've lived b.c.e."

"I think I was in Jerusalem just before I arrived here, but I saw an enormous golden dome where the Temple used to be," he said, as if it wasn't quite right.

"That isn't possible. The Dome of the Rock wasn't there when the Romans were in Jerusalem."

"I didn't notice any Romans, but I was surrounded by all that light so I couldn't see too much."

"But you saw a golden dome?"

"Most definitely. It was magnificent."

"How can that be? The Dome wasn't built until the seventh century. If you came from that time, you would surely know of Christianity."

"My memories of life in Jerusalem are hard to place in time. When you told the tale of the volcano, it opened a door in the recesses of my mind and the memories returned, rushing swiftly like a mighty river. At this moment, it seems as though those events could have occurred yesterday. Yet, I have had innumerable experiences, in many other spheres of consciousness. You will see, Zoee. You have begun the journey, and time as you have known it will soon have little meaning. Appreciate this gift, and believe in your new reality."

She took his hand in hers. "I'm afraid sometimes I find myself doubting."

"You know you must believe. After all, it is belief which makes the journey possible in the first place."

She squeezed his hand. "So, now we're here, at the height of the Keftean civilization. Why?"

"I believe we will soon find out."

"Excuse me," interrupted Lillith, "we must get out here in order to enter Knossis."

They left the vehicle at the plaza, and started up the long, narrow stone ramp to the courtyard. Tall red and black pillars stood on either side of the tunnel-like entryway, and a bullhorn frieze decorated the top. Two more Initiates appeared mid-way, carrying a set of golden robes.

"These are for you," Lillith said. "Please, let us help you put them on."

They emerged onto the central courtyard and found it in full festival swing. Jugglers, dancers and musicians entertained the crowd, and tables offered abundant Mediterranean fare to anyone who wished.

An enormous round tapestry hung from the balcony at the far end. Around its border, a golden snake with bright red eyes encircled the Keftean world. Three tall sailing ships floated on a sea of cobalt blue, and a red octopus, green turtle and white fluked whale swam amidst seaweed and kelp below. A turquoise dolphin leapt into the air, to fly with the seabirds overhead, and thick green oaks grew along the sides, their long roots stretching around the bottom of the sea and tall tops arching into a starry indigo sky.

"Zoee," Inan whispered. "Would you like to hear our mother's poetry?"

"Yes, that would be wonderful."

"She's written a special song for the festival. Come, this way."

They walked over to a large group gathered around three musicians, and listened to Sappho sing.

Sisters, Brothers, gather round this lovely lyre
    and this graceful flute.
Together, we will invoke the gentle Muses.
Let them come, open our hearts and release our inspiration!
Oh, Calliope, and Clio! Euterpe and Erato!
    Call your sisters Thalia and Urania!
Emerge from the ancient waters,
    emerge from Her primal source.
Please, join us here today!
Surround us with your song and laughter, and embrace us
    with your music, sweet like honey from the Bee.
With love we receive your graces and
    we are thankful for your presence.
We know you must soon leave us, so we bid farewell today.
We shall cry to see you go, as our tears fall
    for brilliant silver Moon now waning, slipping into
        Darkness.
It's true, my friends and lovers, the darkest Night approaches
    and we will go to sleep, while careless shepherds

trample through the meadows.
Go to them sweet Muses, caress their angry hearts,
remind them we are the song,
the sacred dance they left behind.
Be our joyful Memory, and we will not slip away.
For we know, the magic crescent will one day wax again,
becoming round and full once more,
to be born with us anew!
And when we do awaken, we shall dance,
again with love and joy of heart!
Our sacred songs will fill the air,
and Life will be renewed!

She raised her arms high and threw her head back, sounding the castanets. The lyre and flute picked up the tempo, and the people danced and sang, "and Life will be renewed! and Life will be renewed!" Their energy peaked, then they quieted back down to hear another poem.

Lillith and Inan waved to their mother, then motioned for Zoee and Joshua to follow. They crossed the courtyard, and entered a wide hallway. Zoee's heart was pounding as they walked up the crowded staircase to a huge, partially covered verandah on the second floor. Everywhere – frescoes, food and festivity. Sunlight streamed through delicate bronze filters, creating stars, spirals and animal shapes on the walls. Hundreds of people sat at round marble tables, enjoying the feast. On one side of the verandah she could see down into the courtyard, and on the other, out to the Keftean Sea.

They followed the twins through the crowd to the large table at the center, where five couples were seated. They all wore fine crimson robes, and each pair donned uniquely patterned vestments which hung gracefully around their necks.

When Zoee and Joshua were seated, the man and woman directly across from them stood, and opened their arms wide in greeting.

The woman introduced herself first. "I am the Asasra of Keftea."

"And I am the Asakra of Keftea," the man said. "Welcome."

"We represent the people of Keftea," the Asasra continued, acknowledging the others as she introduced them. "These are the Representatives of the people of our neighbor islands: Kalliste, Lesvos, Cypri and Nexos. Welcome. We have prepared a wonderful meal in celebration of the Solstice, but before we begin, we would like to tell you our story.

"Many thousands of years ago, our distant ancestors received the gift of consciousness. As they became aware of themselves, and the magical world around them, at first they felt fearful, alone in a vast wilderness of the unknown. Over time, they conceived a story to help them overcome their fear and understand the mysterious energies of nature.

"They imagined the Earth to be their Great Mother, the one who gave birth to them, who fed and sheltered them in life and received them in death. The one who offered the promise of renewal. Sky, who sent the rains to fertilize the Mother, and who sustained them with precious water, was envisioned as their Great Father.

"They knew that without Father Sky to send the rains, Mother Earth would become barren, unable to bring forth life. And without Mother Earth to absorb and transform the rain, the water would overwhelm the land. They saw these two great forces coexisting in partnership, interconnected with each other, dependent upon each other. They called this cosmic union Sacred Marriage.

"The Sacred Marriage became the principle upon which their relationships and societies were founded. Women and men lived in partnership, mutual respect and peace. They valued and respected all life with whom they shared the land.

"They learned to farm sustainably, and when they no longer had to devote the majority of their energy to food production, they were free to cultivate the spirit. The first Temple was built almost seven hundred years ago, when our Awakening began.

"We began to experiment, to express ourselves through weaving, painting, pottery making and theater. We perfected the craft of shipbuilding, creating the opportunity to travel and expand trade abroad, in Egypt, Mesopotamia, Estrucia and Old Europe. Over the generations, we established trade routes across the European, African and Asian continents, which enabled us to share our ideas, customs and goods with many different cultures of the Great Civilization.

"In the beginning, we were wary of those who spoke different languages and told unfamiliar stories. But eventually, we began to recognize the similarities of all of our stories. As we started to see the common themes, we came to understand the Sacred Marriage, Goddess and God, the Allness or Great Spirit, are simply different ways of trying to explain the great mysteries of Life. We accepted each other's view of the world, and were able to live together peacefully for a long, long time.

"Though we no longer fear the Cosmic energies, we still tell our stories of the Sacred Marriage, Mother Earth and Father Sky. They are the golden threads which bind our society together, metaphors to remind us of our connection to the universe and to each other."

The Asakra of Keftea then spoke.

"Many generations ago, nomadic hunters and herders abandoned Mother Earth, and transformed Father Sky into an angry god of war who rules through fear and violence. They broke the sacred trust, and defiled the Sacred Marriage.

"These people came from the steppes in the north, on the fringes of the Great Civilization. At first, they fought amongst themselves, but when they depleted their resources, they went in search of more. The communities of the Great Civilization were not driven by war, so when the barbarians came, there was little defense.

"One by one, Mesopotamia, Old Europe and Egypt have fallen under the power of the sword. They raid the villages and towns, desecrate the temples, kill and enslave the people by the thousands, and still their appetite is not satisfied. The dominators have been coming, wave after wave, for 126 generations. We have resisted them for a thousand years, continuing to live peacefully in our island communities. We may be the last people on Earth who still live in partnership; however, we cannot hold out much longer – we cannot stop the final wave. It is upon us. The Myceneans are now at our doorstep, and our way of life will soon come to an end."

The Asasra concluded. "However, this Solstice Day, we come together in celebration of the Great Civilization. And though we have seen the darkness coming a long time now, we know that, as Sun returns to warm Earth again, so will the light of humanity return to the world one day. Please, celebrate with us, and help bring us full circle."

Zoee and Joshua looked at each other expectantly, then watched as Lillith and Inan approached the table with a large obsidian chalice. The Asasra lifted it up over her head, then brought it gently to her lips. She took a slow sip, then passed it to the Asakra. He repeated the gesture then passed it to the next.

When Zoee received the chalice, for a moment she shared their pain, and the pain of the ages to follow. But then she felt the hope. *So will the light of humanity return to the world one day.* She caressed the smooth curve of the stone, warmed by the hands of the others, then she drank, and passed it on to Joshua. He closed his eyes gently and remained very still, before silently sharing in the spirit.

The cup continued around to the Asasra again, who placed it in the center of the table. "Now let us be grateful for what we have received, and share in the feast of the Solstice. Please, join the others and help yourselves to the food you have helped us prepare."

The Representatives rose, as did Joshua and Zoee. The Asasra and Asakra motioned for them to approach the tables, laden with wine and seafood. Smoked fish and shellfish, octopus and squid were surrounded by vegetables, fruits and breads – the finest they had to offer.

"Please," the Asakra invited. "Select whatever you wish. You are our honored guests." When they were all seated and eating their meal, Zoee found herself speaking.

"I appreciate the honor of being your guest, and have enjoyed the abundance of your table. You are a gracious, loving people, and it has been my greatest joy to experience life with you. Though I've accepted my presence here, I do not yet understand my purpose."

"As the day unfolds," the Asakra of Keftea said reassuringly, "you will find the answers you seek."

Joshua then spoke. "I too am grateful the Allness has brought us here together."

The Asakra nodded graciously, but Zoee sensed the terror beneath his serenity. She looked around the table, at each of the Representatives. Most had taken very little on their plates, and few were even picking at their food. She could see the fear in each of them, but she also felt their collective power, pulling in the cosmic energies, spinning them round their supper circle, magnifying, electrifying, cresting into a whirling vortex...and then a calming silence. No one was moving, not even Joshua, who seemed totally caught up in it all. Zoee took one more bite, set down her fork, and remained very still.

A low, resonating hum rose up from the courtyard, beckoning them over to the balcony. Down below, hundreds of people formed a human corridor, leading from the north entrance into the center, where it opened up into a large circle. The celebrants raised their arms high overhead, casting the invocation skyward. "Aaahhhmmmm. Aaahhhmmmm." Around the courtyard, on every terrace and verandah, thousands more joined in. "Aaahhhmmmm. Aaahhhmmmm." The sound grew louder and stronger – wave after wave, ebbing and flowing, filling the whole of Knossis.

The primal vibration surged through Zoee, drawing her into the Oneness. She raised her arms, and taking a deep breath, added her voice to the call.

Suddenly, a full-grown Bull came charging up the long, stone ramp leading to the courtyard. He trotted through the corridor and into the circle, which quickly closed behind him. Six men and six women came forth from the group, forming an inner circle around him. He bowed his head low and snorted, then reared up on both hind legs. They joined their outstretched hands and began to move around him, bending and curving their ring. He quieted down, prancing slowly around, joining the sacred dance.

The inner circle began the "Aaahhhmmmm," and the outer circle followed. Again, the hum enveloped the entire gathering. As the resonance peaked, the circle broke and a woman approached the Bull. She raised her hands high over her head, gazing deeply into his eyes. He pawed the ground with his hoof three times, then stood very still.

Another woman slowly stepped forward, then knelt down on one knee. She touched her palm to Earth, and bowed her head down low. When she was ready, she launched herself upward, catapulting over the Bull. One by one, the other ten took their turns, hand springing and flipping over his back. As the last one approached, he also knelt down, and prepared himself to go. He lowered his head, paused a few seconds, then propelled himself up. With two mighty steps he cleared the Bull's back, somersaulting three times in the air. He landed squarely, swinging his arms back, then thrusting them high over his head in ecstasy.

The celebrants again held hands, encircling the Bull once more. They danced around him and he pranced in synch, until he was facing the corridor. The inner and outer circles both opened up, and he galloped back through and down the ramp. The music began and the crowd went wild, whooping and clapping their hands.

On the verandah, Zoee and Joshua linked their arms with the Representatives, who linked their arms with the people. As they started to dance, the Asakra of Keftea showed Zoee the steps and she picked them up in no time. Joshua watched her feet, and tried to follow her movements. The first few times he missed the kick, throwing his head back in laughter. He tried again, and again once more, until he finally found the groove. They danced around the verandah and through the tables, in circles, spirals and figure eights. As they swung by the staircase, Cybele appeared and joined the twirling line....

When the dancing died down, Cybele approached the Asasra and Asakra of Keftea. "Good day Representatives, Zoee, Joshua."

"Hello, Cybele," the Asasra said, patting her brow. "We are happy to see you. I trust you have good news?"

"Yes I do. We have evacuated Kalliste, and the people are safe. The ship is secure and we can set sail as soon as the seas have calmed."

"Any word from our friends beyond the Straits?"

"They are expecting us."

"Excellent work, sister Cybele! Thank you," she said, hugging her. The Asasra then called the Representatives together. "Our Kallistean cousins are safe, and our friends on the Isles of Many Stones await. Now we may proceed."

Zoee slipped her arm through Joshua's and followed them down the stairs and into a dimly lit hallway, which turned and twisted out to the theater plaza. The sun was low on the horizon and pink and purple clouds brightened in the twilight. Brilliant Venus hovered in the west, and in the east, Mars and Jupiter aligned.

They entered the open-air theater, etched neatly into the side of a gently sloping hill. Two red and black pillars stood at the entrance way, and fifty rows of gypsum benches cascaded down toward the stage. Two taller black pillars held a blue crescent moon arch, painted with a red triple spiral.

"This play is being performed all over the Islands tonight," the Asasra told them, as they took their seats near the front.

People kept filing in and the sky grew darker. Someone in

the wings gently tapped a little chime and a hush came over the crowd. The stage was dark and a baritone voice began.

"In the beginning, there was Chaos. The Nothingness. The All. Chaos lived alone for a very long time, until out of the void, life suddenly appeared – like a delicate bubble of foam emerging from the sea. Earth and Sky were born."

A woman in a forest green robe and a man in a sky blue robe came on stage from the opposite wings. They each carried a slim white candle, and the low, smooth voice continued. "They joined in the Sacred Marriage."

The couple approached each other slowly, then joined their flames and began to dance. As they whirled around, and around and around, more light started to glow from the wings and above the stage.

"Their love flourished, and six daughters and six sons were born."

Six couples, each wearing robes of a different color, danced onto the brightly lit stage. They spun and twirled to the song of a lyre, laughing and playing games.

"The family lived in peace for many years, until poor, young Kronos fell ill with the terrible Dark Heart Disease."

A male celebrant dressed in red pulled a veil from under his robe, and placed it over his face. He became disoriented and dizzy, collapsing on stage. His family huddled around him, confused about what to do. All eyes turned to the woman in a flowing red robe.

"Kronos' sister Hope knew where to find the cure."

She ran off stage and returned with a glass jar, shaped in the form of a lioness.

"But woe, Kronos went mad before she could give him the medicine. He rose in a fury and lashed out at his loved ones, taunting and calling them names. He captured Hope and imprisoned her in the jar, then hid her away."

Veiled Kronos grabbed sister Hope and dragged her off stage. She screamed for her family to save her, but they were too afraid.

Chaotic music filled the air – strings, flutes and drums rose in cacophonous crescendo as the dancers whirled about in confusion. When Kronos returned, they scattered, trying to escape.

"In his madness, Kronos willed the plague to spread to all of his brothers and sisters. Earth and Sky watched in horror as their children succumbed."

The candles went out. Footfalls were heard on stage as the dancers scurried about in the dark. Piercing shrieks cut through the night air, then silence.

A woman appeared, wearing a long white robe with magnificent wings and a white swan mask. She carried a brightly lit torch, illuminating Sky and Earth, who sat alone in the center of the stage, their heads down. The narration ended and the celebrants spoke for the first time.

"Do not grieve," Swan trumpeted, "for not all of your children have fallen ill."

Sky and Earth lifted their heads and looked to the beautiful bird.

"Your daughter Rhea and your son Oreas are well. Come, let me take you to their island place of refuge."

Swan spread her wings wide as Earth and Sky rose to their feet and held fast. They glided off stage and the house went dark again.

When they reappeared, Swan's torch illuminated a colorful island backdrop, and a woman and man emerged from two invisible openings. Rhea wore gold and Oreas purple.

"Mother, Father!" Oreas began. "Our hearts are gladdened to see you. We had faith you had not succumbed, so we asked Swan to lead you here."

"For the moment we are safe," said Rhea, "though we fear Kronos will not rest until he has conquered us all."

"I'm afraid you are right, my dear daughter," replied Earth sadly. "We must find sister Hope and release her from Kronos' prison. She's the only one who can save us."

"Yes, but where is she?" Sky lamented. "I have searched from the highest clouds, yet she is nowhere to be seen."

Oreas reached into the slender pouch hanging from his belt and retrieved a papyrus scroll. "She's been hidden away in a glass prison, down in the depths of the Sea. With Whale's help, she was able to send this message to us." He unrolled it and read. "'Sail the river Eridanus, brave Oreas, far up into the star filled heavens of Night. Take our parents with you, seek the Great Red Eyed Bull, and wait. You will all be safe. And you, courageous Rhea, must take the path you know, and go to the Outerworld. Kronos will search high and low, but he will not find you there.

"'One day, long in the future, Kronos will look up to the sky and discover Oreas and our dear Parents. He will leave this world and travel the stellar river to try again to capture you. When he does, sister Rhea, you must retrieve me from my lonesome prison far beneath the Sea, and set me free.

"'I will embrace the Earth and spread my cure! When Kronos returns, he too will be well again, and we will live as a family, in peace once more." Oreas rolled the papyrus and placed it back in his pouch.

"May it be so!" Earth and Sky pronounced.

"May it be so!" their children affirmed.

They embraced and a bright flash ignited on stage, then the theater fell dark.

High above the theater arch, Orion the Messenger appeared, sparkling amongst the stars. His parents, the Partners, were rising nearby and the Red Eyed Bull ran toward the horizon.

The applause died down and people started to leave, but Joshua and Zoee remained motionless, lost in the stars overhead.

"Excuse me," the Asasra whispered. "Zoee? Joshua?"

They looked at each other, and then to the Asasra.

"We must go now."

They slowly got up and silently followed the ten Representatives out of the theater. They re-entered the stone tunnel, but this time it took them to a wide spiral staircase, with long, low greenstone steps. Zoee tread lightly on each one, barely noticing her descent. As she slowly curved around and down, the walls grew narrower and narrower. The light became brighter at the bottom of the steps, where the stairs gave way to a room.

The Asasra of Keftea placed her hand on Zoee's arm. "It is our custom to give thanks before entering." With her head lowered, the Asasra approached an altar, tucked into a nook in the far wall. She selected a long slender white candle from a hanging basket, lit it from the single light in the shrine, and gently placed it upright in a small box of red sand. The Asakra of Keftea and the other Representatives followed.

Zoee walked slowly toward the altar. A Snake Goddess figurine stood in the center, surrounded by flowers and sea shells. She selected a candle and looked into the Goddess' ebony black eyes. *Energy of the Universe, connecting all through time and space, I am so very grateful to be here. I continue with humility and without expectation, open to all possibilities.* She merged her candle with the flame, placed it in the sand and joined the Representatives. Joshua selected his candle, softly whispering something as he lit it and placed it in the sand.

They passed through a low, narrow archway and into a small sunken anteroom, ablaze with candles left by those who'd been coming throughout the day. The Representatives fanned out on either side of a darkened doorway, and the Asasra of Keftea spoke.

"Zoee, and Joshua, we are about to enter the most sacred place, but we each must enter alone. Quiet your mind. Feel your connection to the source. Go at your own pace, and follow your invisible thread into the Labyrinth. Your path will lead you to center, where we will meet again. Please honor us by being the first to enter."

Joshua gestured for Zoee to precede him. She took a few deep breaths, then slowly stepped over the threshold.

A solitary lamp glowed dimly at the end of the corridor, throwing long, flickering shadows across the thick stone walls. Step by step on gypsum stones she went inside, directly toward the center. Then she felt the pulling thread, drawing her to the left...

Around a corner, to a curving hallway arching to the right, carrying her out and away from center. She walked and walked through the narrow corridors, winding right again then left...rough stone and feather shadow cleansing away the last grains of dust still lodged in her mind.

Intime she came to another passage, and she felt herself slowing down, approaching this turn with caution. She ran her hand along the wall, taking small, slow steps, feeling the curve of the meander. Around she went, and then she saw a tall stone torch before her. Another step, and then it flared, bringing her to her knees.

She felt the cool, hard floor transforming, turning into a blade of sturdy grass. She inched up the shoot, and into the branches of a juniper bush, enjoying a soft breeze as it blew against her hairs. Her many legs propelled her up the limb; and delicate antennae led her on. When she found the right spot, in a comfortable crook, she stopped. The life thread pulled, round and round, shrouding her in warm silky light.

For sometime, she remained suspended inside the chrysalis, before she felt her skin begin to shed. She quivered and wriggled, and squirmed and writhed, until at last, the old life slipped away. Moretime passed. Then she felt the stirring on her back, and sensed her wings forming, evolving, ready to unfold. She pushed through the fibrous membrane, anticipating flight. As the outer layers peeled away, she came into the light.

Her eyes opened and once again met Joshua's. They were standing together, in the Center of Knossis. Oil lamps burned brightly, illuminating a glorious fresco of griffins and lilies completely encircling them. Incense sticks burned slowly on sleek marble trays, sending up fragrant spirals of smoke. And the Snake Goddess herself was seated across the room.

She wore a purple embroidered bodice laced snugly at her waist, and a crimson double apron over a full-length layered skirt. Her eyes sparkled gold and her curly, jet black hair cascaded down around her exposed breasts and into her lap. A living serpent coiled around the top of her tall headdress.

The Asasras and Asakras sat on long benches on either side of her, and when Joshua and Zoee were seated, the Asasra of Keftea spoke. "This is our Minoa, our link to the ancient wisdom. For many hundreds of generations, our people have been coming here, to this place, to find their connection."

The Minoa rose, and her presence seemed to fill the room. She opened her arms wide and spoke in a low, even voice.

"Welcome to this sacred place. I have been expecting you." The snake hissed. "We are elated and hopeful *because* you are here. As you now know, our way of life is coming to an end, and a long darkness will soon descend. But for every ending, there is a beginning. For every beginning, an ending. With your help, the world will see the end of that which is yet to befall us.

"The partnership way will virtually disappear from the face of Earth, but through stories and Spirit, it will survive in the collective soul of the people. The dominators will suppress it for a very long time, but eventually they will lose their hold, and it will reemerge. We have seen it.

"During your time on Earth, Joshua, there will be a resurgence, a partial enlightenment. Your transformation will have an enormous impact on the world, but it will not overcome the warriors alone. Much time will pass, and many will keep the Spirit alive, until the time enough believe. When Zoee transforms, the cycle will be completed. The Keftean way of life will once again flourish, and the New Era will begin.

"Zoee Nikitas, you are the first human being to transform in a very long time. You represent the future. You have opened the door again for all humanity to step into the Light, and this time they will choose to go through. You and Joshua must bring our Message into the heart and mind of the future."

"Why must a message for Zoee's time come from me?" Joshua asked.

The Minoa glided across the room.

"Come. We will see together."

She took Joshua's hand and then Zoee's, and led them around a stone pillar and down three greenstone stairs. At the bottom, a single candle floated in the center of a large, circular water basin. The two of them stood on either side of the Minoa, and Representatives and Initiates gathered around the pool. The room fell silent as everyone joined hands. After a moment, the Minoa spoke.

"Each has the potential to know the All. To touch infinity. To merge with the collective consciousness of the universe. Joshua, Zoee, will you permit us to see through your eyes?"

They both agreed.

The Minoa's voice suddenly seemed to grow larger, to go beyond the confines of sound.

"Look at the flame, floating on the ocean of existence. Feel its light. Absorb it into your mind. Absorb it into your soul. Allow it to enter you, to surround you. Breathe in the light and feel it become part of you.

"Now, find the light within. See its radiance, feel its warmth. Let it join with the light of the universe." Her voice trailed off.

The water began to glow, and a montage of Joshua's memories appeared in the pool: his birth in a small bed of straw; as a boy in an old olive grove, watching a butterfly fly high in the air; as a young man, talking with a crowd outside the Temple; walking with three Indian men along the River Ganga; living in the wilderness, enjoying the peaceful solitude and beauty; and telling stories to the multitudes on a mountain top. But then the image changed to the inside of the Temple, where Joshua spoke to the merchants about their excessive greed. The doors flew open. Roman troops charged in, with shields raised and swords drawn. People running, screaming, Joshua and his friends escaping to the old meeting place on Mount Tabor. Six women, six men sitting with him, breaking bread and sharing wine, when the light exploded around him.

The pool glowed gold. Ripples of light emanated from the center and began to condense into nebulae, star clusters and galaxies. The universe. Then colors appeared, rushing by, accelerating faster and faster until they blended together to form rainbows of light. They streaked by, curving, twisting, spinning into a vortex of time and space, before dissipating back into the calm lustral basin.

Without saying a word, the Minoa slowly turned away from Joshua, and peered into Zoee. Again a montage of images appeared in the pool. The flash of light disappears, taking Joshua with it. His twelve companions witness the transfiguration and react with awe and confusion – then Mary and Peter are arguing. The split divides his friends. Peter meets with the early fathers and establishes his church. The Christian martyrs suffer and the Roman Empire converts; the Byzantines rise in the east; the Dark Ages descend, with Crusades, Inquisitions and witch burnings; European colonialism spreads its missionaries, slave traders and disease; Native American genocide; the perversions of Nazi Germany, Hiroshima and Nagasaki; Ku Klux Klan with their burning crosses; a Belfast schoolbus exploding; televangelists spewing fire and brimstone; environmental destruction, hunger, poverty and urban hopelessness; David Koresch and Heaven's Gate...

The flash of light broke the spell and returned them to the candle floating on still water.

Joshua dropped to his knees, tears streaming down his pained face.

The Minoa smiled gently, placing her hand on his shoulder.

He looked up at her. "Those were not the lessons I was trying to teach. What happened? What went wrong?"

"The forces of greed, the Dark Heart Disease, has clouded the vision of many."

He sobbed, feeling the agony of 2,000 years of death and destruction perpetuated in his name. She reached out for his hand again.

"These Evils are not your fault. Many have been true to your teachings and they long to hear from you now." She helped him to his feet. "Look again into the pool. These are the people who have been touched by your Love."

Millions of faces flowed through the water, each a gentle soul; Zoee was the last to appear, before the water stilled.

"It is time for partnership to return to the world. We send you, Joshua and you, Zoee as our messengers, to show the world there is another way. But you must be prepared for what awaits. Behold, the future."

They peered into the pool once more.

The Knossos flash illuminates the water, and they see Zoee disappear from the dig site; Joshua appears in the Jerusalem light; people flock to both places in droves; the special report beams the Message far and wide; demonstrations and rallies all over the globe; the Millennium Summit and the final flash.

"When the time comes," the Minoa said assuredly, "you will know what you must do."

Zoee and Joshua silently acknowledged.

"Then let us continue."

The Minoa gracefully walked up the stairs and led them to another sunken antechamber. In the center of the room, a marble gemstone chest rested amongst candles, flowers, statuettes, bullhorns and double axes.

Zoee smiled. "The tablet we discovered just before I came here – the one I was looking for in the cave."

"Yes Zoee, we must now take it there, where Mother Earth will protect it over the eons."

Inan and Lillith presented the Minoa with a small rock crystal rhyton. Closing her eyes, she raised it over her head, then delicately poured three drops of rosewater onto the chest. She stepped back and motioned for the Initiates to approach the tablet. Three men and three women lifted the two long poles supporting the heavy stone vessel. They followed the Minoa into the winding passages, and on out to the courtyard.

A curving, twisting human corridor was ready to receive them. The crowd looked hopeful as their Message passed by, on its way into the future. As the procession moved through the colonnade, the people joined the line, lengthening it, threading it back through itself. They zig zagged out of Knossis and into the open plaza, snaking their way around the fountain, forming circles within circles within circles. The Minoa emerged, delicately pulling the serpentine string down the greenstone staircase and into the forest. Silently, they walked through the wild wood, glowing with the light of a thousand torches. They passed through the roots of the majestic red cedar and crossed over the singing stream. The canopy spiraled upward in fluorescent green reflection, and wise old faces appeared in the gnarly trees.

Once they reached the cave opening, the people fanned out around the chest, held high. The Minoa approached it and raised her arms. After a moment, she spoke, and her voice filled the forest.

"We are the people of Keftea. We are the island communities of Keftea, Kalliste, Lesvos, Nexos and Cypri. We are the people of Gaia, a fragile world adrift on the cosmic sea, blessed with the rare and precious gift of life. Where Mother Earth and Father Sky live in love and peace as do we, in honor of their Sacred Marriage.

"But now the world is changing. The Gods of thunder and war have darkened the hearts and minds of many men. They will transform the world, and there will be much death and destruction as the Evils roam the Earth. Hope will be imprisoned, but she will not be lost forever.

"It will take many generations, but one day, Hope will be set free and our way of life will reemerge. The people of the world have willed it so. We have been teaching and preparing our people for this time, when we must focus the collective thought of a hundred generations and send it into the future; and when the time comes, we know our descendants will bring back the light and pierce the veil of darkness which has befallen us. We send this message to the future, when the world is ready to transform again. Like an ark on water, we cast this vessel onto the Sea of Time."

The Minoa entered the cave, and the Initiates followed her in, carefully carrying the tablet down to its resting place in the depths of the Earth.

When they reemerged, a cheer rose up from the crowd and musicians began to play. Lyres, flutes and castanets created the age old rhythms, and the people danced and sang in the green cathedral. Earth and Sky were alive with their song.

As the cave was sealed, the Minoa's voice rang out. "It is time, the Sun has reached its furthest southerly point. It will be dark for many generations to come, but the Light will one day return."

At that precise moment, a swallow appeared, hovering overhead. It fluttered its feathers, and a tremendous thundering crack broke through the air.

"Kalliste has exploded!" the Minoa proclaimed. "It has begun."

Before they could say a word, a brilliant oval of light broke through the space time continuum and whisked Joshua and Zoee away. The ground began to shake violently, dislodging rocks and debris which tumbled down over the cave.

As it detonated, the top of the mile high volcano was instantaneously disintegrated into billions of particles of ash, dust and gas. The sides of the mountain collapsed in the blink of an eye, and the surrounding sea rushed in, creating gargantuan waterfalls and colossal clouds of steam. A huge, dark mushroom cloud rose high into the atmosphere, surrounding the globe and plunging day into a long, cold night.

CHAPTER NINE
THE MESSAGE

Once again, Zoee was swept away. The points of colored light raced by, streaking together, curving and twisting into currents of energy, pulling her through mind at large. This time she could feel Joshua's presence – not by sight or touch, but as a thread woven into her consciousness as she was woven into existence.

When the flash let them off at the podium, she was calm and centered. She scanned the silent General Assembly Hall, crowded with 4,000 stunned, motionless people. A 'Millennium Summit' banner hung from the gallery over their heads. She glanced behind her, where the flabbergasted dignitaries were on their feet. Above them, the U.N. Earth emblem glowed gold.

She turned back around to face the delegates and television cameras. "I know this is a shock to you all," she said with a strong, steady voice. "But please, hear us out. I'm Zoe Nikitas."

Gasps rose up from the crowd.

"As strange as this may sound, it's *you*, the people of the world, the people of the ages, who have brought us here.

"Three days ago, the translation of the Linear A tablet triggered a complex chain of events set in motion 3,600 years ago by a people you know as the Minoans. They called themselves Kefteans and we have visited their time."

Not a peep from the crowd.

"When the tablet was translated, at that moment when the words appeared on the computer screen, the thought of the Keftean people thrust into our present consciousness. The energy of that collective thought, with the thoughts of those who have kept their beliefs alive through the eons, opened a doorway in space and time. I know this is difficult to believe, but please, it's very important you try to be open to it. After all, it's your belief which makes this possible in the first place.

"The Kefteans were keepers of the ancient wisdom, born from the caves of Earth thousands of years before their time. They had a physical, mental and spiritual bond with Earth, Sky and Cosmos, and their hearts and minds were in harmony with the energies of nature.

"Over a period of 126 generations, the Kefteans saw their world transforming from peaceful coexistence founded on partnership, to a cruel order rooted in dominance and inequality. They began to realize their values, their culture and their very way of life would be destroyed by the warring Indo-Europeans, who were conquering and subjugating the peoples of the Great Civilization.

"One by one, Mesopotamia, Egypt, Estrucea and Old Europe fell under the blade of the warrior; and the Kefteans knew they were next. They cried as their people were murdered, the Goddess defamed, the Earth disrespected. They watched as the old stories were changed and twisted, shifting the people's thoughts from joy to fear, from collaboration to subordination. The Kefteans knew this plague would descend and remain for centuries to come, but they believed our Human spirit could not die. Many generations before they were ultimately conquered, they began to focus their collective vision and hope toward the return to partnership and peace. As the end grew nearer, they conceived a remarkable plan to send a Message into the future. Part of this Message is the written record on their tablet; part of it is our presence here.

"Just before the Santorini volcano exploded, they brought their five, democratic island communities together, and in great ritual and celebration cast those thoughts onto the sea of time. When they sent that tablet into the future, they also sent the essence of their beings, and the power of their belief to us, knowing one day, we would bring back the Light."

Just then, she saw Fiona in the audience, tears streaming down her face. Zoee smiled reassuringly and continued.

"The Keftean spirit has remained alive in the minds and myths of the people throughout the ages, and every so often it bursts forth, gaining momentum with each resurgence – the Classical Greeks stirred the burning embers by cultivating the arts and exploring the sciences. They even experimented with democracy, but it was temporary. After only a few decades, the kings and emperors regained control, and democracy was again forgotten.

During the time of Christ, the light again briefly rekindled, and many felt the love, but it wasn't enough to overcome the dominators. We slipped further backward, into fear and despair. Much later, in the 11th century, we saw another spark flicker, this one amidst the horror of the crusades. Troubadours sang their songs of love, great cathedrals were built for the Virgin Mary, and we began the search for the holy grail once again. This time, the savage wind of Inquisition nearly extinguished the living light.

"But then finally, in the 15th century, a fire ignited in our collective soul. We breathed new life into the arts and sciences, resurrecting them from the dungeon of superstition where they'd been cloistered for well over a thousand years.

"We looked to the ancients, and considered their Utopian ideals, beginning again to believe in the possibility of the Golden

Age. For 300 years this movement grew, ultimately budding with the Enlightenment. Our belief in the power of the mind and our appetite for experimentation and inquiry grew exponentially. Democracy was rediscovered, and for some, political and civil rights rose again as cornerstones of the right to self-determination. We propelled ourselves into the Industrial Age – a phenomenal surge of human initiative, which tragically, has culminated in the most destructive and inhumane period to date, the twentieth century. We have taken technology to the edge, and can now easily eradicate all life on Earth.

"Rousseau was partially right, mankind has become corrupt and greed has darkened our hearts. However, technology is not inherently evil. We have the ability to choose. It's not a foregone conclusion that our sophisticated technology must continue hurtling us toward armageddon. We can choose to direct our technological resources away from the values of the dominator culture and toward economic, social and environmental justice. It's in our human interest to choose to do so, or surely, we will not survive into our own distant future.

"I'm not saying it'll be easy. A real transformation is going to take a sustained, dedicated effort to make the much needed reforms. And, most importantly, you must *believe* such a transformation is possible. I believe we humans can do anything we set our minds to – even create the Golden Age again, as our distant grandparents once did in Keftea. We only need to make the choice and act upon it."

She paused, then stepped back from the podium and looked to Joshua.

He approached the mic, and tapped it. A loud electronic thud resounded around the room. "Hello. I am called Joshua, though you know me by a different name. To you, I am Jesus Christ."

Again, loud gasps from the audience. The cameras zoomed in.

"Please listen to me. Please. With the Keftean's help, I've recently learned of the terrible things which have taken place in my name." He swallowed hard over a huge lump in his throat, and tears welled up and spilled over his eyes. "There has been so much inhumanity, oppression and destruction since my time here." His voice trailed off and he began to tremble. He rested his elbows on the podium, then buried his head in his hands and sobbed. The sound of his anguish filled the room, and many in the audience cried with him.

Zoee put her arm around his shoulder. He took a few deep breaths, lifted his head and wiped away the tears. "It is time to heal," he said, looking into the television cameras, and searching the faces in the audience. "It is time to bring balance back into our lives." He closed his eyes a few moments, breathing deeply and steadily, and the pain in his face began to subside. "I feel the hope here," he again looked to the people. "The grief in my soul is being cleansed away by your hope of a new beginning.

"For the first time in a very long time, many, many of you believe in the possibility of a peaceful way of life that once flourished on this planet – when women and men lived in partnership with each other, and with all life. The Kefteans believe you are ready to choose the partnership way, but it is each and every one of you who must make the choice. You may continue down the path of fear and destruction if you wish, but I beseech you, choose the path of Love!

"This path embraces compassion, forgiveness and kindness as the most important values, and embodies the belief that we are *all* responsible for each other's wellbeing. It recognizes and celebrates the sacredness of all life, and of the small, fragile Earth we share. This path leads us to a place of beauty and grace, of laughter and song. A place of harmony.

"The path of Love is also the path of self-discovery, which leads us to the best inside ourselves. When we embark on this journey, we travel to our center, to the core of our own humanity. It is here we discover the Divine. For Divinity shines within *each* of us, and our greatest gift, our greatest challenge, is to awaken the Divinity within and bring it forth into the world. If we do so, together we can bring back the Light and create a place of joy."

He stepped back from the podium, and as he joined hands with Zoee, the sparkling diamond appeared above their heads. It suddenly exploded into a radiant golden oval, filling the rotunda with Light. Wave after wave of Love Energy flowed from the Cosmic Source, enveloping Planet Earth, and Zoee and Joshua vanished in the glow.

EPILOGUE

Later that afternoon, the CHAOS Chairmen were seen in Central Park, flying big, colorful kites and singing an old Mary Poppins tune.

THE BEGINNING...

THE COMING OF A NEW MILLENNIUM
ORDER FORM

Call Toll Free
1•888•522-7979 (1•888 LABRYS-X)

or e-mail us @:
labrysx@earthlink.net

Via Post:
Labrys
2425 B Channing Way #574
Berkeley, CA 94704

PRICE: $14.95 **SHIPPING & HANDLING:** Please include $3.00 for the first book and $2.00 for each additional book.
SALES TAX: California residents, please add $1.50 per book.

Payment:
☐ Cheque
☐ Credit Card (Circle One): Visa   MC   AmEx   Discover

Card Number _____
Name on Card _____ Exp. Date ___ / ___
Ship to: Name _____
   Address _____
   City _____ State _____ Zip _____
   Telephone Number _____

Thanks for your order!

WATCH FOR OUR WEBSITE COMING SOON!

THE COMING OF A NEW MILLENNIUM

ORDER FORM

Call Toll Free
1•888•522-7979 (1•888 LABRYS-X)

or e-mail us @:
labrysx@earthlink.net

Via Post:
Labrys
2425 B Channing Way #574
Berkeley, CA 94704

PRICE: $14.95 **SHIPPING & HANDLING:** Please include $3.00 for the first book and $2.00 for each additional book.
SALES TAX: California residents, please add $1.50 per book.

Payment:

☐ Cheque

☐ Credit Card (Circle One):   Visa   MC   AmEx   Discover

Card Number _____
Name on Card _____ Exp. Date ___ / ___
Ship to: Name _____
        Address _____
        City _____ State _____ Zip _____
        Telephone Number _____

Thanks for your order!

WATCH FOR OUR WEBSITE COMING SOON!

THE COMING OF A NEW MILLENNIUM
ORDER FORM

Call Toll Free
1•888•522-7979 (1•888 LABRYS-X)

or e-mail us @:
labrysx@earthlink.net

Via Post:
Labrys
2425 B Channing Way #574
Berkeley, CA 94704

PRICE: $14.95 **SHIPPING & HANDLING:** Please include $3.00 for the first book and $2.00 for each additional book.
SALES TAX: California residents, please add $1.50 per book.

Payment:

☐ Cheque

☐ Credit Card (Circle One):   Visa   MC   AmEx   Discover

Card Number _____
Name on Card _____ Exp. Date ___ / ___
Ship to: Name _____
     Address _____
     City _____ State _____ Zip _____
     Telephone Number _____

Thanks for your order!

WATCH FOR OUR WEBSITE COMING SOON!

LABRYS